THE CLEANER
HOULIHAN MEN OF DUBLIN

BROOKE SUMMERS

The CLEANER

Hardmen men of Dublin Book Two

First Edition published in 2024

Text Copyright © Brooke Summers

Edits by Farrant Editing

Proofreading by Author bunnies

All rights reserved.

The moral right of the author has been asserted. No part of this publication may be reproduced, stored in or introduced into a retrieval system, or transmitted, in any form or by any means (electronic, mechanical, photocopying, recording or otherwise), nor be otherwise circulated in any form of binding or cover other than that in which it is published without the prior written permission of the author. Any person who does any unauthorized act in relation to this publication may be liable to criminal prosecution and civil claims for damages.

All characters in this publication are fictitious and any resemblance to real persons, living or dead, is purely coincidental.

They call me The Cleaner.

My job? Make bodies disappear without a trace.
I've done it for years—killed to protect my family, my crew.
And I'd do it all over again without a second thought.

Then there's her—*Lisa Turner.*
She's the perfect storm that I didn't see coming.
I met her years ago, a broken girl with eyes that screamed for salvation.

I thought I could ignore it, push her away, but fate had other plans.
She's back in my life now, and I'll be damned if I let anyone hurt her.
She saved me once, and now I'll protect her from whatever demons still haunt her.

But an unknown foe is coming for us.

Our pasts resurfacing—and it just so happens that mine and Lisa's pasts are on a collision course.

Only one question remains, will we be strong enough to face the unknown together?
Or drown in our secrets?

CONTENT
PLEASE READ CAREFULLY.

THERE ARE elements and themes within this book that some readers might find extremely upsetting.

Please check out my website for that list of potentially harmful topics. Please heed these as this book contains some heavy topics that some readers could find damaging.

www.brookesummersbooks.com

DEDICTATION

No matter what you're never alone....
Reach out for help whenever you need too.
There will be someone to catch you when you fall.

CHAPTER ONE

LISA

"Ma?" I call out as I close the front door behind me and throw my school bag on the ground. "You here?"

"In the kitchen," I hear her reply, and I'm surprised by the cheerful tone she has.

Over the past few months, Ma has been in a depressive state. Her medication hasn't been helping. Doctors have tried various medications at different dosages yet nothing seems to be working. Right now, however, she sounds upbeat—happy even—and that's not something I've heard in a while.

Unable to keep the smile from my lips, I pad toward the kitchen, hoping like hell that she is, in fact, coming out of her depression and this round of medication is helping.

"Hey, baby," she greets me with a smile.

My heart hammers wildly as I take her in. She's clean, and she smells of peaches, so I know she's had a shower. Over the past month or so, I've had to be the one to push her into the bathroom and clean her. Today, she's done it herself. She's wearing a cute summer dress too. I honestly can't recall how long it's been since I last saw her wearing anything other than her nightdress. That's all she's been wearing lately.

"Hey, Ma. Did you have a good day?"

She walks around the counter, still smiling brightly, and presses a kiss against my cheek. "I did, baby. I really did. How about you? How was school?"

I lift my shoulders and shrug. "Eh, it was school. I'm glad it's the weekend."

She runs her hand along my hair. "Your dad will be here to pick you up soon," she says and I roll my eyes. Great, just what I need. Not. "And, honey, I know things have been difficult as of late, but you have to go to your dad's. He loves you."

I can't stop my lip from curling. "Yeah, he loved me so much he screwed his receptionist. He cheated on you, Ma. He broke our family." It makes me sick to know he's living with her and they're happy, all while Ma's suffering. He's the reason she went into a depressive state.

Ma sighs heavily. "Mine and your father's relationship hadn't been working for a long time."

"Ma," I say a lot harder than I had intended. "He cheated on you. If it wasn't working, he should have left you, not screwed a woman young enough to be my sister."

Tanya is nineteen and barely out of school. She goes all doe-eyed whenever she stares at my dad. It's so icky and I don't like her. She tries her very hardest to be a friend of mine, and then in the same breath tries to parent me. I don't go to my dad's house because I don't want to see Tanya. I hate her, and I'm not really liking my dad either right now. Besides, I've had Ma to look after, and I'd rather do that than spend time with two people who hurt us both.

"I know, honey, but he's still your father."

I stare at my ma and see the pain she's trying to hide from me. Her eyes are filled with fear and hurt. "Ma, no lies, remember?" I tell her what she told me when the shit with my dad's affair came out.

"He's threatening to take me to court if you don't see him."

I blink, shocked to my core that my dad would be so callous, but when the shock settles, I realise that my dad is an asshole and this is him to a bloody T. Whatever he wants, he'll get. He's proven that time and time again, but this time, he's pushing me too far. I'll never choose him over Ma, and if he threatens to take me away, I'll make it known how much I despise him and his plaything.

"It's not happening," I snap. "I promise you, Ma, it won't happen."

She pulls me into her arms and I sink into her embrace. "Just for tonight," she whispers. "I want you to go just for tonight. Please, baby, for me?"

I swallow hard. "Fine," I sigh. "For you."

She presses a kiss to my forehead and pulls back. "Dinner will be ready soon. Why don't you go on up and get washed and changed, pack a bag to go to your father's, and we'll have something to eat before you leave?"

I nod, knowing that if I don't go to Dad's, it'll cause an argument. Ma's happy today. She's so damn happy that I won't do anything to jeopardize that. She's worked so damn hard to be where she is right now, and I can't—I won't let Dad spoil that by being a complete dick. She releases me and I give her a quick smile before hurrying upstairs, grabbing my school bag as I do.

The second I'm inside my bedroom, I reach into my bag for my phone and hit dial on my dad's number. The anger coursing through my veins is unlike anything I have ever felt in my life. I was angry, devastated when my dad cheated on Ma, hurt beyond belief that our family had been destroyed by his stupidity and recklessness, but never have I felt such hatred toward him or so much anger.

"Lisa," he greets me with a soft sigh.

"You really think the way to get on my good side is to tell Ma you're going to take her to court for custody?" I ask, still in disbelief.

"Lis—"

"Cut the shit, Dad," I snap, speaking over him. "I'm tired of the lies. I'm tired of listening to you tell me that it's for the best and you only want what's good for me. Well here's the thing, what's good for me is not you and that tramp you call a girlfriend. The two of you have destroyed my life, turned my world upside down, and to make things worse, you want to pull me away from the only stability I have left!" I'm breathing hard, my eyes filling with tears. I'm so damn angry, so hurt by him. I don't know where my dad went but this callous man isn't him.

"Lisa, sweetheart, you're thirteen; you need a family, people who will be able to take care of you. Your mam isn't able to do that."

God, he makes me sick. "I had a family, Dad. I had

my family and you ruined it. I hate you. God, I hate you so much."

"Baby, you don't mean that," he says, sounding defeated.

"I do. God, I do, with everything that I am. I hate you for what you've done to Ma and me. Don't you see? You've ruined every foundation we had. The trust I had in you is gone. You go to court, Dad, and I swear I'll run away. I'd rather be on the streets than be around you and that whore."

"Lisa," he says low. It sounds as though he's on the verge of tears. "I want what's best for you."

"What's best for me is being with Ma. What's best for me is not being around you and the woman who broke up my family. Why can't you see that?"

"I'm so sorry, baby. I never meant to hurt you."

My laughter is bitter. "You cheated on Ma, Dad. What on earth did you think was going to happen? That I'd be okay with being around you and the woman who shattered my world?"

"It's been three months, Lisa."

"I don't care if it's three years; I don't want that bitch in my life."

"Lisa Reanne Turner, you are thirteen years old. You do not speak like that, especially about your elders."

I can't control the laughter that bubbles from me. "Elders? Dad, she's only six years older than me. She's young enough to be my sister. But you know that, don't you? You make me sick. I won't be coming to your house tonight. In fact, I don't ever want to see you again." I end the call, tears spilling from my eyes and my chest heaving. I throw my phone onto the bed, ignoring the incoming call from my father. I can't—won't—speak to him right now. I need to calm down. I don't want Ma to know how upset I am or how I spoke to Dad. She'll be pissed and that's not what I want.

"WHAT TIME IS your dad getting here?" Ma asks me a few hours later. We've had dinner and we're watching TV. She's been happy and I love that. I would do anything to help keep her like this. I love when she smiles. I want to bottle them up and keep them forever. I know that the good days are hard, and they come around so very little, I want to cherish them when they do.

"He'll be here in about twenty minutes. Everything okay?"

She nods. "I'm going to run myself a bath. Shout

when you're going, but I'll say goodbye now." She gets to her feet and presses a kiss to my head. "I love you, my darling girl. I'm so very proud of the person you are. So beautiful, so kind, and so damn smart. You make my entire world. I want you to know that. Without you, I'd be in perpetual darkness. You are my light in the darkest of hours." She gives me a soft smile and runs her hand along my jaw. "Have a good time with your dad, baby."

"I'll see you when I come home," I tell her, my heart bursting at her words. "I love you, Ma, always."

She closes her eyes, her hand pressing against her chest. "Always, my baby. Down to my bones."

As she makes her way up the stairs, I can't help but have hope in my heart that maybe, just maybe, she's on the mend and the new medication is helping her find a way out of the fog she's been in.

I hear her moving around upstairs and leave it ten minutes before I shout, "Ma, I'm going now." I'll hide in my room for the evening. I'll let her have some alone time, but I'll not be going to Dad's.

"Have fun, baby," she yells down to me. "Love you."

"Love you too." I walk to the door and quickly open and close it, giving Ma the impression that I've gone. I quietly make my way up the stairs and step into my room, careful not to make a sound. I don't want to disturb Ma. I climb onto my bed and reach for my book. I'll read. That way, I'm not disturbing her or making any sounds.

I'm so engrossed in my book that I don't notice that it's been over an hour since I settled on my bed and started to read. I frown, sitting up and listening out for noise. I haven't heard Ma make a single noise since I climbed the stairs. I thought for sure I'd hear the bath running, but even that hasn't happened. My gut twists, and I have a sickening feeling. Placing my book down on the nightstand, I rise to my feet.

Walking out of my room, I notice just how eerily quiet everything is. There's not a single sound. Has Ma fallen back to sleep? My heart beats faster as I make my way towards my ma's room, calling out her name with a growing panic in my voice. "Ma? Are you okay?" But my words are met with silence. Pushing open her bedroom door, my heart shatters and my stomach drops as I see her lying motionless on the bed. Her eyes are wide open and unfocused, staring blankly at me. My stomach drops as I spot the bloodied knife on the floor beside her. With trembling hands, I rush to her side. Then I notice it—the deep gash on her wrist that has left a trail of crimson across the pristine white sheets. Tears spring to my eyes as I realise what has happened. She's killed herself.

"Ma," I cry, dropping to my knees beside the bed, clutching at her arm. She's still warm. God, she's still warm. I stagger to my feet and run to my bedroom before grabbing my phone and calling for an ambulance. "Ma," I cry as I race to her room. "I'm going to get you help," I promise her. "We'll get you help. It'll be okay."

The woman on the line is sweet and comforting as she takes all the details that I can give her. "Lisa, the ambulance is minutes out. Hang on; they'll be with you soon. You've done amazingly. Is the door unlocked for them?"

I grasp Ma's cold, lifeless hand in a desperate attempt to bring her back. "It's unlocked," I cry out, my voice shaking with fear and panic.

"That's good. They'll be there any minute," the woman on the phone reassures me, but all I can hear are the distant sirens growing louder and closer. My stomach churns with knots as I realise how serious this is.

"She's not waking up," I whisper, my heart racing. "She's warm but she's not waking up."

"They've arrived," she tells me. "Your mam is in good hands, Lisa. The paramedics are going to do everything they can to save her. Is there someone you need to call?"

"No," I say, trying to hold back my tears as I hear the front door open. "They're here. Thank you."

"You did amazing," she repeats before I hang up.

I step back, my mind going numb as the paramedics rush into the room. I press myself against the wall, sliding down until I'm sitting on the floor. Tears stream down my face uncontrollably as they place paddles on her chest and start shocking her body. Each jolt causes her to convulse violently, but there's no response from her. My thoughts race, trying to make sense of what's happening.

But then it hits me—she's gone. She's really gone.

How could this have happened? She was happy today. She was finally happy. How did this happen?

Did I do something wrong?

Guilt and self-blame consume me as I watch helplessly while the paramedics shake their heads in defeat. In that moment, my world shatters and everything becomes a blur.

How will I go on without her?

CHAPTER TWO

LISA

"Sweetheart," Dad says as he wraps me in his arms, Ma's blood coating my clothes.

I lost it when she was brought into the hospital. I didn't want them to take her from me. I didn't want to be alone. I practically jumped onto the gurney, wanting to be with her. I can't wrap my head around the fact she's gone. That she's never coming back. How do I carry on? She was my ma. I loved her so very much and now I'll never see her again.

"It's going to be okay," Dad promises me.

But I don't believe him. How can it be okay? Ma's not here. What happens next?

"What did you say, sweetheart?" he asks, and I realise I said my words out loud.

"What happens next?" I say. My voice sounds hoarse and it makes me wince.

"You'll be with me," he says roughly. "God, sweetheart, I'm so sorry."

"I don't want to go with you," I say evenly. My heart is broken. "I want Ma."

His arms tighten around me, painfully so, but I welcome it. "I know, baby, I know. I wish she were here."

"Please, Dad, please don't make me come with you."

I can't bear the thought of being around him and Tanya. Not today, not right now. I just can't deal with it. My breathing starts to deepen and my vision begins to blur as I struggle to breathe. The thought of being stuck with them both while my ma is lying in the morgue hurts me.

"It's just me, sweetheart. I promise it's just me." He presses a kiss to my head, rocking me in his arms. "I swear to you, Lisa, it's just going to be me."

I nod. "Okay," I cry against his chest. "Okay."

He doesn't release me. He continues to hold me, to rock me, whispering that everything will be okay. I wish I could believe him. I wish I could trust him. But I don't. I feel so numb and so broken. I don't know what to do.

It takes a while but Dad leads me from the hospital and into his car. I look out the window, watching as the city of Dublin passes us by, but I don't see any of it. My mind is replaying images of Ma lying so lifeless on the bed, blood covering her bedding from where she bled out.

Tears leak from my eyes as I realise that she lay dying while I was reading. Had I checked on her earlier, I could have saved her. I think that guilt will stay with me forever. I could have saved her. I should have.

"We're home," Dad says.

I flinch at his words. No, this isn't home, not my home. Then I realise I no longer have a home. Ma's gone, and so is everything I once knew.

The car door opens and Dad's there, helping me out and putting his arm around me. He steers me into the apartment, not letting me go.

Entering the apartment, I feel a sense of dread. I hate this apartment, this is where dad moved to when he left our home to live with his mistress. Anger rises through me. God, I don't want to be here.

"How could you bring me back here?" I demand, my voice trembling with emotion. "This is not my home. This will never be my home."

Dad's expression softens, guilt flickering in his eyes. "I know this is difficult, Lisa. But we need to stick together now more than ever. Your mother wouldn't want us falling apart like this."

"My mother is dead because of you!" I scream, the words tearing out of me like lave erupting from a volcano. "You left her for another woman, and now she's gone. How am I supposed to go on without her?" I ask, my eyes burning with tears.

Dad winces, taking a step back as if my words physically struck him. "I made mistakes, Lisa, terrible mistakes that I'll never be able to take back. But I loved your mother. I love you. Please, let me try to make things right."

I shake my head, the tears flowing freely now. "You can't fix this, Dad. You can't bring her back. You can't erase the pain you caused by cheating, by being so vile to threaten her with taking me away from her. Now she's gone and I'll never see her again."

He reaches out a hand tentatively, as though afraid I might reject his touch. After a moment's hesitation, I allow him to hold me. "We'll get through this together," he says softly, his voice filled with sincerity. "I'll do everything I can to help you heal, to help us heal together."

I look into his eyes and see the genuine remorse etched in them. Despite the anger and hurt raging within me, a small part of me longs to believe him. I have no other choice. He's all that I have left.

With a heavy sigh, I nod, acknowledging his words. "I don't know if I can forgive you, Dad," I admit, my voice barely above a whisper. "But I'll try."

He pulls me into a hug, holding me close as we stand in the hallway, not having gotten any further into the apartment. "Thank you, Lisa," he murmurs, his voice trembling with emotion. "We'll take it one day at a time."

He rocks me in his arms, just as he did in the hospital. But a sudden crash startles us both. We break apart, and Dad rushes toward the noise. I'm right behind him, wondering what the hell happened.

I skid to a halt in the living room, my heart racing and my eyes wide as I stare at my dad in disbelief. "You lied," I accuse, my words void of emotion. I should have known he was lying. Of course he wouldn't have gotten rid of his whore. My gaze moves to the floor beside Tanya's feet. My stomach clenches as I see a picture frame shattered to pieces. Gingerly, I move forward, reaching out for it.

"Lisa, sweetheart," Dad says softly. "I'll clean it up. Why don't you go on upstairs and rest?"

I ignore his words and lift the picture frame from the floor. I already know which photo lies inside. One of me, my dad, and my ma. It was a picture taken on our last Christmas together—the very last Christmas that I spent with my ma. I spin the frame in my hands and see the picture is still there. Thankfully, it's not destroyed, but the frame is. I clutch the picture to my chest.

God, I miss her. I miss my ma. I can't believe she's gone. How on earth am I supposed to carry on without her? She was my best friend.

"Why?" I ask, my eyes moving to Tanya, whose arms are wrapped around my dad. "Why would you do this?"

She shakes her head, feigning innocence. "I didn't mean to. I was cleaning. I hadn't expected you and your father to be home yet."

"You're not meant to be here," I say. "Why are you here?"

A furrow forms between her brows. "This is my home. This is where I live. Why wouldn't I be here?" she asks, acting and sounding as though she's confused.

I turn my gaze to my dad, whose cheeks are red and his eyes filled with remorse. "I'm sorry, Lisa. I thought she was staying with her parents this evening."

"What?" Tanya says, rocking back on her heels. "You wanted me out of the apartment? Why, Ben? Why would you want me gone?"

"This isn't about you, Tanya," Dad says, running his hand over his face. "Lisa's just lost her mam. She's going through a lot and we all know that the two of you don't get along."

Tanya folds her arms over her chest and starts to tap her foot. "I'm not leaving," she snarls.

I roll my eyes. Of course she's not. I don't bother to talk; I just walk out of the room and up the stairs. I hear Dad calling after me, but I don't look behind me. I don't want to talk to him. I don't want to listen to any more of the lies. I can't do it right now.

I close my bedroom door behind me and climb onto the bed, staring up at the ceiling. My mind is spinning with a whirlwind of emotions, each one crashing into the next like waves against the shore. The image of my mother lying so still in her bed, her wrist slit hits me and nausea crawls up my throat. I could have saved her, I could have stopped it, instead, I was oblivious, lost in a book, and she bleed out. Guilt gnaws at me from the inside out, a relentless beast clawing at my heart.

I clutch the picture frame to my chest, feeling the jagged broken glass pressing against my skin. The photograph inside shows a happier time, a snapshot of a family that no longer exists. Something I'll never get back.

My body trembles as tears cascade down my cheeks, soaking the collar of my shirt. I gasp for breath between silent sobs, feeling an overwhelming sense of loneliness and uncertainty. As I struggle to stay afloat in the depths of despair, I can't help but wonder if there is any hope of escape from this drowning feeling.

"She's not eating, she's not drinking, she's not talking," Dad growls. "She needs help."

"What will people say?" Tanya hisses. "God, Ben, it's bad enough that we've got to listen to people gossip about her mother; the last thing we need is for them to talk about her daughter."

They're speaking as though I'm not here. I hate it. God, I hate her talking about my ma.

"She's catatonic, Tanya," Dad snaps. "This isn't her fault. Her mam's just died."

"Yeah, and had you been man enough, your daughter wouldn't have been the one to find her. Instead, you're too lenient on her. You allowed her to disrespect not only you, but me, and you let her tell you that she wasn't coming here."

"Enough," Dad roars, his voice trembling with anger. "Enough. I'm calling the doctor. She needs help."

I continue to stare up at the ceiling. The numbness I've been feeling has intensified into a fog that seems to blanket me entirely. I can't find the strength to even lift a finger and say something in my defense. Not that I would want to speak to either of them anyway. I just wish they'd leave me alone. I just want to be left alone. I hear Dad leave my room, talking loudly on his cell as he does.

"Are you going crazy like your mam did?" Tanya asks with laughter in her voice. "I think you might be. It's time for you to realise that you're not the most important person in your father's life. In fact, you wouldn't be here right now had your mam not killed herself."

God, I hate this woman. I have no idea what my dad sees in her. I really don't.

"The world would be a better place without either you or your mam in it. You should really do something about that," she taunts.

The sound of the bedroom door opening doesn't faze me. Nothing does right now.

"Ben, she's still the same. She hasn't moved since she came up to bed last night. What did the doctor say?" Tanya asks. God, she's good. She's really good. This act she's got going on would fool anyone. For a second there she actually sounded like she gave a fuck about me.

"He's on his way. He feels as though she needs sleep. He's hoping the sleeping pills he'll prescribe will help her."

Don't they understand that nothing will help?

"Lisa," I hear a deep voice say a while later, but I don't answer. I can't. I'm drowning and there's no way out. "I'm James, a doctor. Can you turn to face me?"

I continue to gaze up at the ceiling.

"I understand that you've gone through something traumatic and you're struggling. I have some sleeping pills here that'll help you sleep. I want you to just take one. They're strong and will put you to sleep almost right away. Can you do that for me?"

Hope blooms inside of me. If they're that strong, will they take me away from here and let me see my ma again? I don't want to be here if it means being around Dad and Tanya. I want my ma. I slowly nod my head.

"Okay, that's good. I'll leave the pills on the nightstand. I urge you to eat," he says, his hand resting on my shoulder. "If she doesn't change by morning after taking the pill, we may have to admit her."

"Admit her where?" Dad asks, confusion evident in his voice.

"To a psychiatric facility," the doctor says cautiously. "Will you follow me out?" he asks. "I'll be able to give you more details. I'd rather not speak in front of Lisa."

I hear the shuffling of their footsteps as they make their way out of my bedroom. They close the door behind them, and I feel relief. A sense of calmness washes over me as I sit up in the bed and reach for the bottle of sleeping pills. This is it. I can sleep and finally be rid of this numbness and pain.

I twist the cap off the bottle and let the pills fall into my hand. They're small white capsules that seem to hold the promise of escape. Without hesitation, I toss them into my mouth and swallow, before grabbing the glass of water and washing them down.

It takes a little longer than I had anticipated for them to kick in, but it's okay. I can wait.

I'm not sure how much time passes until the heaviness of sleep starts to settle over me like a comforting blanket wrapping me in darkness. As my eyelids grow heavy, I lie on the bed, closing my eyes in anticipation of the relief that awaits.

But as I drift into unconsciousness, a flicker of doubt crosses my mind. *Is this really the answer?*

I hear my bedroom door opening and my dad screaming at Tanya. I feel his hands on my body, shaking me. "Baby, please. No, baby, not you too. Please, Lisa, please don't leave me."

But it's too late. The darkness claims me, and I can't help but feel relief as it does.

CHAPTER
THREE
MAVERICK

My gaze lingers on my sister's battered figure as I try to wrap my head around why she didn't tell me about this. I can see the purplish-blue marks marbling her skin, from her neck down to her legs. Her face is a criss-cross of bruises, one eye is swollen shut, and purple splotches cover her cheeks and jawline. Not a single feature remains untouched by the violence done to her.

We're at our parents home, Callie's seated on the armchair beside the fire, it's always been the chair she uses whenever she's home. It's an oversized armchair that makes my sister look small, even more so today than usual.

"Why didn't you tell me?" I ask, trying to tamp down my anger. It's not directed at her. Never at her.

Tears well up in her eyes as she finally meets my gaze. "I didn't want you to worry," she whispers, her voice barely above a breath. "I thought I could handle it on my own." She gives me a shaky smile, but her eyes are filled with so much pain that it doesn't ease my worry.

Callie is more than just my sister; she's my twin. I'd do anything to protect her. Knowing that she's been beaten and this isn't the first time... it kills me. I want to find that asshole, Keith, and put him six feet under. Never, not fucking ever, have I felt so useless. I should have seen the signs. I should have known that something was happening to her. She's my fucking sister, for Christ's sake. My twin. Why on earth did this go on for as long as it did?

"I never liked that fucker," Stephen growls.

I glare at him. This isn't the time nor the place for this shit. I don't care if he's a natural born killer without a heart. The fucker will watch what he says around my sister. She doesn't need us to add more pain onto her.

"I didn't," he says nonchalantly. "He was an asshole. But that remains moot at this stage. How long has it been going on, Callie?" he questions, and the darkness in his voice has my sister shivering. This is who he is, who he's always been. But if anyone knows that, Callie does. She's his best friend. She gave him a home when he didn't have one, even at the age of five. She was always the light in the darkness for Stephen.

"Callie?" Da says, and unlike Stephen, there's no anger in his voice, just absolute devastation.

My da loves his kids. He'll do whatever it takes to ensure we're safe. Finding out that Callie's been in an abusive relationship has rocked him. He feels like he's failed her. Just as I do.

"I'm sorry, Da," she says, her tears falling thick and fast.

He shakes his head. "Nothing to be sorry about, Callie girl. Not a thing. Are you safe?"

She nods. "Yes. I told him it was over and he flew into a rage."

I'm going to kill him. I don't give a fuck; I'll do the time if it comes to it. There's not a chance this asshole is going to get away with hurting my sister. No way in hell.

"How long?" Stephen asks once again.

Callie takes a deep breath. She presses her hands against the arms of the chair and sits up taller, wincing as she does. Pain floods her expression. "It's over," she whispers. "Let it be."

I shake my head. "Callie," I say gently, "you can

barely move. Don't tell us to let it be. How long has he been hurting you?"

"I don't know," she replies, her voice soft and barely above a whisper. "It was fine at the beginning. I know he was worried about our age difference being a factor, but when Mam and Da didn't force me to stop seeing him, he changed. By the time things got bad, I was too far in. I couldn't see a way out."

I bow my head, my gaze on my feet, my jaw clenched tight. Christ, that motherfucker... He did everything he could to ensure he had her right where he wanted her. I hate that she couldn't see a way out. She had so many people who would have helped her, who'd have dropped everything and been at her side. But that motherfucker had her so messed up that she couldn't see the family who loved her, and therefore she couldn't reach out. He had her so scared she had no one to turn to until it was too late.

"You'll stay here," Mam says, rising to her feet. She's been silent since we all sat down. "You'll be safe here."

Callie's gaze turns to me and I see the plea in her eyes. She can't stay here. While we love our mam, she's crazy and will hover over Callie and drive her to the brink. "Mam, Callie wants me to stay with her for a while."

Mam's eyes flash with anger and indignation. "Not happening!" she shrieks. "That won't be happening."

"Yes, it will," I tell her.

Mam shakes her head, her gaze moving to my da. "Eric, you have to do something," Mam says. "You can't let this happen."

"Nic," Da sighs as he rises to his feet and pulls Mam into his arms.

"No," she says angrily. "They're eighteen. This isn't happening."

"Nic, Maverick's been gone for months and Callie moved out three months ago. Callie will be safe with him," Da assures her. I know that he'll be at the apartment every day checking on her. "Trust Mav. He won't let anything happen to her."

Mam presses her lips together. She's not happy, but right now, I don't care. Callie needs space and time to heal. She won't be able to do that with Mam hovering. "Fine, but I am not okay with this."

"We know," Stephen drawls. "But, Nichola, they're growing up and need space."

Her eyes narrow at Stephen, and I see Callie try her hardest not to laugh. "Stephen Maguire, are you trying to insinuate that my children need space from me?"

Stephen doesn't try to hide his laughter. He sits back and grins at her. "Never," he lies.

"When are you taking her home?" Da asks.

"Tonight," I tell him. "She'll have time to rest and recuperate."

He nods. "That'll give your ma some time to be with her before you leave."

Callie flashes me a grateful smile and turns to Mam. "I'm hungry. Is there any soup?" she asks, knowing it'll calm Mam's ass down and she'll get on to making some food for her, not to mention everyone else.

Three Weeks Later

I PULL into the parking spot out front of Callie's apartment and climb out of my car, my gaze moving to the girl who's sitting on the bench across the street. Whenever I come to Callie's, she's here. She doesn't do anything; she just sits down with a book and reads. She looks lonely and broken. I've asked Callie about her, but she doesn't know who she is. All she does know is that she lives across the street in the other apartment complex.

I don't know why the girl caught my attention. It could be the fact that she looks so broken. Her eyes have huge dark circles around them, her cheeks are hollow, and her posture is slumped, as if the weight of the world rests squarely on her shoulders. She's reading a book and seems to have no idea that someone's watching her. Is she oblivious to all that's around her?

No. Her shoulders stiffen and she holds herself tighter. She definitely knows I'm here, and she doesn't like it. That's fair enough. I can't blame her. She's a kid.

I lock my car and make my way into Callie's apartment. It's a good apartment in a great part of the city, and as such it's worth a lot of money. Callie doesn't own it; she rents it, and as the owner is a friend of my da's, he's renting it at a reduced price to her.

"Mav," Callie sighs as I enter her apartment. She's sitting on the sofa, her laptop on her knees as she works. "I'm fine. You don't have to keep turning up. It's been weeks. I'm fine."

I lift my shoulders and shrug. "Never said you weren't," I reply. "Can't I drop by your apartment?"

"If you must," she says, turning back to her laptop and refocusing on work.

When we turned eighteen, our da gave us a pub each. He owns a lot of real estate and wanted to give us a chance to have something we could sell or work to make better. Callie and I both took different avenues with the pubs we were given. I sold mine and made a small fortune, which I've since invested with the help of Da (the man knows the stock market like no one else), whereas Callie has turned her pub into a thriving success. She's got the head for the business side of owning bars and she's turning a great profit on it. Da's encouraging her to purchase another bar. It's something I know she's interested in and is currently looking at to see if it's feasible.

"Callie, it's my God-given right to annoy the ever-loving fuck out of you whenever the hell I want."

She rolls her eyes, but I see the small smile playing on her lips. "Whatever. I hope you're buying dinner."

I chuckle. "If I must."

She nods adamantly. "You must. Now shoo, go do something. I'm working."

It's been a few weeks since we found out that Keith was abusing her and she's slowly getting back to herself. It's going to take a while, but she's not alone and we're making sure Keith stays the fuck away from her. He hasn't turned up at her apartment but he has been messaging her. His messages are all the same: he loves her, he's not letting her go, and he's coming back for her once she comes to her senses. There's not a fucking chance in hell that he will. I won't let him touch her. Not again. Never again.

A few hours later, we settle down to watch Gladiator, our stomachs full from dinner. Halfway through the movie, I swear I start to smell smoke. My brows knit together as I try to figure out where the hell the smell is coming from. Rising to my feet, I stalk through the apartment, looking to see where the fire is.

As I approach the front door, I see thick grey smoke billowing through the cracks. My eyes sting and my throat tightens from the acrid smell. There's a fog of smoke in front of me.

My stomach churns with dread as I know in my gut that Keith has caused this disastrous scene. I run back to the den to get Callie. Her eyes are wide with terror as I approach.

"Mav?" she whispers, her voice filled with fear.

"We've got to go," I tell her as I grab her arm. She comes willingly and I keep her close. Edging out of the den, I'm shocked to see flames licking the walls and floor of the sitting room. Christ, I need to get her out of here. Fuck.

"Cover your mouth and keep a hold of me," I shout over the crackling sound of flames. The smoke grows thicker, making it difficult to see where the hell I'm going. I try my hardest not to panic, knowing that if I do, it'll make Callie panic, and right now, we need to get out of here, so I can't afford to let that fear set in.

Callie coughs, her eyes wide as she nods frantically.

"Don't let go," I tell her, and I feel her hand clenching my tee tighter.

Thankfully, the fire seems to be by the window and not the front door, meaning we have a slither of a chance of getting out of here without being caught by the flames. The heat is intense, scorching our skin even though we're away from the flames.

My lungs are burning and my eyes stinging as I try to breathe, but the smoke is so thick, so powerful, that it's difficult. I splutter and choke while trying to exit the apartment. Thankfully, we're able to escape from the inferno.

"We need to let everyone know to escape," Callie says through her coughs. "Mav, we need to get everyone out." Her eyes are wide and her body is trembling. She's scared, so fucking terrified. I can't look at her. Seeing her so petrified makes me want to track that motherfucker down and kill him.

She's right. We start to bang on doors, getting everyone out of the building before the inferno takes over the entire structure.

The second we're out of the apartment complex, we're gasping for breath, sucking in as much oxygen as we can get. I hear sirens wailing in the distance and know that we were fucking lucky to escape that. If I hadn't smelled the smoke, who knows if we would have made it out alive?

"What happened?" Callie whispers, her eyes filled with tears as she burrows against me, her hand clenching my tee once again. "Mav, what happened?"

I glance away, hating the tears that are falling unchecked down her face. "I don't know," I say, but I'm lying. We both know I am. "We're going to find out. First, we need to get you checked out."

I hear her sharp intake of breath. She hates the hospital. But she needs to go. I want to ensure that she's okay. Once she's in the hospital, I'll be making a stop at Jer's. This shit has gone on for too long. It ends now.

Screw the promise I made Mam. She'll get over it eventually. Callie's more important than that, and if nothing is done about this asshole, he's going to continue to hurt her until he eventually kills her.

CHAPTER
FOUR
MAVERICK

I'VE BEEN SITTING on a shitty chair in Callie's hospital room for two hours when my phone starts ringing, giving me an excuse to stretch my legs. Mam and Da are here too, neither of them willing to leave. The second I called them from the ambulance, they rushed to the hospital. Both freaked the fuck out, and Mam was crying when she arrived. Thankfully, Da calmed her down before she went into Callie's room. Callie's got smoke inhalation and is currently asleep with an oxygen mask on to help with her breathing.

"Yeah?" I answer as I exit the room.

"You were right," Jer says. "We got the footage and Keith was the one who started the fire."

I fucking knew it. That motherfucker. The cameras outside of Callie's apartment building have caught that bastard setting the fire. I fucking knew it was him.

"You have a choice, Maverick. You can stay with Callie at the hospital or you can come with me, Butch, and Stephen," Jer says.

I'm not surprised my uncle Butch is also present. Jer is Mam's brother and he runs the Houlihan Gang, whereas Butch is Da's brother and he is the President of the Dublin chapter of the Devil Falcons Motorcycle Club. Both men are involved in criminal activities, despite neither Mam nor Da being involved, and both are extremely close to Callie and I. Jer even more so than Butch.

"My car's at Callie's and I'm at the hospital," I tell him.

"This mean you're joining me?" he asks, and I know he's talking about joining the gang, not just for tonight. The was a rule Jer put in place years ago. I wouldn't be inducted into the gang unless I wanted to, but if I were to ever purposefully kill someone it would mean that I'd join instantly. No if's, but's, or maybes. I always promised mam that I'd not join Jer's business.

"Yes," I say roughly. It means going against the promise I made, but fuck, I don't care. I will do whatever the hell it takes to ensure that Callie's safe.

"I'll be at the hospital in thirty. Be waiting. Stephen

has a location on Keith," Jer tells me. "Tonight, we're going to make sure this fucker can't get to Callie again."

"See you in ten minutes," I tell him and end the call. I take a deep breath, steadying myself. Today starts a new chapter, one that I'm not entirely sure I'm ready for. But I have no choice. It's now or never and I've chosen now.

"I'm going to head back to Callie's and get my car. I'll swing by again in the morning," I tell my da as I re-enter Callie's hospital room.

He watches me carefully, thankfully not saying anything about the call I've just had, and nods his head. "Is Emmanuel coming to get you or do you need a ride?"

Emmanuel is my best friend; has been since we were kids. His mam and my aunt Patricia are also best friends. It was inevitable that we'd end up being close. "He's coming," I lie. "I'll be back at nine."

He gives me another nod before closing his eyes. I step out of the room as quietly as I can, not wanting to disturb them any more than I already have. The moment I exit the building, I see Jer's car idling at the kerb. I slide into the backseat as Butch is sitting in the front passenger's seat. I grin when I see Stephen sitting beside me. I was sure that we'd be meeting him wherever the hell we're going, but I guess not.

"How is she?" Butch asks, his voice rough and gravelly.

"Asleep," I say evenly. "She's got an oxygen mask on to help with her breathing. She should be able to go home tomorrow."

"Thank fucking Christ you were there tonight, Mav," Butch says thickly. "Who knows what would have happened had you not been."

It doesn't bear thinking about. Right now, we need to focus on Keith and what we're going to do to that motherfucker.

"Where is he hiding?" I ask, needing to know.

"He's in Malahide," Stephen grunts. "Fucker's living it up while trying to kill Callie. Motherfucker."

Malahide is a posher part of Dublin county. The fucker has money, that's for sure. I'm wondering if he's using his parents' wealth to fund his fucked up lifestyle. Hell, do his parents know that he's an abusive asshole?

"What about his parents?" I ask, reaching for my phone and turning it off. The last thing I need is to be traced back to this motherfucker's place.

"Dead. They died years ago. They were filthy rich and left him the house along with some serious cash,"

Jer tells us. I guess it's not just Stephen who's been looking into this fucker; Jer has too. "He's burned through the majority of that cash, mostly through gambling and drugs."

What a useless bastard. "Has he done this before Callie?" I question, wondering if it's a pattern with him. Surely a man like that doesn't just start abusing women. He must have done this before.

"There are no reports with the Gardai, and from everything I've uncovered, he's managed to keep out of trouble for the most part," Jer snarls. "It doesn't mean shit. We all know that it's easy to keep out of trouble as long as you're smart about doing so."

Jer and Butch would know more than anyone. They're both in their late forties and have never been arrested. Hell, they've never had any charges brought up against them despite the work they do.

The rest of the journey is filled with Jer and Butch bouncing ideas around of what they intend to do to Keith once they get their hands on him. Little do they know, I'll be the one killing the fucker.

We arrive at Keith's house and see that his lights are on. It infuriates me that he's at home acting as though he's done nothing wrong. Fucker almost killed my sister and he's at home chilling. Fucking bastard.

It's after two in the morning. It's dark and no one's

around. It doesn't take us long to enter the fucker's home. There's loud music playing and Butch mutters a curse. "Fucker needs to get some taste in music. This is shite."

I move through the house, noting the rubbish lying around everywhere, from newspapers to takeout food. The man's house is a fucking sty. I have no idea how the hell he lives like this. I make my way to the living room and see that he's fast asleep on the sofa. The smell of smoke hits me as I get closer, and it takes every restraint that I have not to kick the fucker to wake him.

"Mav," I hear Jer yell, and I tread back through the house to locate him.

I see Butch at the bottom of the stairs and he nods his head toward the upper level. "You go on up. I'm going to wait here and make sure this fucker doesn't do a runner."

I take the stairs two at a time and when I reach the top landing, I see Jer and Stephen standing in a room. Both of them have the same murderous expression on their faces. "What?" I ask, wondering what's pissed them off.

Entering the room, my heart races as I glance around the walls. Every fucking inch of them has pictures of my sister. There's not a single space that isn't covered.

"Fuck," I say through clenched teeth as I edge closer to the table that's in the corner. It's got candles and pens on it. My jaw clenches even harder as I see that he's got even more pictures of her there. Some are of her in her underwear, taken at her apartment.

Motherfucker.

"He's going to die," I say slowly, my fists clenched. "He's going to suffer for what he's done to Callie."

Both Stephen and Jer nod solemnly. "He will."

"Then let's get this shit done," I grind out. "I want these pictures gone." I don't want anyone else seeing them. If Callie knew he had them, she'd freak the fuck out. That's not going to happen. She'll never know. They'll be gone and no one will know they were here.

"Butch's boys are going to torch this fucking place," Jer tells me as we move down the stairs. "That cunt is coming with us and we're going to make it look as though he was never here."

"We'll take him to the docks," I say, my gaze on the fucker still sleeping on the sofa.

"You got something planned, boy?" Butch asks with a grin. It makes the harsh, weathered lines on his face soften just a bit.

"Yep. This cunt has hurt my sister one too many

times. It ends today. He's going to be in for a world of hurt."

Stephen laughs. "Do you want to use my wood chipper?"

The man is notorious for the way he kills people. There are only a handful of people who know that the Eraser is Stephen, but everyone knows the myth of the Eraser and how he kills his victims—by using a wood chipper and mangling their bodies inside of it until there's nothing left of them but tiny fragments. Most of the time, of the time, his victims are alive as he feeds them to his favourite machine. He loves hearing their fearful screams as the blades of the wood chipper take them.

"No. What I have planned is something that will take time and I need the dock for when I'm finished."

I see the shock on all their faces. Jer's the first one to recover. He grins widely. "Alright, Mav, we'll head to the docks. Anything else you need?"

I shake my head. I saw a hacksaw when I entered the living room. I'll be bringing that with me when we leave. When I get started, Keith's going to be in a world of hurt. "You have somewhere at the docks where we won't be disturbed?"

This time, Jer's smile is huge. "Yup. Trust me, Mav, you can do whatever the fuck you want with him.

Have him make as much noise as you want. We won't be disturbed."

I feel my own smile grow at his words. Good.

Butch and Stephen grab Keith and carry him out of the house. The fucker is out for the count. He doesn't wake up to either of them lifting him. It doesn't take them long to get him into the boot of the car, and once again, we pile into the vehicle, with Jer driving. It usually takes about thirty minutes to get from Malahide to the docks, but it's late at night and there's hardly any traffic on the road, so we'll be there a hell of a lot quicker than that.

I rest my head against the seat and close my eyes. I'm calm, a hell of a lot calmer than I would have expected. I guess that'll come later.

KEITH'S WIDE AWAKE NOW, his eyes huge and filled with fear. I guess this is just a taste of what he put Callie through. "What..." he breathes. "What's going on?"

"Mav," Jer says, his voice filled with pride, "he's all yours."

We're in a secluded part of the docks, in a port-a-cabin, one that I assume Jer owns or has paid someone for the use of. There's clear cellophane on the floor, ready for me to unleash my anger. Keith didn't wake throughout the entire car ride here, but the moment Stephen and Butch threw him to the ground, he woke up and started shrieking like a banshee.

I grip the saw in my hand tighter, glaring at the motherfucker who put his hands on my sister, beat her bloody, and almost tried to kill her tonight. He should have stayed the fuck away from her. Had he done, he wouldn't be here right now.

"This is going to hurt," I say, surprised at the lack of emotion in my voice. I've thought about this day a lot, wondered what I'd do to him. I always thought I'd be angrier, that I'd be reckless, but I'm not. I feel in control. I know what I'm going to do to him. I bend down, my knees pressing into his side, and I hold out his arm. With the saw in hand, I begin to hack away.

He screams in agony as the saw bites into his flesh. I keep my knee planted in his side so he can't escape. The sound echoes through the cabin, bouncing off the metal walls. I don't falter; I keep my gaze on this fucker's arm.

"Christ," I hear Jer hiss. "I didn't expect this."

Stephen's laughter is loud. "We should have. It's always the quiet ones."

"Fucking proud as hell," Butch replies. "I can't

wait to watch the full show. You got any chairs around here, Jer?"

I hear metal scraping and know they have in fact found seats to watch the show.

"I should've done this years ago," I growl. "You should never have touched my sister."

The asshole beneath me writhes on the floor, begging for mercy, tears streaming down his face. "Please, Maverick. Please, I beg of you. I'll do anything, anything! Just let me go."

I ignore him and focus intently on the task at hand. The saw glitters wickedly in the dim light as it slices through skin and bone. Blood spurts from his limb, and I'm grateful for the cellophane. It catches everything. It takes me a while, but I manage to sever his arm from just above his elbow.

I move to his other arm and begin the process all over again. It's methodical, and I won't stop. It's quite soothing being able to hack away at the fucker's limbs. I'm covered in blood, as is the saw and the cellophane, but I don't give a fuck. I have a long way to go yet.

With a shaky hand, I manage to hack away the fucker's arms, legs, and head from his torso. The sound of bones snapping and flesh tearing echoes in my ears as I carry out my task with ruthless determination. It's not a pretty sight, nor is it clean, but I don't give a damn. It's done, and this cunt can never hurt my sister again.

My fingers are coated in slick, warm blood, but I feel a sense of satisfaction wash over me. This is something I never thought I could do, yet here I am, surprised by how calm and focused I feel. As I look at the lifeless body before me, I know that many would question if I am capable of such brutality. But they'd be wrong. I'll prove them wrong each and every time.

I stand up and wipe my hands on my jeans, trying to rid myself of some of the blood that now stains them. The scene around me is shocking, but it's a sight that the fucker deserved. No one else seems fazed by the carnage; they've all seen and participated in acts far worse than this.

"Hey, Butch," I call out to my uncle, "can you bring those heavy bricks over here?"

A round container sits nearby, ready to hold Keith's dismembered body. With the bricks at the bottom, we'll make sure the fucking thing sinks deep into the murky depths of the River Liffey—never to be found again.

Stephen crouches down to help with the heavy container, his muscles straining as he holds it steady while Butch carefully places three bricks inside. When it's finished, I don't hesitate to push Keith's dismembered body into the container. This part is a hell of a lot quicker than hacking away at him.

Jer offers me a bag and says, "Here. It's got fresh clothes inside. I always carry around a second set."

I make a mental note to remember this tip for future situations. Moving away from the blood-spattered ground, I quickly change into Jer's spare clothes while the other men start to clean up, carefully wrapping the cellophane and placing it in the container. I watch as they use super glue to seal the lid shut.

With my new clothes on, the four of us make our way outside and toward the edge of the dock where a small boat awaits us. We load the container onto the boat and Jer takes control, skilfully manoeuvring it out onto the river. In just a few minutes, he dumps the grisly contents of the container overboard. I watch with a grin as the container starts to sink beneath the water. By the time Jer reaches us back at the dock, the container is long gone and hopefully no one will ever find it.

"Let's get the fuck out of here," Jer says, slapping me on the back. "You did good today, Mav. Fucking proud of you, son."

I let his praise wash over me. I did what needed to be done and I'd do it all over again.

"Fucking clean," Butch says, laughing. "Nothing

left over for anyone to trace it back to you. That, my boy, is fucking genius. Well done."

I hear Stephen chuckle. "The Cleaner," he says. "Has a great fucking ring to it, wouldn't you say?"

I see both Jer and Butch nodding in agreement. I guess that's my moniker now. I can't lie and say I'm not thrilled. It's a great name, one that'll have people wondering about me. I hope to be as notorious as Stephen is, but if I'm not, that's all good. I did what I set out to do and that was make sure my sister is safe.

I'll always protect my family. No matter what.

CHAPTER
FIVE
LISA

I SIT CROSSED-LEGGED with my book in my hand listening to the cars go by. It's been seven days since I was released from the psychiatric facility; seven days since I walked back into my dad's home and watched that bitch pretend to give a crap about me.

When I woke up in a hospital bed, my body was extremely weak from my failed attempt to end my life. Anger simmered through me as I realised I was still alive, still trapped in this world that had caused me so much pain. My anger burned toward my dad, who had saved me, but also toward myself for not succeeding. But most of all, it burned toward Dad and Tanya, both of whom I'm forced to live with as I have no one else—neither care about me as much as I deserve.

Being here feels suffocating, like I'm drowning in

their insincerity and lack of empathy, and at the same time I feel alone, like there's no one, not one person, who can offer me a way out. My father cares more about his reputation than my wellbeing, and it shows in everything he does. He doesn't understand or seem to care about the pain and fog I'm in. He's only focused on what others may be thinking about the situation. And now, his overbearing concern means I can't even have my own medications without him monitoring every pill that goes into my mouth.

I'm trying hard, real hard to find a new path for myself, but it's so damn difficult. I find myself tripping over and falling right back to square one. I'm struggling to breathe, struggling to cope with the loss of Ma and the life I once knew. I have no idea how the hell I'm going to continue, but I have no other choice.

The home I have to be in is a living nightmare. Every day, I wake up and wish I could be transported to anywhere else, someplace far away from here. This should be my home, but instead it feels like a prison. Dad and Tanya have made sure of that.

I feel completely out of place, like an unwanted guest in their home. Tanya's disdain for me is crystal clear and her constant snide remarks make me feel like a burden. But I have nowhere else to go and she shows no signs of leaving. We're stuck with one another.

THE CLEANER

The doctors are concerned for my wellbeing, even though I am numbed by the medications they've prescribed. Antidepressants are what's keeping me going; they've lifted the fog somewhat. And twice a week, I sit and talk to Maura, my therapist. She's kind and understanding, never once making me feel stupid for the overwhelming emotions I experience. She knows that coming back to live with Dad and Tanya has only added to my struggles. She has spoken to my dad multiple times about the negative impact of having Tanya around, but he refuses to listen and she remains in our home. That's why I spend most of my time outside.

During my hospitalization, I talked at length about my guilt and anger over my mother's death. The regret eats away at me every day; I should have seen the signs, done something to help her before it was too late. Maura is helping me work through these feelings, assuring me that the anger is natural and will eventually subside so I can fully grieve. But I don't know if I'm ready for that yet. The pain already consumes me; I don't know if I can handle any more. Maura explained that my mother had been battling depression for years and sometimes it's hard to find the right help or escape the fog that surrounds you. In the end, my mother found her only way out: death.

I understand that struggle all too well. My lows are so deep and dark, it's hard to see any light at all. They swallow me whole, leaving me drowning in a sea of despair. I know how my mother felt, or at least I think I do. But I'm determined to find a way out of this darkness, for both my sake and my mother's memory.

My love for reading is what's become my safe haven. I've always enjoyed having my head stuck in a good story, being able to transport myself to another world and forget everything and be able to just be. I was scared when Maura gave me a book at the facility I was in; scared that it would bring back so many memories and guilt, but it didn't. Instead, I could breathe a little freer, knowing that I could escape into a new world and not think about anything for just a little while.

I hear heavy footsteps moving toward me and I pull back from my thoughts. Dad's here. I can tell by the heavy gait of his steps. He's always been a loud walker. Every day, he'll find me outside when he returns back from work. It's become a routine. One that's stupid. I'd rather he just stay in the apartment and leave me be. But he's all about pretences, and being seen sitting with me makes him look good to anyone watching.

"You're going to get cold out here," Dad says as he

takes a seat beside me. "Why are you always outside, Lisa?"

"Where else am I to go? I'm not allowed further than this bench, remember?" I say with a raised brow as I turn to look at him. "That was the rule you set the day I came home from the hospital, right?"

I watch as his brows furrow and he takes a deep breath. "I get the anger. You're pissed that you're here. But, sweetheart, you're my daughter."

Anger whips through me, and I'm surprised by it. Over the past week, I've yet to feel anything other than a complete numbness. I thought the medication I'm on had stunted my emotions.

"Only when it suits you, right?" I fire back. This man shouldn't get into this right now. I'm so angry that I won't be able to control my words, and if what happened the last time I was angry at him is anything to go by, I'm going to hurt his feelings.

"What's that supposed to mean?" he questions, his voice low and filled with confusion.

"Tell me, Dad, when was the last time you put me first? I mean, you tell me I'm your daughter, but you don't care about me. If you could, you would have had me stay in that damn hospital, wouldn't you?"

He rears back almost as though I've slapped him. "No."

I laugh. "I'm not deaf, no matter what you and that whore of yours think. I have perfectly good hearing. I heard everything the two of you said while I was lying in that hospital bed."

"Lisa, sweetheart, I didn't—"

I shake my head. "Don't," I snap. "Don't, okay. I don't want to hear your apologies or hear you say you didn't mean it. Everything that's happened is because of you and your need to break everyone who loved you. Honestly, *Ben*, if I could, I'd be long gone from here. I hate you and I hate that bitch of yours. You've both destroyed my life."

"Where would you go?" he asks, and it once again solidifies everything I've been feeling. He doesn't care about me. I'm truly wondering if he ever did.

"Don't worry about it, *Ben*," I say in disgust. "You'll get your wish soon enough."

He and Tanya have no idea that over the past week I've slowly been stealing money from them. Is it right? No. But I need it. I'm going to escape this awful place and go somewhere I can be free.

"That's not my wish," he says thickly. "I don't know why you believe that I don't love or care for you. I do. Everything I do is for you."

I scoff. Is this man on drugs? "For me? No, everything you do is for Tanya. I hate her, Dad, and I hate being around her, but you chose her. So no, you don't care about me. If you did, you'd want me to be in a safe and happy place. Not with some woman who asked if I was crazy like my ma. Not a bitch who laughed at me when I cried because I was alive. Not a whore who has men coming and going from the apartment every day. You care about yourself and about Tanya. You're a good liar, Ben; so good, I think you've made yourself believe your own lies."

"Lisa," he says sternly, his voice trembling with anger. "How dare you?" he growls. "After everything we've done for you. We've given you a home, a safe place to live, and this is how you repay us? By making up stories to try and tear us apart?"

I stare at him with so much disgust and contempt that he turns away. I'm done. I'm so done. He's proven time and time again that I'm not someone he cares for. What's that saying? *'When someone shows you who they are, believe them.'* Well, Ben has shown me too many times for me to not believe him.

"I'm not hungry," I tell him as I return back to my book. I don't want to talk anymore. It's not productive at all and it just makes me despise my dad even more.

He stays seated for a while longer. I can feel his heated gaze on me but I don't stop reading.

I think I've read the same three lines over and over

again. My mind isn't computing what the words are conveying. But I won't look up. I won't give him that decency.

Thankfully, he rises to his feet and moves away from me. I release a long breath and blink away the tears that are forming. God, why is everything going wrong in my life?

It takes a few moments, but I'm able to gather myself together and continue reading. I only have an hour or so left before it gets dark and I'll have to go inside.

"THERE YOU ARE," Tanya says as I enter the apartment a while later. It's dark out now and it's getting chilly. I didn't bring a jacket or blanket with me so I've had to retreat into the apartment.

"Here I am," I reply deadpan.

She purses her lips together, the disdain for me evident on her face. "Your father told me about your little conversation. I didn't think you were stupid," she says snidely. "Telling your father about the men I bring home... Tut-tut, you are a naughty girl."

I roll my eyes. God, she's so dramatic. "Worried the

money will dry up if he uncovers just how much of a whore you truly are?"

Her blue eyes flash with anger. "Listen here, you stupid brat. Your father and I have a complex relationship. You will not ruin that. In fact, having a daughter as pathetic as you has really bonded your father and I together. You're useless, just like your mam was. It's time you realised that. You are a nobody. If it weren't for your father and I, you'd be dead, but we all know we'd be better off if you were."

"Well tough shit, bitch," I fire back, trying my hardest to not let her know that her words have affected me. "You're stuck with me now and there's nothing you can do about it. I'm going to enjoy making your life a fucking misery."

The smile she has is anything but sweet. "That's where you're wrong, sweetie," she says, her voice saccharine sweet. "You are going to die. In fact, you're going to do what you wanted to do weeks ago. But tonight, you're going to do it right." She walks toward her purse, which is lying on the side table, and I watch as she pulls out a length of rope. "This will do the job correctly."

She pushes the rope into my hands. "What?" I ask, horrified. She can't be serious. Surely not?

"You failed. If your father hadn't come into your room when he did, you'd have been dead. Now, he's gone and he'll be gone for a few hours. Use it, Lisa, and use it well. I never want to see your face again. You don't deserve love. You're a bitch who's taking up everyone's time. You're pathetic and weak, just like your mam was. It's time to put an end to all of our misery."

I stare down at the rope. It's thick and heavy. I swallow hard and think back to the conversation I just had with my dad. Maybe Tanya's right; maybe it'll be better for everyone if I just end it once and for all. The world would be a better place without me. I can be free and be with Ma.

I walk up the stairs. Every step that I take is heavy and filled with dread. I don't want to do this. I don't want to die. Even though I have so much pain and feel as though I'm drowning, I can see a light at the end of the tunnel. Dying isn't something I want. I just want to be free. Glancing down at Tanya, I watch as she glares at me, her foot tapping as she waits for me to end it all.

My hands are shaking, my entire body protesting, but I enter my bedroom and glance around. I see the perfect thing that will end it all. There's a beam above my doorframe. Swallowing hard, I drag the chair over and quickly tie the rope over the beam. I'm breathing hard, my body is heavy, and I'm crying. I really don't want to do this.

"Hurry up, you pathetic bitch," Tanya yells from downstairs.

My heart is racing, but I know that this is it. There's no going back. I need to end the pain and misery. I don't want to be in a world where those who are supposed to love me, don't. Instead, they add to the pain I'm in. I tie the rope around my neck, making sure it's secure. I can hear Tanya's footsteps on the stairs and I tremble with fear. I take one last look around the room. This is it. I'm going to be reunited with my ma once again. I've missed her so much. I just wish Dad would have loved me like she did. If he had, I would have felt safe and secure. I would have been able to overcome the pain I was in and I would have survived. Instead, I'm doing something I don't want to do.

"Get on with it, you little cunt!" Tanya screams, her voice filled with hatred.

I jump at her words, fear coursing through me. I topple the chair from beneath my feet, and I'm suspended with the rope around my neck, the weight of my body pulling the knot taut. My heart races, my vision blurs, and I can feel my breaths growing shorter and more frantic. I don't want this. I really don't.

The world around me begins to fade into darkness

as the rope tightens around my neck. I hear the sound of the front door slamming shut.

"Lisa?" Dad yells. There's worry in his voice. But it's too late. I'm slowly fading. As I begin to lose consciousness, Dad appears in front of me, a mask of horror on his face. "No," he cries. "Baby, please, no. I'm so sorry," he weeps. "Daddy's sorry. I'm so very sorry. Please don't do this."

I feel his hands lifting me up, holding me so the weight of the noose doesn't pull on my neck anymore. But the darkness is consuming me and it finally pulls me under. I welcome it with relief and gratitude.

My last conscious thought is the words Maura said to me this morning. *"You are stronger than you realise. You have the power to heal and overcome this darkness."*

I wanted to be that person. Someone who was able to find the strength to be exactly who she and my ma believed I could be. But it's too late now. There's no going back.

The abyss pulls me under, greeting me once again.

CHAPTER
SIX
LISA

Three Years Later

"You sure you're okay to go?" Orna questions me with a soft smile. "I know what date it is today."

It's three years to the day since I tried to take my own life for the second time. It's been three years of healing and trying to fix what Dad and Tanya broke in me during the three weeks they had me. Orna is my foster mam. She took me in when I needed her. She gave me a home and comforted me when I needed it. It wasn't easy. I was mean and horrible to her, but Orna is sweet and kind. She let me lash out verbally at her and then she'd talk with me.

"I'm okay to go," I assure her.

"Okay, honey, but if it gets too much, just call me. I'll come and pick you up."

I close my eyes and feel the love that she gives me. She's not my real ma, but I know Ma would be so happy that I'm here with her. That I'm finally free and happy. "Thanks, Mamaí," I say softly. "I'll be fine."

She shuffles forward and pulls me in for a hug. It took us eighteen months to get to the point where I'd feel comfortable with any sort of physical touch. My dad and Tanya's treatment of me left me twisted inside. I hated that I didn't have my dad when I needed him the most. I hated that I didn't have someone to protect me. Dad failed me, and in doing so he ruined me. I still have nightmares of that noose around my neck. I wake up gasping for breath and pleading with Tanya not to let me do it.

"Go, honey, have fun, and remember, you don't have to do anything you don't want to do."

I grin at her words, knowing she's saying them for my protection. She's worried I'll fall back into the horrors I was in when I came out of the hospital to live with her. I would get drunk and do drugs. I'd stay out late partying and having fun. I'm pretty sure Orna thinks I used sex as an escape, but I didn't. It was the one thing I didn't do. I'm not sure why. There were plenty of men who wanted it. I just couldn't bring myself to go there. I know Ma wouldn't have been proud had I done that. Orna knows everything that went down with my family. From my ma's depression and suicide, to my own failed attempts, to my dad and Tanya's treatment, and the words that Tanya said to me that night. Orna is my biggest supporter and advocate. Without her, I'm not sure where I'd be right now. She's been my rock, guiding me through the dark times and helping me find the light when I hit rock bottom.

Waking up in the hospital after that fateful night, I was shocked and hurt to find out that I was alone. I thought for sure that my dad would have been there waiting. But he wasn't. That's when a social worker, Eadan, came into my room with a bright smile, took a hold of my hand, and promised me everything would be okay. She didn't sugarcoat anything; she was upfront and honest. She let me know that my dad and Tanya had fled the county as the paramedics turned up, who overheard my dad shouting at Tanya. They heard Tanya confess to giving me the rope and pushing me to do it. It was a punch in the gut to know he had fled with her instead of staying with me.

Maura was a frequent visitor while I was in the hospital. She helped me work through the anger, pain, fear, and disappointment I was feeling. She was there for me to unleash all my inner emotions without judgment. It was day three of being in the hospital when Orna came to visit and Eadan told me that she was going to be bringing me home when I was released. Eadan helped Orna and I transition from strangers to two people who would be living together. Maura also helped me understand what would be happening.

Waking up in that hospital room, I felt alone and confused, but within days I felt as though I had support; people who I could turn to if I needed it.

Some days are hard, even now, three years down the line, but I have a support network around me that I can reach out to if I need it. I feel as though I'm finally breathing and living. I'm happy. That's not something I thought I'd ever feel, but I am. I'm happy and healthier than I've been in years.

THE MUSIC IS loud and thumping as I make my way through the throngs of people. The house party is filled to the brim. Most of the people here are people I don't know. But that's never stopped me from having fun before. Orna and I have an agreement. I don't usually drink alcohol, but if I ever do, I'm not to take any drink from people I don't know and I must always take a can that's unopened. She's strict about that and I respect her rules, so I rarely drink these days, having partied hard for the previous two years.

"Lisa," I hear my best friend, Clodagh, call out to me.

I spin on my heels and see her wearing a bright smile. Her eyes are glassy and she's got a bottle of beer in her hands. Hmm, seems my girl went on a bender today. She staggers toward me in her five inch heels, her blonde hair tied up into a messy bun, yet she still looks so beautiful. There's nothing better than her bright smile. Clodagh and I met two and a half years ago at a bereavement meeting, a place where kids and teens can go and meet others who have been through something similar. Clodagh is also in foster care. She lost her entire family five years ago to a crazed man who wanted to have an eleven year old Clodagh as his own. He managed to kidnap my friend and hold her hostage for two months before the police managed to track him down and find her.

Clodagh rushes toward me, our bodies colliding as we wrap our arms around one another. "You're here," she says giddily.

"I am, and you've been drinking," I say with a smile.

She grins, lifting her shoulders and shrugging. "We

both know what day it is today. How are you holding up?"

Finding someone who knows somewhat what it feels like to go through the loss I did was something I needed. I found Clodagh at a time when I needed a friend. We were both standoff-ish at first. Neither of us wanted to expose what we'd been through—me, because of what happened with Tanya. I don't think I'll ever feel comfortable with people finding out about my suicide attempts, but I know I'm not pathetic and I'm not useless. I've worked hard to know that Tanya was full of shit. She was a jealous bitch who didn't want to share my father's attention. I'm better off without the two of them. For Clodagh, she didn't want anyone to know that a madman had taken her hostage and killed her entire family because he was fixated with her. She's scared that people will think the worst of her. She was eleven, for Christ's sake. She didn't cause that sick fucker to fixate on her.

"I'm good. It's been a long three years, but I'm in a better place."

Her grin widens, brightening up her entire face. "Damn straight you are, girl. So we're partying, right?"

My brows knit together. "Celebrating what?"

"Lisa, it's been three years and this is the first time you're not feeling the pain and grief that awful day inflicted on you. It's time to celebrate the new you. The woman who is strong and resilient, and so fucking beautiful she makes me jealous. So damn sweet that you make me happy. And the best friend a girl could ever ask for."

Tears sting the back of my eyes. Damn her. That is without a doubt one of the nicest things someone's ever said to me.

"Okay," I whisper, trying to beat off the tears. "But you know Orna's rules."

She nods solemnly. "Yes, I know. Orna's got Tammy doing the same. I was warned before I left the house. But Tammy is someone I respect and care about. I won't betray the trust she has in me."

"Same with Orna. We lucked out with our foster parents."

She links her arm through mine. "We sure did. Has Orna thought about fostering more children?"

I sigh. "We've spoken about it. She wanted to wait until I was stable being with her before she reopened her home. I was her first foster child, and I know that she loves me, but she's got so much love to give. I know having another foster child to love would help her too."

Clodagh's arm tightens around mine. "You've also

got a big heart," she tells me quietly. "You'd be an amazing sister."

I laugh as we enter the kitchen, which is also full of people. "I already have one, Clo. You know that."

She rests her head on my shoulder. "You're my sister too, Lis. Mine too." She straightens and I see the joyful girl back again. "Let's get you a drink."

Five drinks later and I'm feeling the buzz. I didn't intend on drinking so much, but the longer I was here, the more I needed to drink, what with dealing with handsy assholes who don't know what the hell no means to Clodagh being so drunk she's barely able to speak without slurring. I'm keeping my eye on her. She doesn't want to leave. Clodagh loves me and she feels deeply for what I went through. While I'm recovering from what happened to me, today marks the day that hurt me deeply, and Clodagh hates it. Just as I do when her day comes around.

"Clo?" I call out as I exit the bathroom and realise that I can't see her. "Clodagh?" I shout.

"Yo, Lisa," I hear one of the assholes from earlier call out. "Your girl is a hell of a lot more fun than you are."

My eyes narrow at his words. "What are you talking about?"

His laughter sends chills down my spine. "She's having fun with three of my boys."

"Where?" I demand. There's no fucking way she's in any way coherent to give consent to that.

"Chill, yeah?" he says, raising his arms in the air.

"Chill?" I growl as I move toward him. "She could barely stand. Where the hell is she?"

"Lisa?" I hear a feminine voice say from behind me. I spin on my heel and see a tiny woman sitting on a guy's lap, his arms wrapped around her and holding her tight. "Is your friend the gorgeous blonde with a beautiful smile?"

I nod. "Yeah. You know where she is?"

"She went upstairs. I'm not sure which room. Freddie, you'll help her, right?"

The man sighs. "Sure."

I shake my head, my gaze moving to the pool stick that's propped up against the wall. "No need," I tell him as I grip the stick in my hand and run up the stairs, my heart racing and my head pumping.

As I reach the top of the stairs, my eyes scan the hallway lined with closed doors. My breath quickens as I realise I have no idea which room Clodagh could be in. The music from downstairs is loud, making it hard for me to hear anything. I'm scared of what could happen to Clodagh.

Without hesitation, I start checking each door, my heart hammering in my chest as each one opens and there's no sign of my best friend.

Finally, on the fourth try, I turn the doorknob and push the door open slowly. The room is dimly lit, the only source of light coming from a bedside lamp. And there, on the bed, lies Clodagh. Her eyes are half closed and she's barely able to keep her head up. I swallow hard as I realise she's naked from the waist down.

My stomach twists into a tight knot as I rush to her side, pushing away the guy who had his hands all over her. "Get out," I growl through gritted teeth.

He stumbles to his feet, a smirk playing on his lips. "She was begging for it," he slurs before stumbling toward me.

I stand tall, my hand tightening around the pool stick. "Come near me, asshole, and you're going to regret it."

I hear laughter and realise too fucking late that I'm cornered, as the three men who came up with Clodagh edge toward me. "Looks like you're fucked, sweetheart," one of them sneers, stepping closer.

Bile churns in my stomach. I haven't been called sweetheart in a long fucking time. The last person to call me that was my dad. Fuck no. This asshole doesn't get to call me it.

I swing the pool stick with all my might, catching one of them across the jaw. His head snaps back, and he stumbles, dropping to the floor.

Another one charges at me and I take a deep breath and raise the pool stick, swinging it with all my might as he draws nearer. The impact against his head sends vibrations along my arm, and I hear a faint cry of pain as he stumbles back.

The third one lunges at me, and I brace myself for the impact, but instead, the door bursts open behind him and three men enter the room. One is the guy whose lap the girl was sitting on downstairs. The other two, I've never seen before. One steps forward and pulls the guy who was about to attack me backward, throwing him to the ground.

"What the fuck?" the new guy snarls, his eyes narrowing as he stares at me. His dark, piercing gaze takes in every detail of my appearance. I feel a sharp jolt in my chest as I meet his intense brown eyes, framed by thick lashes. His hair is dark and tied up at the nape of his neck. He exudes danger, but it only adds to his allure. He's gorgeous. So beautiful.

I lower the pool stick, my heart racing as I take in the sight of the gorgeous man who's watching me with curious eyes. "What?" I ask, as I reach for Clodagh. She's limp against me, but I don't let go.

"Freddie, Emmanuel, take these fucking pricks out of here; teach them a lesson about not touching girls who are drunk and can't say no."

My heart stammers against my chest. Is he for real? He's protecting us? Why?

The three men are dragged out of the room, two of them crying about being hit by a girl. But the guy with gorgeous brown eyes stares at me without blinking. It's kind of unnerving, but at the same time I feel a sense of ease.

"Get your friend dressed, then I'll take you both home," he instructs, turning his back on me and walking out of the room, flipping on the light on his way.

The room fills with brightness and I'm able to see Clodagh better. She doesn't look good. She's got tear stains on her face, her eyes are huge, and she's trembling.

"Are you okay?" I whisper, my heart racing as I take in her sorrow-filled eyes. I hate seeing her like this.

"Thank you," she whispers. "I couldn't fight them off. I don't know what I'd have done if you hadn't come in."

I pull her against me and hold her tightly. "It's okay. You're safe now."

It takes us ten minutes to get her dressed and out

of the room. The man is waiting for us at the top of the stairs. One of his friends is back; not the one with the woman, the other guy. He's also gorgeous. He doesn't have long hair like the first guy, but short dark brown hair and a scar that goes across his eyebrow.

"Emmanuel is going to carry your friend to the car, okay?" the guy tells me. "You're both safe with us."

I nod, then glance at Clodagh, who looks terrified and like she just wants to leave. "Thank you," she whispers, her voice trembling.

The man with the scar half smiles, his eyes full of concern and solely on Clodagh. "You're safe now. Come on, let's get you both out of here."

We leave the house and Emmanuel puts Clodagh in the back seat, before giving a chin lift to the other guy. I watch in shock as he turns and walks back inside the building, leaving us alone with his friend.

"My name's Maverick," the guy who saved us tells me. "What's yours?"

"Lisa," I reply, glad I'm able to keep my voice strong.

I watch as he opens the front passenger's side door for me. I slide into the car, nervous as hell, wondering if I'm making the right choice or if Maverick is a serial killer.

I give Maverick Clodagh's address and he drives in

silence. I'm thankful that it's only a short journey. I turn to the back seat and see Clodagh fast asleep.

"How old are you?" Maverick asks as we get closer to Clodagh's home.

"Sixteen. How old are you?" I ask with a furrowed brow, wondering why he's asking for my age.

"Twenty-one," he says, his voice rough and gravelly. "You shouldn't have been there. You're lucky you weren't hurt or worse."

"I know," I reply, feeling like a small child being scolded.

I watch in fascination as his lips twitch. "Although, for a sixteen year old chick, you're pretty badass. You took down two of those fuckers, and I have no doubt you'd have been able to take down the other without anyone's help."

His praise makes my heart melt. Damn, I didn't expect that.

"Just be careful, Lisa. There are some assholes around," he cautions me.

Little does he know that I know firsthand about said assholes. I've learned a lot over the past three years. One, is to be cautious about people. I don't let many in. Two, is how to protect myself if needed. Orna thought it would help with my anger if I took self-defence lessons. Three, is I've been hurt before, so I won't let anyone do it to me again.

When we pull up to Clodagh's home, the front porch light is on, which means Tammy's asleep. Shit. I'm going to have to wake her up. Clodagh's going to have a lecture when she wakes up in the morning. I also have a feeling that Tammy will be calling Orna in the morning.

Ugh, that's not something I want to experience first thing in the morning, but Clodagh's safe and that's all I care about.

CHAPTER
SEVEN
MAVERICK

WALKING into that room and seeing that asshole advance on Lisa made my blood boil. She's sixteen, for fuck's sake, and that motherfucker Jack wanted to hit her. He and his stupid asshole friends have been wanting to join the Houlihan Gang for some time now and it's a hell no. No man who works for Jer will ever lay a hand on a woman, nor will they rape or attempt to rape one either, and those cunts tried that tonight. When Jer finds out he's going to be livid.

The moment my gaze collided with Lisa's and I saw the anger she had in her eyes, it impressed me, but slowly, the anger faded and I saw something that reminded me of the night at Callie's apartment, of the girl who sat on the bench who looked broken. I know without a shadow of a doubt that this girl is the exact same one. It's been three years since I last saw her and even that was only a glimpse a few times, but I know it's the same one. She's good at putting on a facade. She's hiding her pain, but it's still there; it still lingers within her. I witnessed it tonight.

I glance out the window of my car to the house she's dragged her friend to. She urged me not to get out, not to help; said Tammy wouldn't like it. I have no fucking idea who Tammy is, but if it were my daughter, I'd be the same, except I'd be grateful that someone saved her from those cunts who tried to hurt her. Currently, Lisa and Tammy are having a discussion on the porch. It seems intense from where I'm sitting. Then again, it most likely is.

A few minutes later, Lisa returns and slides into the car. "Are you sure you're okay giving me a ride home?"

"Yeah, of course. How's your friend?" I ask as I pull away from the kerb.

I hear her heavy sigh. "She's okay. She'll have a headache in the morning and will probably get a lecture from Tammy. But she's okay and she'll be okay."

I have a feeling there's a lot more to her words than meets the eye, but I leave it. It's not my monkey, not my circus.

"You'll be home soon, Lisa. Just sit back and relax," I urge her.

I glance over at her a few minutes later and see that she's got her eyes closed and is breathing softly. I have no idea if she's asleep or not, but she seems peaceful.

Forty minutes later, I'm pulling into a familiar street. My body's tense. Fuck, it's been three years since I've been back here and I didn't think I would be. The last time I saw this place, I was pulling my sister from the fire. I roll the car to a stop outside the bench I saw her sitting on and gently push her shoulder. "Hey, Lisa, we're here."

She sits up straight, her eyes wide and alert, watching me carefully.

"Hey, it's okay. You fell asleep. I didn't mean to scare you. We're here."

She blinks, shaking her head slightly. "Sorry," she says sheepishly, giving me a wry smile. "Thank you, yo—" Her words cut off as she stares out the window, her entire body shaking.

"Lisa?" I ask, my voice filled with confusion and concern. What the hell just happened? One moment she was fine, and the next she was trembling uncontrollably. I quickly reach out and grab her shoulders, shaking her gently in an attempt to snap her out of it. But instead of a response, a piercing shriek escapes from her lips, cutting through the air like a knife. It echoes around the car and sends chills down my spine, causing me to pull back in shock. Something is definitely wrong.

"Why?" she cries. "Why would you bring me here?" she asks, hurt and anger lacing her words.

"This is your home..." I say, wondering if I'm wrong.

She glances between the apartment and me. "How did you know?"

"My sister lived there," I tell her, pointing across the street. "I saw you reading on the bench a few times."

She continues to tremble. "That was years ago," she says angrily. "How did you know it was me?"

I pause, unsure of how to respond. Lisa's eyes bore into mine, searching for answers that I'm not sure I have. Taking a deep breath, I decide to be honest with her. "Your eyes," I tell her honestly. "Three years ago, you looked lonely and broken. Your eyes had huge dark circles around them, your cheeks were hollow, and you looked as if the weight of the world rested squarely on your shoulders. You were reading a book. It looked as though you had no idea that someone was watching you."

I watch her pull in a sharp breath. "It was you. You

were the man who got out of the car the day the apartment complex was on fire." She's slowly starting to stop trembling, her breathing is evening out, and she's no longer looking so scared.

I nod. "Yeah. I guessed you knew in the end because you tensed up. So, you don't live here anymore?" I surmise.

She shakes her head. "No. God, no. I had hoped to never come back either."

She's not alone in that thought. If I had a choice, I wouldn't have come back. The memories of what happened that night still linger with me. The constant what if's play on my mind. What if I hadn't been there? What if I hadn't smelled the smoke?

"Okay, so tell me your address. We'll go and you never have to come back."

I want to ask what caused her to fear her old home, but that's her story and I'm not entitled to it.

I have no fucking idea why the hell I'm feeling so protective of her. I've felt that way since I saw her reading her book on the bench three years ago.

She rattles off her address and I realise that she's actually close to my own home. It's late and it shouldn't take us too long to get there.

She's silent once again for the ride and I leave her

be. She's still trembling every so often and I don't want to upset her any more than she already is.

My phone rings and I hit the answer button on the Bluetooth. "Yeah?" I answer.

"Mav, fuck, man, where are you?" Emmanuel asks, sounding panicked.

"Driving Lisa home," I say, glancing at the woman in question, who's tense as a fucking bow. "Why?"

"Tommy is looking for you," Emmanuel says. "He and his boys are out looking for you."

Fuck. This is not what I fucking need right now. "Christ, where are they?"

"Dunno," he replies unhelpfully. "But I wanted to call you and warn you. Jer's on the warpath and he's wanting everyone to be on the lookout for Tommy and his boys."

Tommy Jennings is a forty-three-year-old wannabe gangster who's pissed that Jer's recruited more men, which means our patch is bigger and better than ever before. Tommy believes this is my fault as the new recruits have joined since I have. I call bullshit, but whatever. If Tommy's looking for a fight, then he'll get one. But first, I need to get Lisa home. The last thing I need is for her to get caught up in this bullshit.

"Thanks for the head's up, Man. I'll call you in a while." I hit the end call button.

"Are you in trouble?" Lisa asks, and I'm surprised to hear her voice is calm and stable.

"Don't worry, everything will be fine."

She releases a heavy breath and I aim my grin out the front window.

I stop at a red light close to her house. I'm on edge since Emmanuel's call. Tommy is unpredictable and the fucker doesn't give a fuck about collateral damage. I drum my fingers against the steering wheel as I wait for the red light to change to green.

I reach for my phone and send a text to Jer, letting him know that I'll be home in about fifteen minutes. Once I'm there, I'll call him.

The sound of squealing tyres hits me, and I lift my head and realise there are two cars in front of me, blocking my car from going anywhere. Christ. Tommy and his shit heads have found me.

I take a deep breath and climb out of the car, needing to ensure that no matter what happens, Lisa isn't brought into this. "Stay in the car, Lisa," I order, my voice firm as I walk toward the men who have now stepped out of their vehicles. Tommy stands in front, his sneer evident as he cracks his knuckles menacingly. His cronies flank him, eyeing me with malice.

The street is eerily quiet, the only sound being the distant hum of traffic in the background.

"Well, well, well, look who we have here," Tommy sneers, his eyes glinting with rage. "Maverick, thought you could run and hide from us, huh?"

"Really?" I drawl. "You think I'm running and hiding?" I can't help but laugh at his words.

His face reddens, his eyes practically bulging out of his face. "You think you can just waltz in here and take what's rightfully mine?" Tommy spits out, his words dripping with venom. "Jer made a big mistake trusting you."

Does he think this is the first time I've heard that shit? No one knows what I'm capable of. No one knows what I've done, the people I've killed. I'll always have my doubters claiming that I shouldn't be so far up the ranks within the gang, that it's nepotism at its finest, but I don't give a fuck about those people.

"You really want to do this shit?" I growl, watching as his cronies step closer. "You think the four of you can take me?"

Tommy chuckles darkly, taking a step closer. "You think you're better than me?"

I stare at him, my gaze unwavering. "I don't think it, Tommy, I fucking know it."

With a swift movement, Tommy lunges at me, aiming for my throat. I dodge just in time, his fist grazing my skin as I sidestep. His cronies move in, fists clenched and ready for a fight. Adrenaline courses through my veins as I assess the situation, calculating my next move.

As Tommy regains his balance, I deliver a powerful punch to his gut, causing him to double over in pain. One of his lackeys rushes at me from the side, but I anticipate his move and quickly sweep his legs out from under him, sending him crashing to the pavement.

Tommy rights himself and charges at me again, this time with a ferocity I didn't know he had in him. He lands a blow to my ribs, knocking the wind from me. I dodge the next blow and follow it through with a punch of my own. My skin is red and raw from the blow, but I smile as I watch Tommy spit out blood and teeth from his mouth.

Tommy tackles me, sending the two of us sprawling to the ground. My back crashes against the hard ground, and I have no fucking doubt that I'm going to have a fucking road rash on it come morning. Tommy grabs a fistful of my tee, trying to pin me down, but he's too old and slow for that to happen. I kick out at him, my foot connecting with his chest. I use as much force as possible and it sends his ass crashing backward.

My ribs are smarting. I have a feeling one or two are bruised, maybe even broken. Fuck.

The sound of a car revving catches my attention and I watch in fascination as Lisa races toward Tommy's fucking men. I'm shocked to see her take all three out as she perfects the most spectacular doughnut. I gingerly rise to my feet and move toward the car.

"You okay?" she asks as I slide into the passenger's seat.

"Grand. How the fuck did you learn how to do that?"

She smirks, gripping the wheel tightly. "The last three years have been..." she pauses for a moment. "Hard. I've given my mamaí more than a few grey hairs. I learned how to street race, drift, and do the perfect doughnut." She says the Irish word for mam, which isn't something I've heard in a while.

I chuckle, running a hand through my hair as she places the gear into drive. "Well, I'm glad you did. Maybe you should teach me."

She rolls her eyes, but a small smile tugs at the corner of her lips. "Maybe one day. Now, what's going to happen with these guys?"

She doesn't seem to be afraid as she pulls away from the scene. She's confident in her driving skills, which is surprising seeing as she's only sixteen. "Don't worry about it, Lisa."

"What are you going to do?" she asks, her voice harder than it had been.

"I'll handle it, don't worry. Nothing will come back on you. I'll fucking guarantee it."

Her brows furrow. I've noticed she does that a lot. "I wasn't worried about me."

"I'll be fine," I assure her.

Her shoulders are tense, but thankfully she doesn't say anything. She drives, and the silence is thick as she does. Soon, she pulls into a cul-de-sac. The street is quiet and empty. Lisa cuts the engine outside of a detached house and turns to face me, her eyes searching mine.

"Be careful," she says softly, her voice laced with concern. "I won't be around to save you the next time."

I chuckle at her words, reaching out to squeeze her hand. "I saved you; you saved me. I say we're even."

She grins. "We both know that we didn't need the other to do so." She shrugs. "It sure as hell felt nice to have it though." She slides out of the car. "Be safe, Maverick..." She leaves her sentence hanging, wanting my last name.

I grin at her as I get out of the car, ignoring the

pain in my ribs. "O'Hara. And the same goes for you, Lisa…"

Her laughter is low and silky. "Turner. I'm sure I'll see you around. Bye, Maverick."

I watch as she walks toward her front door, not once turning back to me. The moment she's inside, I slide back into my car, this time into the driver's seat, and pull away from the kerb.

My mind whirls with everything that's just happened. I dial Jer's number, my thoughts a mix of relief and concern. "Hey, Jer—"

His voice cuts me off, his tone urgent. "Jesus, are you okay? I heard what happened. Are you hurt? What the fuck, Mav, you ploughed through Tommy's men?"

I can't stop the laughter that bursts from me. I wince as it pulls at my ribs. Christ, they're fucking sore. "Not me. I'm fine, just a little banged up. I'm on my way to yours. I won't be long."

"Alright, Mav. Just be careful, alright? See you soon."

As I hang up the phone, I know that tonight will be a night to remember. It's not every day that a sixteen year old girl saves your ass.

I have a feeling that this shit with Tommy is just the beginning. *Fuck*.

CHAPTER
EIGHT
LISA

My head is pounding as I make my way downstairs. I got very little sleep last night and it's all thanks to Maverick O'Hara. I don't know the guy. I only met him last night and yet I feel as though I've known him a hell of a lot longer than that. He's gorgeous, and while I felt safe around him, I couldn't deny that he's dangerous. He took on the man he called Tommy last night and was more than capable of taking on the asshole's friends too. I have no idea what caused him to get into trouble with them, but I do know that the fighting seemed to come naturally to him.

"Morning," Orna greets cheerfully as I enter the kitchen. "I've toast made. Do you want jam or chocolate spread?"

I shake my head. Neither sound appealing at this moment. "I'm good with butter, thanks."

I slide onto the chair and reach for the glass of water that's placed in front of me. I take a sip, loving the coldness of the water as it hits my throat.

"Here," Orna says, handing me two painkillers. "For your head. We both know what you're like when you have little to no sleep. You were tossing and turning all night. Are you okay?"

"Grand. I just had a lot of things on my mind," I mutter as I throw the two red capsules into my mouth and wash them down with water. "You were up late too. Everything okay?"

"We'll come to that later. Right now, I'm more concerned about you and what happened last night. Want to explain in more detail?" she asks with a raised brow. She has that authoritative tone that she rarely ever uses with me.

"Let me guess, Tammy called?"

She nods as she takes a seat opposite me. "What the hell happened, Lisa?"

I sigh. I knew this would happen. I quickly explain what went down with Clodagh and the party.

"Jesus," Orna hisses. "Do you have any idea what the hell could have happened to you? To the both of you?"

"I know, but what was I supposed to do? Leave her there?" I ask, getting annoyed. I know what could have happened, but I did the only thing I could and that was to protect my friend before those bastards did anything else to her.

"No," she says, her shoulders sagging in defeat. "You shouldn't have left her, and I'm glad you didn't, but I worry about you, about the two of you. Who was the guy who saved you both?"

"Maverick," I tell her. "I don't know him. He was at the party and gave us both a ride home."

Her eyes narrow. "Maverick O'Hara?" she asks, sounding horrified.

I nod. "Yeah. Do you know him?"

"Lisa," she whispers, her eyes wide. "He's a criminal. He's part of the Houlihan Gang. His uncle is Jerry Houlihan, and his other uncle is Butch O'Hara of the Devil Falcons Motorcycle Club. What the hell were you doing with him?"

I grin. It's not often that something can freak her out. "He was the guy who saved Clodagh and I," I say dramatically. I didn't need saving, but as I said to Maverick last night, it sure did feel good. "He gave us a ride home. Why are you freaking out?"

"Just stay away from him, honey, okay?"

I raise a brow. "You're actually telling me to stay

away?" She's never, not once, told me who I'm allowed to be around and who I'm not.

She presses her lips together. "I trust you," she says quietly. "I trust your judgment. If you think he's okay, then I'll be fine."

"So you don't know him; just what you've heard?" I ask, wanting to understand where she's coming from.

I grin as she holds up her hands and laughs. "You're right," she says, even though I didn't say anything. "I judged him without knowing him and that was shitty of me to do."

I wave her off and reach for a slice of toast. "So, back to you. Why were you up late?"

Orna wrings her hands together. It's something she does when she's nervous or when she wants to talk about something. "I got a call last night," she begins. "There's a little boy who needs to be housed. He's been abused and needs safety."

"Okay..." I whisper, my heart hurting for that little boy. God, I hate that he's been abused. What the hell is wrong with people?

"He can't be around men. He's too afraid of them. He can only be around women. They want me to house him, and I told them that I would have to speak with you. This is your home, Lisa. I don't want you to feel uncomfortable at all."

"I'll be fine," I assure her. "You've helped me so much, Orna, so, so much. Without you, I don't know where I'd be. I know that your dream was to open your home and heart to as many kids as you could, and I love that you gave me time to get used to the new normal, but that little boy needs you, just like I did. Don't turn him away, call them. Tell them that you'll take him."

Tears swarm in her eyes. "Are you sure?" she asks, pressing her hands to her heart. "I don't want anything to hurt you."

"I'm sure. Call them, find out what we need to arrange before he arrives. He'll need new clothes and we'll have to get the room ready."

I remember how Orna set my room up for when I arrived. It wasn't pink as I had thought it would have been, but a pale yellow that made me smile. It wasn't a childish room, nor was it one that made me dread coming into it. It felt homely and welcoming, not to mention the books that were stacked on the shelves. Orna had taken the time to ask her friends, who were also foster parents, if they had any books she could have as she was getting a foster child. At that stage, she didn't know how long I'd be in her care. She just wanted me to feel comfortable.

She reaches across the table and pulls my hand into her own. "Thank you," she whispers.

I close my eyes and nod. Things are going to change, but I know I'm safe here no matter what happens. It's time for Orna to offer that safety, that sanctuary, to someone else too.

I'M PERCHED on the edge of the plush sofa, my knee bouncing nervously. My eyes are glued to the little boy crouched behind the chair in front of me, his face contorted with fear and pain. My heart aches at the sight. He is so tiny, yet he looks as though he has been through hell and back. Black and purple bruises mar his delicate features, causing my protective instincts to kick into overdrive. How could anyone harm someone so young and innocent? I can only imagine the extent of his injuries beyond what I can see on his face. It takes all my willpower not to gather him into my arms and shield him from any further harm.

I reach out a trembling hand toward the boy, my heart breaking at the thought of the pain he must have endured. His eyes flicker toward me, wide with a mixture of fear and uncertainty. I can see the wariness in his gaze. I want to wrap him in a hug and hold him tightly, promising him that everything will be okay.

"Hey there," I say softly, trying to keep my voice gentle and reassuring as I crouch down onto the floor beside him. "My name is Lisa. I'm a foster child too."

He flinches at the sound of my voice but doesn't retreat further behind the chair. He watches me carefully, his gaze bouncing between my hand and my face.

"You're safe now, okay? No one is going to hurt you here."

He tilts his head. The look of disbelief in his eyes is heartbreaking, but I know it's going to take time for him to trust; time for him to understand that not everyone is as bad as the person who hurt him. I stay where I am, not moving my hand nor moving forward. I'm going to let him come to me, hopefully.

It takes fifteen minutes before he slowly and cautiously inches forward, his small hand reaching out to grasp mine. I can feel the tremors running through his body, and it makes me want to hurt whoever put those bruises and the fear on his face.

"My name's Lisa. What's yours?"

"Devin," he says slowly.

"I love your name," I tell him with a smile. "I'm sixteen. I've lived with Orna for three years. Since my ma died."

He blinks, tears building in his eyes. "My mammy's dead too."

I close my eyes at the sound of the sheer brokenness of his voice. "I'm really sorry."

"She was a good mammy. Was yours?" he asks, and I'm so glad that he's speaking. He's been here for four hours and this is the first time he's spoken to any of us.

"My ma was the absolute best. I bet your ma was pretty, just like you?"

He gives me a shy smile and ducks his head. My heart aches for him. He's so young and is feeling so much pain.

I squeeze his hand gently, feeling the fragile bones beneath his skin. "Devin, I promise you that things will get better from here on out. You're safe now," I murmur, my voice filled with sincerity. Devin looks up at me with those big, haunted eyes and nods slowly. I'm so happy Orna has taken him in. I can't imagine what would've happened to him if he hadn't come here.

A sudden noise from the hallway startles us both, and Devin flinches, his grip on my hand tightening. I shoot him a reassuring smile before turning toward the doorway. Orna stands there, her face etched with concern as she takes us both in. I watch as she slowly eases from concern to gratitude. She gives me a small nod before moving forward slightly, careful not to spook Devin any further.

"Lis, is everything okay here?" she asks softly, her gaze shifting from Devin to me.

I nod, giving her a small smile. "We're getting to know each other. Right, Devin?" I say, looking down at the young boy beside me.

Devin nods hesitantly, his eyes darting between Orna and me. He's uneasy around her, and I'm wondering if it's because she's an adult or not. I gently squeeze his hand to reassure him. Orna takes a step closer, her expression softening as she crouches down beside us.

"Hi Devin, I'm Orna," she says warmly, giving him a kind smile. "I'm here to help take care of you and make sure you're safe."

Devin studies her for a moment before turning back to me and whispering, "Is she gonna hurt me too?"

My heart clenches at his words. God. Oh God, the poor boy. What on earth has happened to him?

Orna's eyes widen in sadness at his words, and she shakes her head gently. "Oh, darling, never. I'm here to protect you, just as I protect Lisa. We're both going to care for you. This is your home now, Devin."

Devin's grip on my hand relaxes slightly as he looks

between the two of us. The vulnerability in his gaze tugs at my heartstrings, and I know that building trust with him will take time and patience. Just as Orna did with me. I just pray it doesn't take three years with Devin. I don't want him to feel alone anymore.

Orna stands up and extends her hand toward Devin. "Would you like to come with me and I'll show you your room?" she questions him.

Devin looks at me, almost as if he's searching for an answer. I give him a quick nod as I release his hand. "Go with Orna, Dev. She's excited to show you your new room."

He's hesitant, but I give him one more nod and he gets to his feet and takes Orna's hand. I watch his entire body tremble as he stands beside her. "Would you like me to go ahead and you to follow?" Orna asks.

I watch as he nods quickly before ducking his head in shame.

"That's fine, darling. No worries. Come on, we'll go upstairs."

I watch as they both make their way up the stairs. I can hear Orna talking to him constantly, and I know she'll win him over soon. She'll never harm him, that's something I know, but he doesn't, and until he sees that we're not going to hurt him, he'll be terrified and afraid.

We'll just both have to be here for him whenever he needs us. I remember the feeling of coming to someplace new and not knowing anyone and feeling afraid. It was terrifying to a thirteen year old. I can only imagine what a four-year-old is feeling.

I just pray that whoever hurt him is behind bars, because if I ever saw them, I don't think I'd ever be able to control myself. I want to kill them.

CHAPTER NINE
MAVERICK

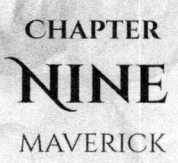

"Tell me what the fuck happened last night," Stephen snarls as he lowers himself onto the sofa.

We're at Jer's house. He's gathered me, Stephen, and Emmanuel here to discuss Tommy fucking Jennings and the bullshit crusade he's on.

I quickly give Stephen the low down of what happened. After I dropped Lisa home, I came here to Jer's and the doctor was called. I have two bruised ribs, thankfully. It could have been a hell of a lot worse.

Emmanuel leans forward, his eyes flashing with anger. "Tommy Jennings is out of control," he begins, his voice low and intense. "Last night, after his show down with Mav, he showed up at Callie's pub, completely wasted."

I grit my teeth. This is fucking new information.

Had I known that bastard had gone looking for my sister, I'd have ended him then and there.

"The fucker started picking fights with everyone, accusing people of being in Jer's back pocket and that they were pussies if they were. He said if they wanted to be respected, they should come and work for him. It didn't go down well, I can tell you that."

Stephen's jaw clenches as he glances at Jer. "We need to do something about this before this asshole does anything more. Tommy's not a man who will go down without a fight. He came after Maverick last night thinking he was the weak link in your organization."

I chuckle. "We all know damn well that's Thomas," I say, grinning. Thomas Grace is a motherfucking asshole who's married to my aunt and is the father of my cousin, Jessica.

"Stephen's right," Jer gripes. "That fucker isn't going to stop. He's going to stir up so much fucking trouble. It's the last thing we need. Tommy is on the police's radar. He's reckless, stupid, and an imbecile. I'll be damned if his stupidity drags us down with him."

"He comes for me again and I'll put an end to this once and for all," I say thickly. Let that motherfucker underestimate me again, and he'll live to regret it.

"We'll be sending a message to him today. No one

hurts my nephew and gets away with it," Jer grunts. "Now, these girls that you dropped home last night, I had someone check into them. The two of them are foster children."

I feel my gut twist at his words. "Why are they in foster care?" What the hell? Have they always been in there?

"That's not something I'm going to tell you," he says. "But I will tell you that you did a good job saving them last night. They've both had a rough few years. But that leads me to my next point. Those motherfuckers who were at that party last night, who allowed those assholes to take a clearly drunk girl up to their rooms, will be put on notice. If I find out that they've done anything like this again, they'll be in serious trouble. I don't tolerate this shit."

"What about those three fucking bastards?" Emmanuel questions. "The beating they took last night isn't enough."

Jer's grin lets me know that he fully agrees.

"Trust me," he says, leaning in closer to emphasize his point. "Those fuckers are in for a world of hurt. They're being taken care of as we speak." His cold, calculating gaze flicks over the three of us. "I need you guys to find one of Tommy's men and send a message to that motherfucker."

I sink back into the sofa, my mind racing with potential targets. "Any man in particular?"

Jer's eyes narrow, his grin growing more sinister. "Preferably one who was with him last night," he says, a dangerous edge to his voice. "But honestly, any one will do. I don't give a fuck."

Jer's gaze locks onto mine, and I can tell he means business. He doesn't tolerate anyone hurting his family or any of his men. I know better than to argue with him when he's in this state. Not that I would. He's right, it's time to send a message, and it gives Emmanuel, Stephen, and I time to play.

I rise to my feet, and I'm followed behind by Stephen and Emmanuel. We say our goodbyes to Jer as we step outside. The tension in the air is almost palpable. This isn't just about getting back at Tommy Jennings and his cronies; it's about sending a message that this kind of behaviour won't be tolerated in our town.

I roll my neck, letting out the anger I feel. We've got a long night ahead of us, but one thing's for sure: when we're finished, there's going to be a war.

"Bingo," Emmanuel says with a grin, as he watches two of Tommy's men exit the pub.

We've been sitting outside The Hanged Man pub for the past four hours. Emmanuel's been on edge. The fucker kills people for a living and he's scared about sitting in a car that Jason stole a few weeks back. Jason is a car thief that Jer has on his books. He's one of the more well-liked guys within the gang. He not only boosts cars, but anything that you'd need. He's the go-to guy to get whatever the fuck you want.

"Is that Paddy?" I ask, leaning forward a little. "It fucking is." I turn to Emmanuel and see that he's rubbing his hands with glee. "Follow him," I instruct. "I'll call Stephen and tell him to have everything ready."

Paddy is Tommy's son. The fucker has two boys and one girl. The last I heard, his daughter married a rich fucker and they moved out of the county. They're currently living down the south of the country. Paddy is his eldest boy, and then he has Tommy Junior, who hasn't long turned eighteen.

Emmanuel nods in agreement and starts the car, smoothly pulling out to follow Paddy discreetly.

I pull out my phone and dial Stephen's number, excitement coursing through me. This is what I live for. It's been three years since my first kill and I've honed my skills, learned the best way to do what I do best, and have even concocted my own acid that will destroy skin and bones and everything in between. It's stronger than hydrofluoric acid and it's something that took me a while to find the right mixture. Now, I'm able to be rid of every single one of my enemies.

Stephen picks up after the second ring. "You good?" he asks.

"We'll be with you soon," I assure him. "We've found the perfect target."

"Good," he says thickly. "Whoever it is, they'll be regretting ever getting tangled up with Tommy."

He has no idea just how true his words are. Paddy's going to be in for a world of hurt. He'll be left with scars and lifelong pain when we're finished with him, and he'll only have his dad to blame for his bullshit.

"See you soon," I tell him and end the call.

We tail Paddy through the winding streets of Dublin. It's late, almost midnight, and there's still people milling about. Emmanuel follows at a safe distance behind. Paddy has no idea that he's being tailed—fucking moron. He's going to be surprised when we finally get him.

We keep tailing Paddy. It doesn't take long for Paddy to stop along a dark street. I watch, shaking my head, as the fucker unzips his pants to take a piss.

Emmanuel cuts the engine and we sit in tense silence for a moment. I nod at Emmanuel. "Let's get this shit done," I tell him. The sooner we have this fucker, the sooner we get to play.

As Paddy continues to relieve himself, we cautiously exit the car, careful not to make a noise and alert him that we're here. I quickly position myself behind Paddy while Emmanuel stays hidden nearby in the shadows, keeping an eye out for anyone else. When Paddy is done, he zips up his pants and turns to walk away—not noticing our presence. Without hesitation, I lunge at him from behind, grabbing him in a bear hug and holding him tight. Paddy struggles and tries to break free, but it's no use—he's trapped.

"What the fuck?" he yells, his voice muffled by my grip.

Emmanuel emerges from the shadows, a sinister grin on his face. "We've a message for Tommy and you're going to be the one to deliver it."

Paddy's eyes widen in terror as he realises that he's fucked in this situation. "What do you want?" he manages to stammer, his voice shaking with fear.

I release him just enough so he can turn around and face us. "We want you to bring a message back to your old man," I say, my voice dangerously calm. "Tell him that we're coming for him next, and we won't stop until we've taken everything he holds dear."

Paddy's face contorts in pain and frustration. "I don't know anything about this! Why are you doing this?" he practically yells at me.

Emmanuel steps forward, his expression cold and merciless. "Do you really think we're stupid enough to believe that you have no idea what criminal activities your dad's involved in?" he asks, sneering. "You're his son, his second in command. We know everything about you, Paddy, and we're going to make sure that we send this message correctly."

I rear my arm back and let fly. Paddy's head snaps back violently as my fist connects with his nose, the sound of breaking bones echoing through the night. A sickening gurgle rises from his throat as blood spills from his lips. He lurches forward, trying to steady himself.

"Alright, message received," he groans, spitting out the blood that's now coating his lips.

A chilling smile curls on my lips as I let out a low, menacing laugh. "Oh no, Paddy. We've barely scratched the surface." Paddy's eyes widen in terror as he stares at me, his body trembling with fear. I nod to Emmanuel, and he steps forward, rolling his shoulders as he does. Mimicking my actions, he delivers a swift punch to

Paddy's face, sending him crashing to the ground. I chuckle when I realise it took Emmanuel one punch to knock the fucker out.

We quickly load him into the boot of the car, careful to ensure that we're not seen. We have a forty minute drive to get to the farmhouse that Stephen owns, a place where he does the majority of his killings. When Tommy realises that we were the ones who hurt his son, he's going to lose his mind. He'll be beyond pissed. He came for me, but he should have known better. He started this war, and I can guarantee we'll be the ones to end it.

When we finally arrive at the farmhouse, Stephen is waiting for us, his expression focused and cold. He's been doing this shit longer than most of us. He's the one who helped me hone my skill. While we've never been as close as he and Callie are, he's my friend, one of my closest, and I know if shit goes south, I can rely on him to help and vice versa.

"Everything's ready," he says. "Are you ready for this?"

My smile is wide. "I'm always ready." I never expected to enjoy the thrill of the kill but I do. It's a shame that we're not killing Paddy, just maiming him today. But either way, we'll all unleash some pent-up frustration on the fucker.

"What are we thinking?" Emmanuel asks. "Who's going to have fun?"

I laugh as he glances between both Stephen and I. It's a good question. Will Stephen want to use his wood chipper?

"How about we both have fun?" Stephen grins. "We'll take the fucker's arm and leg. It'll show that motherfucker that we're not to be messed with."

"I see you have the tarp waiting for us. You've got a chainsaw set up too?" I note, as I look at the set up on the grass area. It's seen a hell of a lot of deaths over the past few years. Many of which have been violent and loud.

"Two," he replies with a grin. "I'm not letting you have all the fucking fun."

We move to the car and we drag Paddy's unconscious body to the grass. His weight is almost unbearable, and I can't help but think that perhaps he needs to lose a few pounds. Of course, that won't be an issue once we start cutting off his limbs.

"We should probably gag him," Emmanuel suggests as we reach the grassy patch near Stephen's shed. "I don't want him screaming when he wakes up and realises what's happening."

"Good idea," I reply, nodding in agreement. "Get some tape from the shed."

Emmanuel returns moments later with a roll of tape and I take a long piece, wrapping it around Paddy's mouth to ensure he won't make a sound. The thought of the pain he'll soon endure brings a twisted smile to my face.

"Are you ready?" Emmanuel asks, his voice filled with excitement. He rarely gets this close and personal when it comes to taking out targets. As the Silencer, he's known as one of the best sharpshooters in Europe, hired for high-profile hits that come with a hefty price tag.

"Let's do this," I respond eagerly, grabbing the chainsaw and ripping off the cover. Adrenaline rushes through me as we strip Paddy of his clothes, leaving him exposed and vulnerable on the tarp Stephen had brought along.

It's deep into the night, and Stephen's farm is secluded enough that it'll be difficult for anyone to find us or hear us. Or even see what we're doing. It's one of the reasons Stephen purchased this place. It's far enough from the city that it won't be happened across and there's no one close enough to wonder what the fuck is going on.

The moon is bright in the sky, illuminating the farmhouse, so we're able to see everything, which is perfect, as I'm able to see the moment that Paddy wakes up. His entire body freezes; it's subtle but I watch it. The fucker's probably realised what happened and now he's scared shitless.

We all know this will be a turning point in our feud with Tommy. He crossed a line by coming after me, and now he'll pay the price for his foolishness. If only he had kept away from me and the rest of the Houlihan Gang; none of this torture would have been necessary.

"Welcome back, Paddy," I sneer as Stephen chuckles beside me. "Remember what I said, this is a message to your father."

I turn to Stephen and watch as he grins, his eyes glinting with sadistic pleasure. In his hands, he grips a chainsaw. This is who we are—depraved killers who seek nothing but the thrill of inflicting pain.

"Have at it," I tell Stephen.

Stephen doesn't hesitate. He powers up the chainsaw and it roars to life. Paddy begins to wriggle, trying to escape, but Emmanuel is there, holding him down. Stephen gets to work on Paddy's leg first, pressing the saw against his kneecap and slicing through the bone with ease. It's messy and bloody, but Stephen doesn't give a fuck.

Paddy screams and writhes in agony, but they're muffled due to the tape over his mouth.

"My turn," I goad as Stephen rises to his feet. He's got blood splattered over his face and clothes. Something I'll have over me when I'm finished no doubt. Tears stream down Paddy's face as I get closer to him. He's terrified. I have to admit, seeing the fear on people's faces is something that'll never be topped. It's such a rush, having them look at me as though I'm the monster, as though I'm some sort of demon sent from the bowels of Hell. I suppose to them, I am.

Just as Stephen did before me, I power on the chainsaw. It vibrates in my hands, but I hold it steady as I bring the blade down onto Paddy's arm. He once again howls in pain, struggling to get free. I laugh. "Struggling only makes it worse," I tell him. "But I like it."

That has him stilling, his body taut and his eyes wide as he watches me. "The question is," I muse aloud. "Do I take the entire arm or just from the elbow down?"

He shakes his head, groaning, his eyes pleading with me not to do this. Does he not realise that nothing he says will ever stop me? He's in for a world of hurt. For the rest of his life, he's going to live with the knowledge that he lost his limbs due to his dad. That's going to be a bitter pill to swallow.

I slice against his skin. It's rough and the vibrations

get stronger, but I push through it, push harder down, and it cuts through his skin like it's nothing but a piece of paper. The lines are jagged. The scar he'll have will be hideous. Blood splatters against my face. My hands are slippery due to it, but I don't stop. It'll only take a few more moments before his limb is completely severed.

I stand back once I'm done, marvelling at my work. It's bloody and gruesome.

"He'll need to be cauterized," Stephen drawls. "Otherwise he'll bleed out."

Emmanuel chuckles. "We wouldn't want that now, would we?"

I hear Stephen's laughter as he moves back to the shed. That man has everything he could ever need in there and then some. He returns a few moments later with a blowtorch. He turns it on and I stand back and watch as the flames lick at the jagged wounds of Paddy's now missing limbs.

The sound of his muffled scream is chilling as he thrashes on the tarp beneath him. It takes twenty minutes, but Stephen manages to stop the bleeding by burning his wounds closed. It's a fucked up thing to do, but it was the only way we could guarantee that this fucker remains alive.

"Eman, you call Jer to have someone do the drop

off," I mutter as I watch Paddy. He's silent, unmoving. I think he passed out from the pain. I'm impressed that he hadn't done before now. "We need to get rid of our clothes and the tarp."

Emmanuel chuckles. "Don't forget the limbs."

He's right. I had forgotten about those. Once the asshole is couriered out of here, I'll fix everything to ensure that no one will ever know what happened here. As Emmanuel calls Jer, I bring the chainsaws to an outbuilding around the other side of the farmhouse. It's got everything I need to clean. I begin by spraying the chainsaws down with disinfectant, followed by bleach, ensuring that they're sparkling clean and like new.

By the time I'm finished cleaning the chainsaws, Paddy is long gone. Whoever came to get him did so while I was busy in the outhouse. Maverick hands me a bag, and I see that Stephen's already changed into new clothes. I quickly strip down and clean off the blood from my hands, face, and anywhere else it may have gotten.

"Ready?" I ask Stephen once I'm dressed.

"Let's get this shit done," he replies, his words low.

He has a barrel waiting for me, along with my acid concoction. Half of the barrel is already filled with it. I'll top it up once we have everything placed inside.

Our clothes, the tarp, and the limbs are placed inside the barrel carefully. Once they're in, I pour the remaining mixture of acid inside. Within forty-eight hours, everything inside of the barrel will disintegrate into nothing. Just the way I like it.

We seal the lid and Stephen and I carry it to the underground bunker he has. It houses guns, barrels, and a lot of bomb making materials. The only way inside is to be Stephen. It uses his biometrics to gain entry. Meaning no police or anyone sniffing around could enter.

Finally, after what feels like a fucking week, I'm done. It's time to go home and sleep.

Tomorrow will be exciting when Tommy finds out what happened to his son. That'll be fun, and I can't wait for the fall out.

CHAPTER
TEN
LISA

Four Months Later

I FEEL the bed dip beneath me and instantly I'm awake. For the past four months, it's been the same every single night. Devin has night terrors. They're horrendous and they're loud. The first night he had them, I thought someone was trying to murder him. I made it into his bedroom before Orna did, and what I walked into is something that's etched into my brain forever. Devin was fast asleep, tears spilling from his eyes as he tried to fight off someone. He was pleading and begging them to stop, promising whoever was hurting him that he would be a good boy, that he'd be better.

I was stuck, frozen on the spot. I know from my own experience with night terrors that waking the person up could be detrimental to them. Thankfully, Devin woke up, panting and crying. I climbed onto the edge of his bed and sat with him. I held his hand and talked to him as he calmed down from his nightmare. He had wet the bed and himself during his terror, and he was so ashamed, so embarrassed. I think he thought we'd be upset. I promised him we weren't, that we were just glad he was safe. Orna took him and gave him a shower as I cleaned his bed and changed his sheets. Thankfully, Orna had purchased multiple protective sheets that stop bedwetting from seeping through to the mattress.

That was the first night that Devin crawled into my bed and slept. He didn't have any more nightmares while with me, but each night, he goes into his own room and tries to sleep. He's not had a huge terror like that in about a month, which is huge progress and it means that he's feeling safer with Orna and I. He also has an amazing support system around him. He has Orna and me, along with social worker, Meg, and his therapist, Gillian, who's one of the best when it comes to children. He's not alone, and I truly hope that he sees that and feels it.

"Hey, Dev," I whisper softly, not turning over.

"I'm sorry," he replies just as softly.

"What are you sorry for?" I ask, a furrow forming between my brows.

"For being here. I know I should be in my own bed."

"You're fine. I don't mind. Sometimes we need support." I turn in the bed and see that he left my bedroom door open. The light from the hallway shines in and I'm able to see the tears streaming down his face. "What's wrong?"

He buries his head against my shoulder, his fists clenching in my sleep shirt. He shakes as sobs wrack through his tiny body. "Dad," he gasps. "He wants me back."

"What?" I gasp, unsure that I've even heard that right. There's no fucking way that monster is to be anywhere near Devin. He's beaten him and landed him in hospital. There's a court order for him not to be anywhere near Dev.

"He was at my school," he says, still whispering, his body trembling with fear. "Lisa, he's going to get me."

"He won't," I promise him. I'm going to make sure that he doesn't.

"Promise?" he asks, trembling against me.

"I promise," I vow. I won't let him down. No way. Fuck no. The fear he has seeps from him. I can feel it against me. I won't let anything happen to him.

"Gilly told me what my dad did to me was called rape," he says a little while later. Gilly is what he calls his therapist. It helps her seem friendlier to him and it really helps him settle around her and open up.

My entire body freezes at his words. They're so small, so terrified, yet sound so fucking loud.

"I didn't know what it was. It hurt so much. I kept bleeding."

I close my eyes tight, breathing hard through my nose, trying to stop the tears from falling. Oh my God. That monster. That fucking animal.

"Gilly told me that no one had the right to do that to anyone. She was really upset when I told her what happened."

I swallow hard. I have no doubt she was. I don't know all the details nor do I want to, but I can guess that it rocked Gillian to her core, as it has done me. "She's right, baby. She's so right. No one has the right to hurt you and no one has the right to rape you. Ever. I'm so very sorry that your dad did that to you. But let me tell you something," I say low, but my voice is clear and full of conviction.

"What's that, Lisa?" he asks, his hands still clenched around my sleep shirt.

"Our families are who we choose, not who made us. We get to choose who we want to be our parents and our family. I love my ma. She was the best and she'll always be my ma. I don't have a dad, not anymore. Ben doesn't deserve to be called that. So I call him Ben. If you want and you're ready, you don't have to call the man who hurt you your dad."

He looks up from my chest, his eyes bright and soaked with tears. "Really?"

I nod. "Really. Our family doesn't hurt us, Dev. They shouldn't. And we finally have the power now that we're free of them to make that decision for ourselves. It hurts knowing that we don't have them anymore, but when you're ready to make that decision, let me know and we'll think of a name to call him, yeah?"

I have a lot of names that spring to mind, but Dev's so young, so sweet, and so fucking caring. His father hurt him. God, he hurt him in ways no one should ever be hurt, especially at such a young and vulnerable age; an age when kids love their parents unconditionally and will do anything to please them. That fucker hurt Dev so damn much.

I wish I could find him. I wish I could track him

down and kill him, make Devin never have to worry about him coming near him again.

"You're safe here, Dev. Orna and I will never let anything happen to you," I promise him. But tomorrow, I'll be having a conversation with Orna about Dev's school having that motherfucking creep in such close proximity that he actually spoke to him. That should never have happened, and until Orna has a guarantee that it won't happen again, Devin won't be going back. There's no way Orna would allow that to happen.

"I don't want to leave," he tells me, his voice losing some of the terror and fear that he had.

"You don't have to," I say. "This is your home." I pull him into a hug and press a soft kiss to his head. "Sleep, Dev. Tomorrow's a new day."

I hold him in my arms and rock him softly. In doing so, it brings back memories of my dad doing this to me when my ma died. I hate that I was so weak and vulnerable that I allowed him to fool me into trusting him. It didn't take long for him to dash every last hope I had for him. I'm just glad that I never have to see him again or that bitch of a girlfriend of his. I just pray that Devin gets the same peace with his father. That he'll never have to deal with him again either.

"Is everything okay?" Clodagh questions. "You've been quiet all night."

We're currently sitting on the side of an old bridge. It's fairly secluded here. It's a place where both Clodagh and I always come to collect our thoughts when things are tough. Today, I needed to come here and just process everything. When I first met Clodagh, I used to unleash my anger by smashing shit and just being a general bitch. I'd lash out and let the anger consume me. Now, I tend to process it and work through it.

I release a long sigh. "Devin's going through a lot and I feel useless. I don't know how to help him."

The school apologized but claimed there was nothing they could do as it happened outside of the school grounds, and they told Orna that they weren't able to police what happens outside of school. I call bullshit as Devin assured us that he was still in school when it happened and that fucking bastard was talking to him through the fence. That's on school property, so why can't they do anything about it? It pisses me off that they're so fucking blasé about it. Thankfully, Orna lost her shit and pulled Devin from the school. She also put in complaints with the school board, the council, social services, and the police. That school is under investigation as it's considered a safeguarding incident, one in which they failed in. They have a duty of care with all students and they let Devin down.

"Is he okay?" she asks, watching me carefully.

I lift my shoulders and shrug. "He's not having nightmares, not that I know of, but he still lies in bed with me every night. His dad is back and it scares him."

I watch the anger seep into her features. "That motherfucker," she hisses. "How is he allowed back?"

Clodagh doesn't know everything about what Devin's been through. That's not something that I'd ever share with anyone. Devin trusted me with that and I'll never break that trust he has in me. But Clodagh saw Dev when he first came to live with us. She saw the bruises and the fear. She knows that he abused him physically and that's enough for her to be pissed on Dev's behalf.

"He's safe with us," I tell her, my voice filled with conviction.

"Girl, I know that," she says with a laugh. "I've seen you with a pool stick. Imagine what you'd be like with a baseball bat."

"Fuck that, a hurley stick would hurt more," I chuckle. "But that bastard comes near Devin, and I'll unleash my anger on him. Thankfully, Orna loves golfing. I'm pretty sure there's a five iron beside the door."

She shakes her head. "That asshole won't know what's hit him if he comes looking for that boy."

I pick up a stone and throw it into the water, my gaze focused as it skims across the waves. "How are you feeling?" I ask her. She rarely talks about that night at the party and I know she's still affected by it.

"I feel stupid. I know better than to do what I did. We didn't know anyone at that party. Honestly, Lis, if you weren't there, I don't know what would have happened. I just feel so stupid and idiotic for letting myself get into the situation in the first place."

I rest my head against her shoulder. "It was a lesson. A hard one but a lesson nonetheless. I think we've both realised that it's time to stop binge drinking and going to parties. I'm too old for this shite."

She laughs, just as I knew she would. "Old? Girl, we're almost seventeen."

I nod. "Right? And we've been doing it for the past three years. Others our age are just starting, and I can't be arsed with it to be honest."

"Okay, grandma," she laughs. "But I get it. It's exhausting having to be constantly aware of our surroundings. Constantly on edge."

She's right. We're both like that, and I have a

feeling it's due to our past. I'm not sure if the feeling will ever go away. I sure as hell hope so, but I doubt it.

"Tammy's got me on a tight curfew," she sighs. "I need to regain her trust and have to be back by nine. Are you staying here a little longer or are you going to head home?" she asks as she rises to her feet, brushing dirt from her pants.

I hear a car pull up close by and ignore it. There's a main road just beyond the thick line of trees. It could be anyone, though there's rarely anyone who comes here. "I'm going to stay here for a while."

Orna and Devin had a night planned for themselves. I'm sure Devin's fast asleep by now, but I don't want to go home just yet. I'm still reeling from Devin's confession about his father, and I need to unleash the anger. I need to be alone for a while.

"Alright," she says. "Let me know when you get home."

I nod. "I will do," I assure her and watch as she leaves. It'll take her ten minutes to walk toward the nearest bus stop. Once she's away from this deserted place, there'll be enough lighting that she'll be safe. I continue to watch her walk away, not moving my gaze until she's no longer in view.

I throw more stones onto the river, watching as they skip along the water. It's soothing. I'm able to just be and let my mind wander, sifting through everything. Tears leak from my eyes as I replay Devin's words over and over again. That poor baby has been hurt so horrendously that it makes me sick to my stomach. I don't understand why that animal was allowed to stay with Dev. Surely there would have been welfare checks on him. But the social workers are understaffed, and there are just so many families that fall between the cracks. Devin is safe now and he'll be able to heal as much as possible.

Sighing as I wipe my tears from my eyes, I can't help but feel that Devin's dad isn't finished yet. A man that not only physically but sexually assaults their child, or anyone for that matter, isn't going to let go of them, ever. They're going to do whatever the fuck they can to get them back. I just want to know why he's not behind bars. Surely with Devin's face and the fact that there's a court order dictating that he's not allowed near his son, that would be enough to have him sent to prison?

I hear footsteps grow closer and turn to see a drunken man stumble from the thick bushes. I roll my eyes. This isn't uncommon. There are a lot of homeless people around, and as this place is secluded, I know they tend to frequent this spot to lay low when needed. I rise to my feet, knowing that it's time to go.

"Where are you going, bitch?" I hear the man slur from my right.

I glance at him and wonder how the fuck he got so close to me. He's quick on his feet.

"Home," I reply, picking up my pace and moving away from him. My heart's racing as I hear his footsteps get louder, faster, closer.

"Not happening," he sneers. "I know you've been keeping him from me." The coldness of his tone makes my skin crawl. "I won't let you keep him. No way. I need him."

I spin on my heels, wondering what the hell he's talking about. Who does he need? The moment I catch a glimpse of him up close and personal, I don't need to wonder. It's so very clear who he's talking about. God, he's Devin's dad. He's the spitting image of this man. My stomach churns as I look at the man who hurt that poor baby.

"You," I snarl, my anger whipping through me thick and fast. "How dare you? You deserve to be six feet under after what you did to that poor boy."

"I do what I want. He's my boy. You've taken him. You've ruined everything," he growls. "Everything. He was my money maker. Now you will be."

This man is fucking delusional. There's no way in

hell I'll ever do anything for this prick. "You're crazy. Devin is better off without you."

He steps forward, his hands reaching behind his back. My heart races as my gaze moves to the side, trying to find something, anything, that'll help me fend him off.

I only see small rocks and tree sticks. Nothing to help me. Crap. What the hell am I going to do?

CHAPTER
ELEVEN
LISA

I swallow hard when I turn back to him and see that he has a thick rope in his hands and a sinister smile on his face. "You'll fetch a pretty penny," he says, still grinning like a madman.

My blood runs cold at the thought of being sold like some kind of animal. I can't help but feel sickened at the thought of him doing this to Devin. His words are clicking in my head. He was planning on selling his child. I can't believe this shit.

"Not happening," I snap, unable to keep my anger from bursting out. "You're a sick motherfucker. You're disgusting."

His face contorts with rage, and my heart skips a beat as he edges closer to me. "You think you're better than me, bitch?" he spits out, his voice dripping with malice. "I'm going to make sure you wish you'd kept your mouth shut." He lunges toward me, his hand reaching for my throat.

I stagger back, tripping on a nearby rock, and I hit the ground hard, the wind knocked out of me. He looms above me, his eyes promising destruction.

Fuck, I'm not going to let him win. I claw at the ground, searching for something, anything, to use as a weapon. My fingers brush against something heavy and jagged, and I grab it, my heart pounding in my chest.

As he nears me, his eyes never leaving mine, I leap up, the heavy rock in my hand. I smash it against his chest, hearing the sharp crack of bone. He stumbles back, his hand flying to his chest, a look of shock and pain crossing his face.

I don't hesitate. My adrenaline pumping, I swing the rock again, this time hitting him in the temple. There's a sickening thud as his head connects with the rock, and he crumples to the ground like a broken doll.

I stand over him, panting heavily, my heart still racing. I can't believe I just did that. But I did. My breaths come in ragged gasps as I lean down, almost afraid to check for a pulse. Relief rushes through me when I feel the faint beating against my trembling fingers. Hatred mixes with my relief as I realise he's still alive. Fuck. Fuck. Fuck. He's still alive.

Shit. What have I done? Panic sets in as I try to figure out my next move. Do I run?

If I do that, it'll mean Devin will continue to be in danger. Hell, maybe even me. But what other choice do I have?

Sinking to my knees, the reality of the situation hits me like a ton of bricks. My hands tremble as they rake through my hair. Crap. How do I end up in these situations?

I glance around, my eyes landing on the rope. Fuck. A plan forms in my head. I'm not sure if I'll be able to do it, but I have to do it. There's no other choice. I can't afford to waste any more time. With a deep breath, I push myself up from the ground and rush toward his prone body. Reaching for his feet, I manage to drag his unconscious body to the edge of the old bridge. I'll only have a matter of moments to get this done before he wakes up. I can't let him survive. I hate that I'm doing this, but for Devin, I'll do whatever it takes to keep him safe. I need him to be safe.

Over the past four months, I've grown to love that boy. He means the world to me and I want to protect him. Doing this? Killing the man who raped and abused him, it may hurt me, but I'll do it, and I'll do it over and over again if needed.

Taking a deep breath, I drag his body so that his legs are hanging over the edge of the bridge. It's not a big bridge. It's fairly small, more like a walk bridge, but it'll do what I need it to do.

I ignore the barrage of images that hit me of the last time I had rope in my hand. I won't ever go back to that time in my life. I won't ever allow anyone to make me feel as lonely and useless as Tanya did. Right now, I'm in control. I'm doing this to save a boy who's been through enough. I'm doing this to ensure that his future is bright and filled with happiness.

I wrap the rope around his neck, making sure it's tied tightly. I need to ensure that it's done correctly. The noose I've created is strong and fits perfectly around his neck. I tie the other end around the iron of the bridge. I pull it taut, making sure there's no way it'll come undone.

As I step back, taking a moment to catch my breath, I can't help but think about what this means. I'll be a killer. There's no two ways about it. I'll be a murderer.

I take another breath, try to calm my racing heart, and remind myself of the reason I'm doing this. For Devin. For his happiness and safety.

With that thought in mind, I step forward, and with my entire weight behind me, I push the man off the edge of the bridge. He falls fast, and I know the instant he wakes up. I hear the muffled scream just as he comes to a stop, the noose tightening around his neck. I watch in horror as his body twists and turns, fighting for his life.

I close my eyes, unable to watch any longer. My heart feels heavy, but I don't feel remorse. I know that what I've done isn't right, but what that monster did to Devin wasn't right either. He would have continued to come for him. He wouldn't have stopped until he got him back, and that's not something I could live with.

Glancing down, I see that he's stopped fighting. His body is swinging in the wind, and there's no fight left in him. He's dead.

I'm a murderer. I thought I'd feel something. Instead, I feel relief. Justified and glad.

Suddenly, I hear a rustling in the bushes behind me. My heart jumps into my throat as I spin on my heel and see a man walking from the bushes.

Crap. Fuck. What have I done?

"I'm not here to cause trouble," the man tells me, and I frown at hearing the English accent. From what I can tell, he's from London.

"You know?" I ask, unable to keep the fear from my voice.

He nods. "I do. You did a good job. I watched, ready to step in if needed. You're Lisa Turner, right?"

I step backward. What the fuck? "How do you know my name?" I ask, my body trembling.

"Shit, let me introduce myself," he says with a warm smile. "Travis James. I'm sure you have no idea who I am and I can't blame you. I don't live in this country, but what I do for a living is what brought me here. You see, someone had a problem with the asshole you killed. Seems the man makes enemies wherever he goes."

I cross my arms over my chest, wondering where he's going with this.

"I co-own The Agency. It's a site where you can go and order hits, and you'll be told when and where so you'll know to have an alibi. It's a website for the elite. Not just anyone can stumble upon it. You have to be given a card, and that card has a code, one that's only good for you. I also take some of those jobs and kill whoever the intended target is. Today's lucky guy was Shane Larkin."

Oh, so that's what his name is. I hadn't known. This all sounds so confusing and fanatical.

"I didn't realise things like The Agency existed in real life."

He chuckles. "Oh, darling, there are so many things that would scare the fucking life out of people if they found out they were real."

"So I killed him. What happens now? Am I going to get into trouble?"

Travis shakes his head and steps closer to me. "No. In fact, the opposite. No one is going to know that you were here, that you were the one to kill this fucker. Darling, I doubt anyone would think this was anything other than a suicide, especially as this asshole's van is parked on the other side of those trees," he says, pointing his thumb in the direction from which he just came.

I stare at him in disbelief. "You... you mean I'm safe? No one's going to come after me?"

Travis gives me a small smile. "Not if I can help it, darling. You did what you had to do, and in the end, you saved Devin, right?"

I stare at him in shock. "You know about Devin?"

He nods. "I know everything there is to know about Devin, Shane, and even you. By the way, your father is a fucking prick."

I'm freaked out that he knows about me, but I'm not surprised. "Yeah, I learned that a while ago."

He nods. "I bet. Fucker needs to be castrated."

I smile at the thought. "Thank you, Travis, for this." I thought for sure I was going to have to be looking over my shoulder for the rest of my life, wondering, waiting for someone to uncover what I've done.

He shakes his head. "No need to thank me. I should be thanking you. I don't need to get my hands dirty. You've done my job for me."

I lift my shoulders and shrug. "I suppose I have, not that I meant to. It just happened."

"Trust me, that's what happens to the majority of us. We don't intend to turn into killers, it just happens," he tells me. I watch as he reaches into his pocket and pulls out a small, black card. "This is your pass to The Agency. Keep it safe, and if you decide that doing what you did tonight is something you want to continue, just give us a call."

I hesitate, not sure if I should take it or not. "You can't be serious?"

Travis shrugs, waving it at me. I reach out and clasp it in my hands. "Not many people can do what you did tonight. You need to think of a better way to incapacitate them, but the final product? Fucking inspired. Then again, knowing what I do about your past, I'd say it was."

"I feel normal. I know I should feel guilty, but I don't," I confess.

He nods. "That's because you know what he would have done had you not killed him. He was never going to let Devin out of his sight. His end game was to get that boy back and you stopped it. You could stop more men and women like him."

I swallow, wondering if I could do it. Would I be able to? "How would you incapacitate them?"

His grin is full of triumph. "That's easy," he says as he turns on his heel. I follow behind him, needing to know the answer. "A drug—something that we can easily supply to you. It'll be out of the victim's system within hours of being administered. It will make them sluggish, giving you the opportunity to get them in position, to tie the noose around their necks and throw them off the bridge."

It sounds so easy when he's saying it. Like it's the most natural thing to do in the world.

He stops and turns to face me, his expression serious. "Do you want the job?"

I look down at the card in my hand, feeling the weight of my decision. Do I? Could I live with the guilt knowing there are other kids out there like Devin who are stuck at home with monsters because they've fallen through the cracks, and I've not done anything to help? No, I couldn't live with the guilt.

"I want it," I say quietly. "I want to ensure there's no one helpless like Devin was."

Travis grins at me. "That's really good, Lisa. I think you've found your calling." He reaches for his phone, and I watch as his fingers move over the screen. "I'll meet you tomorrow," he says as I feel my phone vibrating in my pocket. "Don't be late. We've a lot to discuss. If you change your mind, that's okay. There will be no hard feelings and no one will force you to do this job."

I breathe a sigh of relief. I have said yes, but I'm still not sure. I have some time to make a decision. Some time to find out if this is really what I want.

"Tomorrow," he says, and I nod. "Now, it's time to leave, Lisa. We don't want to be caught here. Go straight home," he instructs.

I turn on my heel, not saying goodbye. It's time to get the hell out of here. I've a lot of thinking to do.

I'm scared of what the future holds for me now that I've killed someone.

CHAPTER
TWELVE
MAVERICK

"We're missing a shipment," Jer says to me, and I can hear the anger in his voice. He's currently in Spain, where he's trying to sort out the drug shipments he has coming from the south of Spain through France, then the United Kingdom, before it lands in Ireland.

"How much?" I ask, wondering just how much money is now gone. How much we've lost.

"Six mil," he grinds out. "We started sending them out in smaller shipments since the Gallaghers started taking over the majority of mainland Spain. I thought we'd only have to worry about them. But we both know whose name is written all over this shit."

He's full of shit. The man who runs Spain for the

Gallaghers is his biological son, something we only found out recently. It's also one of the main reasons that Jer's spending more time in Spain. Malcolm is the second son of Denis Gallagher. It's a fucked up situation for my uncle to have found out he has a son, but knowing he'll never be able to have his son call him dad as he's so close to Denis. But Malcolm and Jer have managed to forge some sort of relationship, and Denis is all for it.

I think it also helps that he's now dating Callie, something I wasn't too fucking happy about, considering the asshole was married when he and my sister got together—something Callie had no idea about. But my sister is happy and in love, and Denis has vowed to love and protect her. And I know he will. I watched him kill his wife—the woman who had a man break into Callie's home and try to kill her. Not to mention, the woman was a fucking awful wife and mother. She cheated on Denis throughout their twenty-two year marriage, and out of the six children that she birthed, only two were her husband's biological children. Denis loves his kids and he loves my sister. We can't lie, the relationships he has with both Callie and Malcolm have only helped strengthen our hold on Dublin and Europe. Having such close ties to one of the biggest Mafia families in the world is always a fucking bonus.

"You really think that the missing shipment is down to that cunt, Tommy?" I ask, not believing that he'd have the power or knowledge of how to pull something like this off.

Over the past four months, shit has hit the fan with regards to Tommy Jennings and his cronies. It took Tommy ten weeks to figure out that it was me and Stephen who took his son's arm and leg. I'm not sure if it was because Paddy was afraid, or if he couldn't speak, but we heard all about the shit that happened the day he found out we were responsible. He was in The Hanged Man pub and was not quiet about the plans he has for us.

He's trying to mount a coup, which is fucking laughable. There's not one of Jer's men who would ever turn their backs on him. Not even Thomas Grace would be that fucking stupid. But Tommy can try. He can work as many avenues as he likes. None of it's going to get him far. The only thing it'll do is piss us all off even more than we already are. He has another son we can go after next if it comes to it.

"What are we going to do about the shipment?" I ask Jer. There's a fucking lot that we should do, but Jer's all about keeping things close to his chest, making moves without them being flashy. He likes to slide under the radar. The only time he'll go big and bold is if someone comes for family or one of his men.

"We need to act fast," Jer says, and his voice has a lethal edge to it. "I have a contact in France who might be able to help us track down the shipment. Word on the street is that Tommy's brought his daughter into the fold. Apparently, she's manipulative as hell. She's sadistic, and she's all about power and money."

Sounds like a Jennings alright. They're all power and money hungry bastards, but not one of them have a brain cell between them.

"Last I heard of Tommy's daughter, she was living down south of the country with her new husband."

I hear Jer's scoff. "That woman broke up a marriage. They both did. Her now husband was already married, had a kid and family. They fucked up the mam and daughter with their bullshit. His ex-wife had bipolar and was struggling to find the right medication to help her through her depression. From what Niall found out, Tommy's daughter was switching the pills. The poor woman couldn't even get the help she needed."

That's beyond fucked up. Why would you destroy a family and then continue to destroy the wife's life? You've got what you want, so why continue? It's all down to the power. That fucker wanted to show she had the power to take everything. Narcissistic bitch.

"What happened to the ex-wife?" I ask, wondering if she got the help she needed.

"She committed suicide. Her thirteen year old daughter found her."

Christ.

"Then the thirteen year old went home with her dad and that bitch of a girlfriend. She was there all of two days before she tried to take her own life too."

Fuck. Fuck. That's heavy. Christ. What the fuck was her dad doing?

"Tommy will no doubt expect us to retaliate to this," Jer says. "But I'll be fucking damned if I give that man anything he wants. No, we're going to play this smart. That fucker will be waiting for us, so we'll ensure that we don't do a fucking thing."

While I understand why, it's not in my nature to sit back and do fucking nothing. This is not how we operate. It never has been. Someone sends a shot at us, we fire one back ten times harder and we do it so they don't see it coming.

"Let me call my guy in France, see what he knows. The shipment should have reached Calais port two hours ago, but hasn't. I'll let you know when I do."

"What do you need from me?" I ask, knowing he wouldn't have called me if he didn't.

"Thomas Grace," he says thickly.

Ah, his brother-in-law and my uncle. The man is a bastard, always has been, always will be. No one but my aunt Patty likes the man. I have always wondered what the hell she saw in him. He's creepy as hell and loves money and power. Many nights I'll find him at the local underground poker ring and watch as he blows through thousands of euros nightly. He's also very handsy with the women servers that work there—something that both Jer and I have warned him about. I laughed when Jer broke his arm when he brushed his hand along one of the server's breasts as he tried to put money into her bra. He's lucky that's all that he got. He'd have had every fucking finger broken, along with his jaw. But Jer sent his message and the man's on his best behaviour—around us, that is. I don't trust him, however, that's for fucking sure.

"What about the cunt?" I ask with a snarl.

"Thomas Grace needs to disappear for a while. I need you to make sure he stays out of the picture until we figure out what Tommy Jennings is up to. Keep an eye on him. Tommy may try to use him against us," he seethes. "There are things not adding up with Thomas, things I can't put my fucking finger on. I don't trust him, Mav, not at fucking all. I need you to ensure that he stays far a-fucking-way from Tommy."

Jer has always had trust in every single one of his men. He'd give them the benefit of the doubt if anything went wrong. He'd never doubt them–publicly at least. But Thomas... Christ, whatever that fucker is up to, it isn't making him look good.

"You know I'll ensure he's gone. I'll have him go to Portugal. He can take Patty and Jess with him for a few weeks. I'll tell him we're looking at purchasing property out there."

I hear Jer's chuckle. "Smart. It won't piss him off. We don't need Thomas Grace acting more suspicious than he already is. Keep him far away from anything to do with the Jennings. He might try to play both sides, and we can't take that risk."

He'll be pissed that I'll be delivering the message that he'll be going to Portugal, but there's nothing that can be done about that. Jer wants me to take over from him when the time's right. He wants to move me to be his second in command, something that Thomas thinks he is.

"And, Mav, keep an eye on your sister. I don't trust Tommy's daughter one bit. If she's as cunning as they say, she might try to use Callie-Girl to get to us," Jer says thickly.

If those fucking Jennings' even think about coming for Callie, they'll die. Not only from us, but from Denis too. Going after Callie would be the wrong motherfucking move.

"She'll be safe," I vow and end the call.

No one is coming for my family. I'll take them out before they even try.

CHAPTER
THIRTEEN
MAVERICK

"Where the hell have you been?" I ask Emmanuel as he slides onto the barstool beside me.

It's been nearly two weeks since I last laid eyes on him, and he's looking more tan and refreshed than ever in his crisp white T-shirt and black jeans.

With a smug grin, he replies, "Jer sent me on a top-secret job in Italy. And while I was there, The Agency had a few assignments for me as well."

We all do side work for The Agency. It's easy money, especially in our line of business. But for Emmanuel, it's a bit trickier. His jobs are always high-profile, like taking out a corrupt politician or a ruthless mafia boss. As a sharpshooter working from a distance, he has to be meticulous and have every detail planned perfectly. But it's no surprise—he's one of the most skilled sharpshooters in Europe and highly coveted by The Agency. Clients specifically request him for their dangerous missions.

"So you decided to top up your tan while you were there?" I ask with a raised brow.

Emmanuel's smile widens. "Jealousy is an ugly look on you, man."

I shake my head and reach for my pint. "How long are you in town for? Or do you have more jobs lined up?"

"Nothing for the next month or so. Jer asked me to stick around, said he may need me," Emmanuel replies. "What's going on?"

I sigh and give him the lowdown on what Jer said about Thomas. "The man's a fucking prick, but thankfully he'll be flying to Portugal tomorrow." I take a sip of my beer. "He can't be trusted."

Emmanuel nods knowingly. "I've known that since the moment I met him. He's a fucking snake. What about Tommy? Has that fucker resurfaced again?"

"We think so," I answer. "Jer called this morning. One of the shipments has gone missing and he's beyond pissed. He thinks it was Tommy and his daughter who did it."

Emmanuel raises an eyebrow in surprise. "Daughter?"

"Yeah. Apparently, she's been brought into the fold and is working with her dad," I say bitterly. "That should be fun. But she's a narcissistic bitch, and from what Jer told me, she's ruthless. But she's a Jennings. I doubt they have a working brain cell between them." I tell him about what she and her husband did to his family and what that bitch did to his ex-wife. She's seriously fucked up for that shit.

"We shouldn't underestimate them," Emmanuel warns. "If that bitch is that manipulative and so casual about it, she may be smarter than we're giving her credit for."

"That's true," I muse. "But so far she hasn't shown her face in Dublin. I doubt she'll come back. She'll probably continue causing chaos from wherever the hell she is down the country."

Emmanuel chuckles. "She'll probably stay down there until something else happens with her family. Who knows when Jer will lose his shit and give us the go-ahead to deal with another one of Tommy's men."

I won't be going after his men the next time Jer lets me at them. Fuck no. I have my sights set firmly on his other son.

"Have you seen that girl again?" Emmanuel asks me with a sly grin, interrupting my thoughts about revenge.

My brows furrow and I turn to him. "What girl?"

He laughs, amused by my forgetfulness. "Forgotten her already?" he quips. "The girl who saved your ass."

Lisa Turner. Of course I haven't forgotten about her. I've tried to push her out of my mind, knowing she's just a young girl and not my concern. But it's not every day you meet someone who'll run down fully grown men to try to save you.

"She didn't save my ass," I snap defensively. "But you could learn a thing or two from her about driving. You drive like your granny."

He flips me off playfully. "I was curious about her friend."

I did notice the lingering look he gave the young girl.

"She's just a kid," I tell him, getting annoyed that he's even going there. "Too fucking young for you."

"I know that," he snaps back defensively, his tone softer now. "The girl was almost raped. Who knows what she went through before we showed up? I was just wondering how she's doing."

I ease up a little, understanding where his concerns are coming from. "I don't know, Eman. Maybe ask Jer. He seems to know their backgrounds pretty well."

"You don't know?" he asks quietly, his eyes avoiding mine as if trying to hide something.

"Know what?" I ask impatiently, wondering what the hell he's talking about.

"That girl, Clodagh?" he says in a hushed voice so that only I can hear. "Her parents were killed and she was taken hostage."

I blink in surprise at his words. Never in a million years did I think that would be what he'd say. "Fuck, are you sure?"

He glances away, the tips of his ears turning red with embarrassment. "Yeah, I'm sure. Jacob Dellinger was the man who killed her family and kidnapped her. He held her captive for two months."

I grit my teeth in anger at the mention of that name. Fucking Jacob. That bastard is a sick, twisted monster, and I would gladly slit his throat if given the chance. "Emmanuel," I say through clenched teeth. "It wasn't your fault."

He nods, his expression heavy with guilt. "I know that, Mav. I do. But Clodagh was only eleven when he took her. And he became fixated on her because of me."

"Fuck that," I snarl, my own anger rising to match his. "He's a sick motherfucking asshole who had an affinity for young girls. It's not on you, and the fact that he tried to blame it on you is fucked up. You were barely seventeen at the time. You wouldn't have done what that cunt did."

"Hell no," he fires back vehemently. "I'm no fucking paedophile. I don't touch kids."

No, he wouldn't. Emmanuel is nothing like his biological father, despite what that prick claims. He may be ruthless and willing to kill for money or thrills, but he would never harm a woman or child. He's not like Jacob.

"Your mam and step-dad raised you right, Eman," I remind him sternly. "You are them, not that sperm donor."

"Genetics can be a fucked up thing," he confesses with a heavy sigh. "I think she recognized me that night. When I looked into her eyes, she froze. But when I spoke, she seemed to relax a bit. I scared her for a moment."

It's hard to deny that he has the exact same eyes as Jacob, but he couldn't be any more different from that bastard. Emmanuel may share DNA with him, but he's nothing like Jacob. He'll never hurt an innocent like his father did.

"You probably won't see her again," I tell him truthfully. "But if she was scared of you, I think she would have made it known. Both Lisa and Clodagh seem to have strong wills and aren't afraid to speak their minds."

"I just want to know what the fuck Ava was playing at that night," he seethes, his anger directed toward my sister's best friend, who had been at the party the night we met Lisa and Clodagh. "She watched Clodagh go upstairs with those assholes. She knew she was drunk and did nothing," he spits with disgust. "What the fuck was she doing?"

"Freddie was beyond pissed," I growl, remembering the conversation we had the next day when he told me what happened; how he'd arrived just as Lisa had started looking for her friend. Ava was sat on his lap and asked her if she meant Clodagh and then told her where she was. "Ava was ripped a new asshole by Freddie and Jer. I have no doubt that Callie also lit into her too."

A smile plays on his lips and he nods. We drink our drinks and change the subject, talking about the football game last night. I hear the door of the pub swinging open, and I am taken aback by who walks in — Travis James. It's been years since I've seen him.

"Well, well, Maverick, just the man I was hoping to run into," Travis greets me with a charming smile. He's not changed over the years. He's gotten older, sure, but he's still the same man I met eight years ago with Jer.

I raise an eyebrow in surprise. "You have my number. You could have called."

Travis laughs as he takes a seat next to me and orders himself a beer. "True, but you know me; I enjoy the element of surprise. I actually have a favour to ask you," he says, his English accent thicker and more pronounced than I remember.

"Oh really? And what might that be?"

"I have a new recruit for The Agency. They're young, but she's incredibly talented," Travis explains, resting his hands on the bar in front of him.

"Travis," I say low. "You can't be serious? I'm not going to babysit someone, especially a female, as they kill someone." Is he for fucking real with this shit?

"I'm not asking you to babysit her, Maverick," Travis replies, a hint of annoyance creeping into his voice. "She's young but she's not stupid, nor does she need to be handheld. I trust her, but just as you had Stephen and Jer when you started out, she needs someone too."

He's right, I did have Stephen and Jer when I killed first, but having to watch over someone I don't know isn't on the top of my list of things to do.

"Is there no one else?" I ask, hoping like fuck that there is.

His jaw clenches, and I watch as anger flashes in his

blue eyes. "There is," he snarls. "But I had hoped I could have someone I trust fully to watch over this girl. Mentor her, so to speak."

I sigh. "With all the shit that's going on with the Jennings' right now, Travis, I don't think I'll be the right person to mentor her."

"Alright," he says, bringing his glass to his lips. "But if you change your mind, let me know."

I nod, knowing I won't. I know it's not what he wants, but I can't and don't want to do it. Even though he denied it, it is babysitting and I've not got time for that shit.

"I can see that it's a firm no," Travis says. "I'm in Dublin for the next week or two. I want to get her settled in. I have to admit, her technique needs some adjusting but it was fucking inspired. She's going to make a name for herself."

"How exactly did you meet this woman?" I ask.

He grins wide. "I met her this evening. Flew over to take out a target. Let me tell you, this asshole was the lowest scum to walk the earth. I would have done it for free, he was that much of a fucking shit. Anyway," he says, taking a sip of his drink, "I followed him to a secluded area. I couldn't believe my eyes when I watched him confront this girl. He was out of his mind, the fucking dick, but she took no shit. She overpowered him easily and then killed him. All without breaking down. The kid's good, so good, in fact, that I offered her a job on the spot." His voice is filled with glee.

"You watched it happen?" Emmanuel asks in surprise. "You let a woman fight off a fucking crazy man?"

"If she needed me to, I would have stepped in. She didn't. So now I'm taking her under my wing and getting someone to mentor her."

I give him a pointed stare. "If you like her so much, why don't you do it?"

"She lives here in Ireland. I don't, nor do I want to. I have my own business in London. So I need someone I can trust to help her hone her skills. I have a few people in mind. I'll give them a call this evening."

I can't lie, I'm intrigued. I'm curious as to what method of killing she uses. I haven't heard Travis praise someone in a fucking long time. I guess if she's as good as he claims, I'll be hearing about her a lot more.

CHAPTER
FOURTEEN
LISA

I KEEP my head down as I walk along O'Connell Street. It's busy, people walking by without a care in the world. It's the way to be; to not see the horrors that lurk in other people's worlds. I thought my dad was an asshole, but Devin's father took the cake, and yet people have no idea what the hell the person beside them is like. They're oblivious to the depraved assholes that walk this earth. It's been almost twenty-four hours since I killed Devin's dad, and I'm scared. Not because I'm worried about what'll happen to me. No, it's the opposite. I'm scared of myself. I feel no remorse for what I've done. I thought for sure that when it sunk in what I had done, I'd feel something. But there's nothing, not even guilt or repulsion.

I'm a murderer, and right now I'm on my way to

meet a man who's going to give me more jobs. I have no idea what to expect, but I know deep in my bones that this is the right thing for me to do. I don't know why; it's just a feeling I have, and I've learned to trust my gut. It hasn't led me wrong thus far. I also know not to speak a word of what's gone down or will go down. If anyone found out what I'd done, they'd be repulsed, disgusted, afraid. No matter what that cunt did to Devin, I'd be made out to be the bad guy. I can't lose my support system. They've helped me so much and I'm not ready for them to go away.

Pushing open the door to the pub, I'm surprised to find Travis seated in the corner booth, his gaze squarely on me. I watch as the haggard lines on his face transform as he smiles widely at me. I didn't have a chance to really look at him last night. I was more focused on trying to get out of the situation I was in. But looking at him now, I see that he's in his mid-to-late forties. He's got jet black hair and a goatee; his blue eyes are bright and piercing.

Taking a deep breath, I walk toward him, noticing that he's not alone. He's got a blonde guy sitting with him. Both of them stand as I reach the table. "Travis," I greet with a small smile.

"Lisa," he replies. "I'm glad you came. Let me introduce you to Ciarán. He's someone who's agreed to help you hone that technique."

I turn to the blonde guy. He's got a cheeky smile on his face, and his green eyes are filled with a hidden darkness. I can't help but wonder what scars he's hiding that caused that darkness.

"Lisa," he greets, sticking out his hand for me to shake. "It's nice to meet you. Travis has told me a bit about last night's situation. I've got to admit, I was surprised when he told me what you did. It was fucking crazy, but then again, aren't we all?"

I flinch at the word crazy. It's been over three years since Ma died and I still hear Tanya calling Ma and me crazy. It's something I think will always stick with me. I know Ma wasn't crazy and neither am I.

"It's nice to meet you too," I say quickly, recovering from the flinch. I take a hold of his hand and we shake. "Do you work for Travis?"

He laughs. "Yeah, I do. Come sit with us," he says, his voice soft and gentle. "Have you eaten?"

I hear Travis chuckle and I turn to him with a raised brow. "I told him he'd start to feel protective of you when he met you."

I roll my eyes. That's utter bullshit. No one other than my ma and Orna has ever felt protective of me. I'm not the type of girl anyone cares about.

"He's right," Ciarán tells me as I slide into the booth between him and Travis. "You're young, and I'm going to ensure that your safety is paramount when you're on the job. Which means until Travis and I believe that you're more than capable of doing it alone, I'll be with you whenever you have a job."

"Great," I mumble. "A glorified babysitter. Surely you have something better to do than that?"

Ciarán laughs. "Trust me, from what Travis has told me, this'll be fun."

"Christ," Travis hisses. "You're like a child, Ciarán." He turns to me. "What he means is that we want to ensure that you're well equipped and are comfortable to go out on your own and do this. We're not babysitting you. We're just giving you the chance to do what you want but with the right tools."

I release a deep breath as I press my hands flat against the table. "So, how does this all work?"

Ciarán rubs his hands together with glee, a wide smile on his face. "Told you she'd be game."

Travis glares at him. "Shut it," he snaps. "So, you'll be added to the system. When someone who matches your requirements is put onto the system to be taken care of, you'll be notified with the time, date, and price. It's not something you have to do. You'll be given the opportunity to accept or decline. If you accept, you'll be given the target's name and the location they'll be in. You'll then have to take out the target."

I drum my fingers against the table. "It sounds very covert," I tell him. "How long have you had this Agency?"

"Over a decade," he answers honestly. "We've got some of the very best killers working for us and we want you to join the ranks of The Agency."

"Do you have women work for you?" I ask, needing to know I won't be the only one.

Travis' grin widens. "Oh yes. My daughter works for us. She doesn't take on as many as she used to, but the money from the job set her up nicely."

I rear back, surprised by his answer. He let his daughter kill people? I shouldn't be shocked, but I am. "Okay, so how do I get paid?"

"Ah," Travis begins with a slight pause. "As you're a ward of the state, I took it upon myself to set a bank account up for you. This one only you will be able to access." He reaches into his pocket and pulls out a phone. "I also purchased you a new phone."

I blink. "Why?" I ask, wondering why he's done that.

"Last night, you took care of something that I was meant to. I owe you, so take the phone as my thanks."

I reach forward and see that it's the latest model.

He must have spent a lot of money on it. "Thank you," I say softly. The phone I have is old and belonged to Orna before she upgraded her own. I was grateful when she gave it to me, knowing how tough it is to have me and Devin to take care of.

"You'll see an app for banking," Travis says, pushing a piece of paper across the table. "Here's the details to enter it. Once you've got it sorted, change the pin code. It's all yours, Lisa. Everything in there is too."

I pause at his words and stare at him. "What have you done?" I ask, unable to keep the horror out of my voice. "Travis?" I ask, needing to know what the hell is going on.

"Christ, Lisa, just look at the bloody app," Travis replies, running his hand through his hair. "You're going to be a pain in my ass, aren't you?"

I ignore him and input the details he's given me, my heart stammering against my chest as I log in. I'm beyond shocked to see the amount on the screen.

"Why?" I ask, swiping my tongue along my bottom lip. "Why on earth does it say there's two-hundred-thousand euros in my account?"

"Welcome to The Agency, Lisa," Ciarán tells me with a smile. "It's not some shitty agency; it's high-end contract killing. You have to pay handsomely for it, and let me tell you, that's one of the lower sums I've seen."

I blink, unable to believe what I'm hearing. "Are you for real?"

He nods. "I've been paid into the millions for a job," he says with a laugh. "But of course, the higher the profile you take out, the more you get paid. Remember that."

"So," Travis says. "Are you ready to accept the job?"

"Yes," I reply without hesitation. My mind is whirling with all the things I can do with the money. "So what's the next step?" I ask, wondering where we go from here.

"Are you sure you don't want some food?" Ciarán asks. "Have you eaten?"

"What are you, my da?" I ask with a raised brow. Hell, even Orna doesn't ask if I've eaten anymore.

Travis chuckles. "Let the man worry," he tells me. "This is new for him too. He's going to be your mentor, Lisa, which is a role he's taking seriously. If you need anything, you call him."

"Him?" I wonder how old he is. He looks barely old enough to drink let alone be a mentor. "Sorry," I say, realising just how bitchy that sounded.

Ciarán waves me away. "Trust me, I get it. I'm eighteen, Lisa, so I know what it's like to be where you are now. In fact, I was also sixteen when I started working for The Agency."

Now I'm intrigued. "You recruit young, don't you?" I say to Travis, who laughs. "Is it a front for a cult?"

Travis and Ciarán burst out laughing. "God, you're hilarious, Lisa," Travis says through his laughter. "No, we're not a cult, and the reason Ciarán started working for us is because of his brother. My son recruited him."

"So it's a family business then?" I ask, knowing that he owns it and both his son and daughter work for him.

"Yes, so to speak. We all co-own it. Melissa—my daughter—coded the website and has ensured that it's secure. She's a fucking genius."

"Okay, so Ciarán's my mentor. What does that entail?"

"He'll be contacted first to ensure the date works for him, and if he says yes, you'll receive a message. I urge you, Lisa, to call Ciarán when you get that message. It opens a line of trust between the two of you. When you both give the go ahead, together you'll travel to the mark. Ciarán will only be there to assist if needed as well as give pointers on what you can do. He's solely there to help you, not take over. This is all on you. Your mark, your kill, your life. Ciarán will probably be present more than not because that's just who he is. He's going to worry about you and no doubt wants you to check in with him every so often, just as my son did with him when he mentored Ciarán."

I take a deep breath. It's a lot to take in, but I have realised that it means I have support, and as annoying as Ciarán seems, I can tell that he has a good heart. "Okay, I agree to those terms. But if Ciarán interferes in my personal life, I'm not going to be happy."

Ciarán smirks. "Worried I'll run off all the boys?"

I roll my eyes. "Ass," I bite back.

"Okay, children," Travis says with exasperation. "I forgot how annoying kids are. Thank fuck mine are adults."

"I am an adult," Ciarán grunts.

"Then bloody act like it," Travis hisses. "So, Lisa, we have a mark in Belfast who needs to be taken care of this evening. We don't want to rush you, but as both Ciarán and I are here, we're more than happy to come along with you if you accept."

Can I kill someone again so quickly after killing Devin's father?

"Sure, why not," I reply. It's not like I have anything else planned. "Oh, I do have one last question," I say. "With Ciarán being my mentor, does he get paid?"

Ciarán shakes his head but it's Travis who answers. "No, it's free. Ciarán knows that and is happy to be your mentor. Now, we really do need to get moving. We need to drive to Belfast and get in position."

I'm shocked Ciarán is doing this for free. I'm grateful he's wanting to take me under his wing and show me the ropes. I follow both men out of the pub and down the street to the car park where Travis' car is parked.

"You're in the back," Travis instructs. I do as he says and slide into the back seat. It's around a two hour journey to Belfast from here. I'm just hoping that whatever's about to happen isn't going to be hard. I don't want it to be messy either.

I'M STANDING against the car. Ciarán stands in front of me, blocking my path so I don't lose my shit. I watch as a man backhands his daughter. Her eyes are red raw from the tears that are streaming down her face. She didn't even flinch, which lets me know this isn't the first time she's been hit by that bastard.

"That is our target," Ciarán tells me, his voice low

but vibrating with anger. "He's going to send his daughter into the hotel and he's going to go for a walk. To his wife and daughter, it's to work off his anger—something he does a lot of—but the truth is, he's going to find his friend who works in trafficking, and that man has three young girls for this asshole to choose from."

I cross my arms over my chest, my nails biting into my skin. What an animal. God, I hate him. I'll happily take him out. In fact, I want to do it right now.

"Focus, Lisa," Travis says from beside me. "This is why we have someone mentor you. Ciarán is going to walk you through what you need to do. You need to listen to him. Listen to every word he tells you."

I take a deep breath, tearing my gaze away from the man hitting his daughter once again. "Okay, what's the plan?"

Ciarán grins. "Atta girl." He reaches into his back pocket and pulls out a needle. "This has a drug that'll knock him out, and by the time the asshole's found hanging from the bridge, the substance will be gone."

"You managed to get that quickly," I comment.

Both Ciarán and Travis laugh. "You'd be surprised what you'll be able to get when you look in the right places," Travis says. "Now, he's on the move. We're going to follow behind him. I need you to inject him in his palm, Lisa. That way, it'll be harder to decipher the pin prick he'll have.

Ciarán hands me the needle, pulling the top off the pin. I grip it between my fingers tightly.

We follow the man through the almost empty streets. I keep the needle gripped firmly. I can't help but feel determined. I'm glad I'm not the only one who wants this monster taken down. I'm beyond relieved that someone has put a hit out on him. It's dark out, the only light from the streetlamps. I keep my gaze on the man ahead of me.

I need to get to him before he meets his friend and takes one of those young girls.

The man leads us to a nearby alley, where he takes out his phone and makes a call. I listen as he confirms the rendezvous with his friend. Ciarán and Travis begin whispering to each other, talking about the plan, but I blur their words out. I have to focus on the man in front of me.

I can't lie, having them by my side is such a relief. I know they'll be here if I need them. It's a comforting thought.

"Okay, Lisa," Ciarán says, breaking the silence. "You ready?"

I grip the needle tightly, my hands shake slightly,

but I know I have to be strong. I can do this. I won't let that animal hurt a girl.

"Yeah," I reply, my voice steady. I'm more than ready for this.

As the man rounds the corner, I increase my speed, easily catching up to him. I step beside him, feeling the heat radiating off his body, and the adrenaline pulses through my veins. With a steady hand, I reach out and brush against his palm, concealing the syringe in my grip. In one swift motion, I plunge the needle into his skin and inject him with the drug, watching as his eyes widen in shock and he mutters a curse.

I pull the syringe from his palm and carry on walking, acting as though nothing has happened. My feet move quickly to the nearby alleyway, where I lie in wait for him to stagger past.

As I stand against the alley wall, my eyes flicking toward the street, I watch in anticipation for the man to appear. I know Travis and Ciarán remain close by, ready to act if need be.

The man turns the corner into the alleyway, stumbling slightly. His eyes dart about, wild and unfocused. He reaches out, his hand brushing along the wall as he staggers toward me.

I step out from the shadows, my hand extended toward his. I can see the fear in his eyes as he grabs my arm, his grip tightening. "What do you want?" he rasps, his voice strained.

"Nothing," I reply, my voice steady and calm. "I just wanted to make sure you understood the consequences of your actions."

I release his wrist and he stumbles back, tripping over his feet. He collapses to the ground, and I know that now is the time.

"Travis has gone to get the car. He'll be here any second," Ciarán tells me. "I'm impressed," he praises. "You did that effortlessly and without hesitation. I'd say you have a good career ahead of you."

I hear the sound of Travis' car pulling up outside the other end of the alleyway. "Let's get him out of here," I say, my voice calm and steady, but I can feel the adrenaline coursing through my veins.

Without hesitation, I reach for his feet and drag him toward the car. He's heavy as hell, but thankfully, I'm able to load him into the boot of Travis' car. The moment Ciarán slams the boot closed, I feel a sense of relief and satisfaction.

I'm surprised at how easy I'm finding this. I thought I'd be terrified but I'm not. I'm at ease, especially knowing that we've saved at least one young girl from a horrific fate. I wish I could have taken the friend out too, but I know there's a process, and today

I'm focused on the asshole who's currently in the boot of the car. I can live in hope that his friend will be taken out next.

Travis drives us to the nearest bridge. Thankfully, with it being late at night there's hardly anyone around. I know that once Travis parks, I'm going to have to go as quickly as I can. I won't have much time to linger. I guess that's for the best. The quicker I do this, the better.

The second Travis pulls up on the bridge, we're all out of the car, Travis keeping watch to ensure that any cars that come near us don't stop, and Ciarán at my side in case I need help.

Pulling the asshole from the car is hard work, and God, I wish for once there'd be some skinny asshole, who I'd be able to manage easier. Once I have him out of the boot, I reach for the rope Ciarán brought with us. He came prepared, which is great. I tie a noose on the end of the rope and wrap it around the fucker on the ground's neck. Once I've done that, I drag him to the side of the bridge. There's enough room for him to fall between the gaps. I take it that Travis did his homework and found the best place to do this.

Tying the rope to the bridge takes a lot longer than I had anticipated. Thankfully, Ciarán's there. "Think of it like your shoes," he instructs. "Tie, loop, pull.

That's it," he encourages as I do exactly as he says. "Now do it again. Double knot it, Lisa. We want to ensure that fucker doesn't escape from the rope."

I tie it three times around the bridge, pulling it taut so it tightens impossibly. Once I'm done, I take a deep breath and push the asshole from the side of the bridge. Just as Devin's father did before him, he falls at rapid speed, but the rope stops him and he begins to swing. Ciarán helps me to my feet and keeps his arm wrapped around my shoulders as we watch the fucker below us.

Within minutes, he's dead, his body still swinging in the wind.

"Let's get the fuck out of here," Travis says, his gaze searching the road, checking to ensure no one's coming. I slide into the back of the car, pulling on my seatbelt as Ciarán jumps into the front passenger's seat.

"You did good, kid," Travis praises me. "Once again you didn't falter."

"Yep," Ciarán says, nodding his head. "You just need to work on your strength. You need to be able to carry them sometimes. Having scrape marks on their bodies may not be the best thing."

"Noted," I reply, my hands shaking as the adrenaline rush I felt starts to crash.

"Let's go home and get you some food." Travis

smiles through the rear-view mirror. "It'll be a while before you'll have another job. Just remember what we said. Keep in contact with Ciarán."

"I will," I vow, knowing I can learn a lot from him. A hell of a lot. "By the way, what was the price for this job?"

I hear Travis' deep laughter. "Half a million," he tells me through his laughter.

Holy hell. What do I do with that much money?

Fuck. I'm rich.

I'm only sixteen. Imagine how much I'll have by the time I hit twenty-one.

A smile forms on my face. For the first time in a long time, I'm looking forward to the future. I can't wait to see what life has in store for me.

CHAPTER
FIFTEEN
MAVERICK

Five Years Later

"Are you going out tonight?" Jer asks with a raised brow.

I shake my head. "Christ, old man, I'm twenty-seven years old. I don't need to ask permission."

He chuckles. "Not wanting you to ask for permission, asshole; just curious if you're going out."

I narrow my eyes at him. "Oh, and why is that?"

"You see, every time you or Emmanuel go out and party, you end up fighting with one of Tommy's men."

I sigh. "That's not our fault. They start that shit

and you and I both know I'm not going to let some punk start a fight and let it slide."

Over the past five years, Tommy and his family have kept a low profile. He's careful not to start shit with Jer or Denis Gallagher. His men, on the other hand, don't know how to stop themselves, and we find ourselves showing those assholes their places. Many nights I've ended up sending someone to the hospital because they couldn't control themselves.

Just because Tommy and his family have kept a low profile, it doesn't mean they're not doing things. From what our sources tell us, they're focusing on working down the country where his daughter is spearheading things. As long as they're not coming at us, we'll let them be for now.

"I think Tommy learned his lesson when he tried to take your drugs," I remind him. After that call about the shipment going missing, Jer made a call, and within four hours he had his drugs back. It showed Tommy that it doesn't matter how big he thinks he is, we've got a bigger reach. Jer has worked in this industry for decades. He's forged relationships and made strong allies. People are loyal to him, and in return he's just as loyal to them and their families.

"True," Jer agrees. "But don't forget, this ain't a

game. We're dealing with serious people here, and one wrong move could cost us everything."

"I know," I say, my voice low and filled with anger. "That's why we've been playing this carefully, keeping our distance. We're following your lead, Jer. Had it been down to me, I'd have taken Tommy down the moment he fucked with our business."

Jer leans back in his chair, his gaze fixed on me. "I know you would, kid. But patience is key in this game. Revenge can wait as long as we're still standing strong." He pauses, taking a puff of his cigar before continuing. "But speaking of taking someone out, there's been some chatter lately. Rumours swirling about a new player in town, and they're making a name for themselves."

I raise a brow. That's news to me. I haven't heard shit. "Any idea who it might be?" I ask. "What are they doing?"

Jer shakes his head. "Not yet. But I've got some feelers out, trying to uncover what this new player wants. They're taking out some big names in our world, Maverick, so I need you to keep your eyes open and stay sharp."

"They're doing it under the radar, aren't they?"

Jer's lips curve into a smile. "Yes, and they're

fucking clever about it. Not even the cops have caught on to the murders. They just see them as suicides."

It clicks in my head what he's talking about. I saw on the news two nights ago that the rate of suicides has risen over the past year compared to the last ten. Knowing someone's murdering these people and making it seem as though it's a suicide just adds a whole new layer to the mix. This person's either stupid or very, very fucking smart.

"Stay smart and stay alert," Jer instructs. "The last thing I need is for your mam to lose her shit if you're mixed up in this shit."

I laugh at his words. My mam is the only one who scares him.

"I'll be stopping by to see Jess tomorrow," I tell him. "Want to come?"

My aunt Pattie died almost four years ago. She was shot while out running errands when Jess was fourteen. My cousin is quiet and reserved. She keeps everyone at arm's length. It's her eighteenth birthday soon and I want to get her a present.

"You know that Jess doesn't like me, but I'll ensure that she has her birthday present. I try not to piss her off with my attendance more than I have to."

I chuckle. He's an ass, but he loves Jess and wants

the best for her. "I'm going," I tell him. "I'll see you tomorrow."

Over the past five years, my role within the Houlihan Gang has grown. The people within the gang know that I'm someone they come to if they need anything, especially if Jer's out of town. It used to be Thomas Grace, but that cunt has been even more of an asshole since Aunt Patty died. He's an insufferable asshole, and the only reason we keep him around is because of Jess. If he weren't her father, he'd have been dealt with a long fucking time ago.

"Be safe, and don't do anything I wouldn't," Jer shouts as I exit the house, his laughter following behind me.

"Fuck." I hear Emmanuel's low hiss. "Christ, is that who I think it is?"

We're at the back of Callie's pub in Temple Bar. It's crowded, as it is every weekend. Everyone is out to have a good time and let loose, to forget about their troubles and just have fun.

My head snaps in the direction of Emmanuel's gaze, and my whole body locks up. It's been five years since I've seen her, but there's no mistaking that it's her. Lisa Turner. Fuck, she's beautiful. Her dark brown hair is now streaked with blonde. She's got a bright smile on her face, making her beauty stand out. I watch as she moves through the throngs of people with ease and grace, drawing attention from every guy in here.

I swallow hard as I see her wrap her arms around a tall, muscular guy. My eyes narrow as I catch a glimpse of his cut. He's a prospect with the Fury Vipers MC, the new motorcycle club in town. The president, Pyro, is dating Callie's step-daughter—my niece–Chloe.

"Is that fucking Cowboy?" Emmanuel questions.

I nod. Yes, it fucking is. The guy got his nickname due to the fact he's got his hands in everything. The mafia, the Fury Vipers MC, drugs, guns... Anything he can, he's involved in. He's a fucking cowboy, hence his moniker.

"How the fuck does she know him?" I ask, my voice low and filled with anger.

She's pure. He shouldn't touch her. He shouldn't be anywhere near her. I can't stand back, not anymore.

I push through the crowd, determined to get to her. Cowboy's gaze lands on me when I'm five feet away. I see the surprise register on his face. He mutters something to Lisa and she spins on her heels to face me. The moment her gaze collides with mine, I see the recognition hit her. It's mixed with surprise and heat. That's fucking good, because the way she looks, there's no way I wouldn't be interested in her. She's always intrigued me and even more so now.

"Maverick," she breathes, her voice barely audible over the music.

"Lisa," I reply, my own voice rough. I didn't expect to want her. But Christ, I do.

She moves away from Cowboy and practically throws herself into my arms. "How are you?" she asks. "It's been so long."

I wrap my arms around her, pulling her close to me. "It's been too long," I reply. Too fucking long. She's what, twenty-one now? She's fucking gorgeous. She still has that glint of sadness in her eyes, the same as I saw almost a decade ago when I first met her.

She looks up at me, her eyes searching mine—for what, I don't know. I glance behind her to where Cowboy is standing a few feet away, his expression unreadable, but there's a dangerous glint in his eyes that doesn't go unnoticed. He's watching us both, almost as though he's her bodyguard.

"I didn't expect to run into you here," Lisa says, her fingers absently playing with the collar of my leather jacket. "How have you been?"

"I've been keeping busy. What about you? What

brings you here tonight?" I ask, loving that she's touching me without realising it. It's been a while since I've been with a woman. I'm not a one night kind of guy. I've always felt as though there's something missing with the women I've been with.

Lisa hesitates for a moment before glancing back at Cowboy, who is now making his way over to us. "I'm out to have fun," she tells me with a bright smile. "I didn't know he'd be here. He's just a friend."

I'm glad as fuck that she clarified that he's just a friend, although I don't think he knows that. I can feel the tension radiating from him as he approaches, his eyes locked on mine.

"Maverick," Cowboy greets with a nod, his voice low and filled with barely concealed anger. "Long time no see."

I nod back, my jaw clenched tight. "Cowboy."

Lisa looks up at me and then back to Cowboy. "You two know each other?"

"Yeah, we go way back," Cowboy answers cryptically, his gaze never leaving mine. He's always been an asshole, but he's pushing his luck right now.

Lisa steps back, her eyes narrowed as she stares between Cowboy and I. "How do you two know each other?"

Cowboy clenches his jaw, his gaze solely on me. I

ignore the jackass and focus on Lisa. "The motorcycle club he's affiliated with?" I say, and she nods. "My niece is the president's old lady."

"You're Chloe's uncle?" she asks, her eyes bright. "Callie's your sister?"

I grin at her. "My twin sister, yeah. You know Callie?"

She nods. "She's sweet. So tell me, have you managed to stay out of trouble?"

I can't help but laugh. Christ, she's fun. "Not really. Have you?"

She giggles. It's soft, and my cock stirs to life. "Not really," she says, copying my answer.

"Lisa," Cowboy says, interrupting us, and I want to smash my fist into his face. "Call me if you need me," he tells her. "And be careful."

"Why is he warning you about me?" I ask, wondering how close they actually are.

"He's a friend, Maverick. Just a friend. Now, I'm parched. Why don't I get us drinks and we can catch up? It's been too long since I've seen you. I'm guessing there's a lot that I've missed."

I bite back a retort and reach for her hand. She doesn't hesitate and curls her fingers around mine. "What are you drinking?" I ask and smile. "You are legal, right?"

She sighs. "I'm twenty-one, Maverick. I've been legal for a while. I'll have a beer, please."

I order our drinks, noting that Emmanuel is gone. I lead her to the corner of the pub, where I was sitting when she arrived. "So, how have you been?" I ask once we're seated.

She takes a sip of her beer. Her eyes still hold that sadness that once looked as though it would consume her. "I'm good. I can't believe it's been five years since I saw you. Tell me everything. Did you get in any more trouble with those assholes?"

I laugh, remembering the night we met and Tommy fucking Jennings and his cronies came after me. "No more trouble. What about you? Have you put your street racing talent to use since then?"

Her smile is wide and my cock stirs to life once again. Christ, I want her. I've never felt this way before. I want her, but it's not just about sex. I'm not a virgin, and I've had my fair share of women, but there's something about Lisa that makes me want a fuck of a lot more than just sex.

"No," she laughs. "I've been on my best behaviour. I think Orna would lose her shit if the cops came to the door again." Her smile lights up her entire face. Christ, she so fucking beautiful. "So, have you settled down?" she asks while glancing down at her hands, which are tight around the glass of beer she's holding.

I can't help but smirk. "No, I've never thought about it."

She raises an eyebrow, a small smile playing on her lips. "So, there's no one special in your life?"

I pause, my eyes locked on hers. "I wouldn't say that," I reply, my voice low and intentional. "I've never thought about settling down with anyone until about twenty minutes ago, when this gorgeous brunette walked into the bar. Gotta tell you, babe, it was like being struck by lightning seeing you again."

Her cheeks flush. "Mav—" she whispers.

"You gonna tell me you're not feeling the same?" I ask her with a raised brow.

She shakes her head and her eyes dart away, her fingers tracing the condensation on her glass. "I... I can't deny there's something here, Maverick. But it's complicated."

I lean in closer, my voice low. "Complicated how?"

She takes a deep breath, meeting my gaze again. "I'm not the same girl you met five years ago. A lot has changed. I've changed."

"Babe, you think I don't know that? You think that we've not all changed?" I shake my head. "We were never going to be the same as we were five years ago." I reach across the table and take her hand. She doesn't pull away. Instead, her fingers curl around mine. "This thing between us..." I begin, and she nods, her eyes wide and filled with hope and a little fear. "We're starting out. You don't know me and vice versa. It'll take some time to build trust. You just gotta take the chance."

Lisa nods slowly, her thumb absently stroking the back of my hand. "You're right," she says softly. "It's just... I've been hurt before, Maverick. I'm scared of letting someone in again."

I squeeze her hand gently. "I get it, babe. I've got my own scars too. But sometimes you've gotta take a chance, right?"

She gives me a small smile, vulnerability shining in her eyes. "Yeah, I suppose you do."

"Do you have any plans for tomorrow?" I ask, a plan forming in my head.

Her brows knit together. "No. Not that I know of. Why?"

"Then how about we have dinner? Tomorrow night?"

My heart begins to race. Fuck, what if she says no?

A small smile tugs at the corner of her lips. "Dinner sounds nice."

"Good," I say, feeling a wave of relief wash over me.

I want to woo her. I want her to feel comfortable around me. "I know a great little Italian place not far from here. I'll pick you up at seven?"

She nods, her smile growing wider. "I'd like that."

My heart rate settles as I stare at her. She's so fucking beautiful, so damn sweet. I want her. I want her so badly I can't fucking think straight.

A date? I've never been on one before, but I know that Lisa deserves to be treated like a fucking queen. *So a date it is.*

CHAPTER
SIXTEEN
LISA

I'M GIDDY. There's no other way to describe it. I've never felt so wanted or as beautiful as I do tonight. This date is anything but ordinary. The food was amazing and the company even more so. There's always been something about Maverick that makes my heart go crazy and I've never been sure what it is, but being with him this evening has made me understand just what it is. I'm attracted to him, and I think it's more than that.

He's been the perfect gentleman. He holds my hand tightly, keeping me close to him as we walk. He's so bloody tall, somewhere over six feet. It makes me feel small despite me being five-foot-six. He stands between me and the road as we walk, as well as shields me from people walking past. Throughout dinner, the conversation was easy and didn't feel uncomfortable at all. We didn't delve into our family dynamics, which is great as I'm not sure I'm ready to open up about my family just yet. Hell, if ever. But being with Maverick feels good, feels right. That's not something I've ever felt before, and I want to keep it.

"You okay, babe?" he asks, and my stomach clenches, as it has every time he's called me babe.

"Yeah," I reply. "Thanks for this evening. It was the perfect date."

It really was. I couldn't have asked for a better date. I had been nervous all day—something I hadn't felt in a long time. My world upended when I killed Devin's father and it's been a rollercoaster since. I've had to be strong and take charge, something that hasn't come naturally. I've had to become someone different. But tonight, I could be me. I could relax and just be who I really am. It's been amazing.

"I'm hoping the night's not over yet," Maverick says with a grin as he pulls me close to him. I collide with his rock hard body, my hands resting against his chest as I look up at him. "Stay with me tonight," he whispers, his lips ghosting against my own.

My heart races. Stay the night? I've never done anything like this before. I'm still a virgin. Am I ready for this?

"Hey," he says softly, his hands framing my face. "No pressure, Lisa. Just spend the night, nothing else."

I look up at him. Those gorgeous brown eyes of his are filled with such tenderness, it's a wonder I can breathe. "Okay," I whisper, praying I'm not making a mistake. I trust Maverick. I want this with him. I'm just not sure that I'm ready for the next step.

His smile grows and my breath catches at how beautiful he is. God, the man is drop dead gorgeous.

I'm so turned on it's not even funny. I can barely speak. The entire drive to Maverick's house, his hand was on my leg, his thumb running along my thigh where the slit in my dress sits.

The feel of his skin against mine was almost too much to bear. He's gotten me worked up and he's grinning. Does he find this funny?

"I'll show you around tomorrow," he tells me as he leads me to the bedroom. My stomach flips as my nerves start to kick in. Am I really ready for this?

"I'm not sure if I told you this or not, babe, but you are so fucking beautiful," he growls low in his throat.

I turn to stare at him, my mouth dry and my heart pounding. "Really?" I whisper.

No one has ever looked at me the way Maverick does, and it sends shivers of anticipation down my spine.

I step closer to him, my heart racing as I reach out and lightly brush my fingers over his forearm. A shiver runs through his body, and I can see desire ignite in his eyes.

When I reach for his zipper, he doesn't stop me. My nervousness melts away as I free his hardening cock from its confines. It's a sight to behold—thick, long, and pulsing with need. The veins stand out against his smooth skin, and my eyes are drawn to the neatly trimmed patch of dark hair at its base. As I wrap my hand around him and begin to stroke, I can feel him getting even harder. Encouraged by his sharp intake of breath, I lean forward and run my tongue along the tip of his cock, tasting his salty pre-cum.

As his hips push forward, I struggle to take him in my mouth. The thickness of his cock fills and stretches my mouth, causing it to water and my jaw to ache. He grabs handfuls of my hair and pulls me closer, and I can't help but moan against his cock.

His thrusts become more urgent, and I feel myself gagging, but he doesn't let up. With determination, I create a rhythm and work to swallow past the thickness in my throat. My cheeks hollow as I suck and slurp, trying to accommodate his size while also fighting the urge to choke.

His rough, calloused hand slips down the front of my dress, the fabric bunching and sliding under his touch. His fingers find my nipple and begin to play with it, sending sparks of pleasure straight to my core. Each rotation and pinch elicits a sharp gasp or moan from me, my body responding eagerly to his skilled touch.

As he continues to tease and torment me, our panting breaths mix together in a symphony of desire. I am lost in the sensations he is awakening within me, wanting him to explore every inch of my skin.

But just as I start to reach a new level of arousal, he suddenly pulls back. Confusion floods my mind, until he grabs my hands and pulls me to my feet. My dress is quickly discarded on the floor, leaving me standing completely naked before him. The cool air kisses my exposed skin, but all I can focus on is his hungry gaze as he takes in every inch of me.

I can feel the anticipation building between us, the arousal hanging heavy in the air. Maverick's eyes are locked onto mine, and I can see the desire there; the need to possess and explore every part of me. It should scare me. I should be fearful. But I'm not. I want this. I want him.

He pulls me closer to him, our bodies pressed together from head to toe. I can feel the heat radiating off his skin, the hardness of his erection against my belly. My breath catches in my throat as he gently runs his fingers over my skin, tracing the curve of my hip, the dip of my waist, the swell of my breasts.

He leans down, his lips grazing my earlobe, his warm breath sending shivers down my spine. "I want you so bad," he whispers, his voice deep and husky. "You're so fucking beautiful, Lisa. You take my breath away."

I close my eyes and feel his hands sliding around to my back, his fingers gently unhooking my bra. My breath hitches as his hands cup my breasts, his fingers brushing over my nipples, sending bolts of pleasure radiating through me.

"You're so beautiful," he murmurs, his voice thick with desire. "I need you."

His hands leave my breasts and move down to the waistband of my panties. He hooks his thumbs in the elastic and slowly pulls them down. His fingers graze the soft skin of my inner thighs, sending shivers throughout my body.

"Spread your legs for me," he commands, his voice low and gravelly.

I obey, opening my legs to him, feeling vulnerable and exposed. But there's a thrill in that, a desire to be claimed by this man who makes me feel so alive. This man who makes me feel special and wanted; who makes me believe things that I haven't believed in a long time.

"You're so wet for me, Lisa," he growls, his fingers tracing the lines of my folds. I can feel the slickness against his fingers.

"I want to taste you," he says, his eyes never leaving mine.

I nod, my breath coming in short pants, my body trembling with anticipation.

He helps me onto the bed and positions his head between my legs. His tongue darts out to taste me, his lips brushing against my clit. I gasp, my body arching upward as a wave of pleasure washes over me.

"Oh, Maverick," I moan, my hands gripping the sheets beneath me.

He continues to explore me with his mouth, his tongue flicking and probing, his lips sucking gently. His hands move to my hips, pulling me closer to him, deepening the sensation. I can feel his breath against my pussy, and I'm lost in a wave of pleasure. I writhe beneath him, my moans loud and long, his name a plea on my lips. I'm so close, I can feel it.

His fingers slide inside me, thrusting gently, stretching me as I cry out his name.

"Maverick," I beg, my body trembling with need.

He continues to work his fingers and tongue, his every touch awakening new sensations, driving me closer and closer to the edge. I can hardly breathe at the intensity of it all. My body is shaking and quivering with each flick of his tongue.

"I'm going to come," I whimper, my voice hoarse with desire.

"Come for me, baby," he growls, his voice gravelly and low. "Come for me now."

And with that, I shatter, my body writhing and convulsing as wave after wave of pleasure crashes over me. I cry out his name, my body screaming with sensation as I come hard, my climax shuddering through me.

As I come down from my orgasm, I lie there, panting and shaking, completely spent. Maverick's hands are still between my legs, his fingers gently stroking me, stilling the last tremors.

He pulls his head up from doing his very skilled work and looks me in the eyes, his own filled with hunger and satisfaction. He brushes my hair back from my flushed face and leans down to kiss me, gently at first, then deepening the kiss as I reach up to wrap my arms around him. The kiss is hard and passionate. I get lost in everything that is him.

Pulling back slightly, he gazes into my eyes, his expression tender and possessive. "That was amazing," he whispers. "You're so fucking beautiful, so fucking responsive."

"It was," I agree, my voice ragged and filled with heat. I've just had my first orgasm and it was amazing, but I want more. I want him.

My heart races as his body hovers over mine, his eyes locked with mine in a moment that feels both exhilarating and terrifying. The rest of the world fades away, leaving only him and me.

I can feel my own body responding to his, my thoughts fading, and all I can feel is the pleasure he brings me.

He positions himself at my entrance, the pressure of his cock against me causing my breath to catch in my throat. Slowly, he begins to push forward, stretching me in a way I've never experienced before. The sensation is overwhelming, a mixture of pleasure and pain that makes me gasp for air.

"Relax," he murmurs, his voice husky with desire.

I try to comply, willing my body to loosen up

under his touch. But as he continues to press into me, the discomfort only intensifies. I bite down on my lip, refusing to cry out and reveal just how much it hurts.

But he misreads my silence as enjoyment and picks up his pace, thrusting deeper and harder with each movement. The pain becomes sharp now, bringing tears to my eyes. My nails dig into his back instinctively, unsure if I want to pull him closer or push him away. A whimper escapes from between my gritted teeth before I can stop it.

He stops suddenly, concern etched on his features as he looks down at me. "Are you okay?" he asks gently, furrowing his brow.

I nod frantically, not trusting my voice to speak. I don't want him to stop, to think that I can't handle it. But a single tear betrays me by sliding down my cheek.

His face softens at the sight. "You're a virgin," he says quietly, more of an observation than a question.

Shame and embarrassment wash over me, and I turn my head away, unable to meet his gaze. "I'm sorry," I whisper, feeling small and inadequate.

But to my surprise, he doesn't withdraw or push me away. Instead, he cups my face gently in his hands and turns me back to face him. "Hey, it's okay," he murmurs soothingly, brushing a gentle thumb over my cheek. "We'll go slow. Let you get used to me."

A wave of relief washes over me at his understanding words. As he starts to pull out, I instinctively wrap my legs around him, holding him in place. "No, please," I plead softly. "I want this. I want you."

He searches my eyes for any sign of hesitation before nodding and leaning down to kiss me deeply. As our tongues caress, I feel myself relaxing into his touch, the pain fading into a dull ache.

He begins to move again, but this time with deliberate slowness and care. With each gentle thrust, sparks of pleasure shoot through my body like electricity. I moan into his mouth as my hips rise to meet his in a perfect rhythm.

"That's it," he encourages in a husky voice, his hot breath tickling my ear. "Just let yourself feel the pleasure." His lips brush against my earlobe as he whispers sweet words of encouragement that only fuel the fire within me.

With every thrust, I'm moaning, groaning, and crying out with pleasure. I've never felt so alive, so wanted. I arch my back, pressing my breasts against his chest as I wrap my arms around him.

My hands roam freely over his muscular back. My pleasure rushes through me as he pounds into me. The way he bottoms out inside of me ignites a fire within me.

"Oh God," I moan, overwhelmed by the new sensations flooding my body. Every nerve ending feels alive and electrified.

He picks up the pace slightly, still mindful of my comfort. His lips trail kisses along my neck and collarbone, sending shivers down my spine. I tilt my head back, giving him better access as I lose myself in the moment.

"You feel so good," he murmurs against my skin. "So tight and wet for me."

His words send a fresh surge of arousal through me. I rock my hips to meet his thrusts, craving more friction. A coiling tension builds low in my belly with each thrust.

"Faster," I breathe, digging my nails into his shoulders. "Please."

He obliges, increasing his pace as he drives deeper into me. The new rhythm sends shockwaves of pleasure through my body. I cry out, overwhelmed by the intensity of the sensations.

"That's it, baby," he groans. "Let me hear you."

His encouragement spurs me on. I moan loudly with each thrust, no longer caring about holding back. The tension inside me builds to a fever pitch as he hits a spot deep within that makes me see stars.

"Oh God, oh God," I chant, feeling myself teetering on the edge of something monumental.

He senses how close I am and slips a hand between our bodies. His fingers find my clit and begin to rub tight circles. The dual stimulation is too much to bear.

"I'm gonna... I'm gonna..." I can't even form the words as the pressure inside me reaches its breaking point. With a cry of his name, I shatter. Waves of intense pleasure crash over me as my body convulses. My inner walls clench around him as the orgasm rolls through me.

He groans at the sensation, his thrusts becoming erratic. "Fuck, I'm close," he pants.

I feel him swell inside me as his movements become more urgent. His grip on my hips tightens as he thrusts into me with a newfound energy. The intensity of his thrusts prolongs my own orgasm, sending aftershocks of pleasure rippling through my body.

"Come for me," I whisper, wanting to feel him lose control.

With a guttural moan, he buries himself deep inside me one final time. I feel the warm rush of his release as his body shudders above me. He collapses onto me, his weight pressing me into the couch cushions as we both struggle to catch our breath.

For several long moments, we lie tangled together,

our sweat-slicked skin cooling in the aftermath. His fingers trace lazy patterns on my arm as my heartbeat slowly returns to normal. I've never felt so utterly satisfied and complete.

Eventually, he lifts his head from where it had fallen to my shoulder. His eyes meet mine, filled with a mix of satisfaction and tenderness that makes my heart skip.

"Are you okay?" he asks softly, brushing a strand of hair from my forehead.

I nod, not quite trusting my voice yet. My body feels both utterly relaxed and hyper-sensitive. Every nerve ending is still tingling.

He carefully pulls out, and I wince slightly at the feeling of emptiness. As he rolls to the side, I become acutely aware of the sticky wetness between my thighs and the slight soreness. But any discomfort is overshadowed by the lingering waves of pleasure still coursing through my body.

He pulls me against his chest, wrapping his arms around me. I nestle into his warmth, feeling safe and cherished in his embrace. His fingers trail up and down my spine, sending little shivers through me.

"That was..." I trail off, unable to find the right words to describe the intensity of what we just shared.

"Amazing," he finishes for me, pressing a soft kiss to my forehead. "You were amazing."

I blush at his praise, ducking my head against his chest. "I didn't really know what I was doing," I admit shyly.

He chuckles softly, the rumble vibrating through his chest. "You could have fooled me," he says, tilting my chin up to meet his gaze. "You were perfect."

His words make me glow with pride, erasing any lingering doubts. I lean in to kiss him, savouring the gentle press of his lips against mine. When we part, I can't help but smile.

"So what happens now?" I ask, suddenly feeling a bit uncertain about where we stand.

He pulls me closer, nuzzling into my hair. "Now, we rest for a bit," he murmurs. "And then, if you're up for it, I'd love to explore your body some more. There's so much I want to show you."

A thrill runs through me at his words, desire already stirring again despite my recent release. "I'd like that," I whisper. "But that's not what I meant."

His eyes darken as he looks at me, and my heart batters against my chest. "You're mine, Lisa. The moment you walked into my sister's pub, I knew you were mine."

"Yours?" I whisper, searching his eyes. What the hell does that mean?

He nods, his gaze never leaving mine. "You're mine, and I'm not letting you go. I don't think I could even if I tried. There's always been something about you, Lisa. From the moment I met you there was something different. You were too young back then. Now?" He grins, and it's filled with satisfaction. "Now I have you, I'm not letting you go."

His words send a shiver down my spine, with equal parts excitement and trepidation. There's an intensity in his eyes that both thrills and unnerves me. I search his face, trying to understand the depth of what he's saying.

"What exactly do you mean by 'yours'?" I ask hesitantly. "I've never done this before."

He runs his fingers through my hair, his touch gentle but possessive. "I mean that I want you in my life, Lisa. Not just for tonight, but for good."

My heart races at his words. It's overwhelming, especially considering we've only just had sex, not to mention it's been years since I last saw him. But I can't deny the pull I feel toward him; the rightness of being in his arms. I've always felt a pull to him.

"This is all happening so fast," I whisper.

He nods, understanding in his eyes. "I know it might seem sudden, but I've never felt this connection to anyone before. There was always something special about you. Now that you're an adult and you're here, I don't want to waste any more time."

His words make my heart flutter. I can't deny the intensity of what I'm feeling, even if it scares me a little. "I feel it too," I admit softly. "But I'm not sure I'm ready for anything too serious right away."

He cups my face gently, his thumb stroking my cheek. "We can take things as slow as you need," he assures me. "I just want you to know that I'm all in. I'm not letting you go."

Relief washes over me at his understanding. "Thank you," I whisper, leaning in to kiss him softly. As our lips meet, I feel a spark of electricity run through my body. The kiss deepens, his tongue gently probing as he pulls me closer. My hands roam over his muscular back, feeling the strength beneath my fingertips.

When we finally part, both breathless, he rests his forehead against mine. "You're incredible," he murmurs.

I blush at his words, still unused to such praise. "So are you," I reply softly.

He grins, a mischievous glint in his eye. "Ready for round two?" he asks, his hand sliding down my side.

I think he may just kill me. But oh, what a way to go.

CHAPTER
SEVENTEEN
MAVERICK

I HEAR the sound of her soft footsteps along the floor. I turn from the newspaper I'm reading and see Lisa walking toward me. The moment she spots me, her steps falter and she ducks her head. "Come here, babe," I say loud enough for her to hear me.

She's beyond fucking gorgeous with her hair tousled from last night while wearing just my T-shirt. Her legs are tan and she's got pink nail polish on her toes. She hesitantly walks toward me, and I can't lie, I love how shy and nervous she is, especially when she's so confident around others.

The second she's within touching distance, my hand clasps around her wrist and I pull her into me. Finding out she was a virgin was unexpected, but fuck, it means she's all mine and will always be mine. The moment I saw her again, I knew I wanted her. Spending time with her just cemented that fact. Our date wasn't what I had expected. Having never been on one, I had thought it would be awkward and long. Instead, I enjoyed spending time with her and getting to know her. The moment I fucked her, I knew without a shadow of a doubt that I wasn't letting her go. Fuck, she was pure, and now she's mine.

"Morning, baby, you sleep okay?"

She nods against my chest. "Yeah," she whispers. "Sorry, it takes me a while to wake up," she murmurs against my chest.

"What are your plans for today?" I ask as I hand her my cup of coffee.

This is so natural, so easy. She just fits. I never thought that would be the case. I didn't think I could find someone who made me want what my parents have, what my sister has. But I guess I was wrong.

"I've got to visit Mamaí and Devin," she says as she takes a sip of the coffee. I grin as she grimaces at it. "Jesus," she cries. "Where's the milk?"

"Too fucking early for milk," I mutter as I rise to my feet, setting her down onto the stool I was on, and fix her a cup of coffee. "Who's Devin?" I ask as I place the cup in front of her.

She blinks, her hands stilling around the coffee cup. "Oh, um, my brother."

"You have a brother?" I ask. I hadn't realised.

She lifts her shoulders and shrugs. "I mean, sort of. He's my foster brother. He's ten and the best kid ever."

Now that's not what I had expected her to say. "Your parents foster kids?"

She swipes her tongue along her bottom lip. "Um, not exactly. I'm a foster kid. Have been since I was thirteen."

The fuck? Shit. Fuck. I remember now, Jer explained the night that she and her friend were at the house party that they were both foster kids. "What happened to your parents?"

I watch as she shuts down. Her expression blanks and her eyes close. "Ma died and my father left. I'm glad he did. He's a piece of shit. I got to live with Mamaí and then Devin came along."

She has a lot of affection for her foster mam. I can hear it every time she talks about her. I had assumed when she said Mamaí, she meant her birth mam. Now I know that it's her foster mother. "I'm sorry about your ma," I say softly.

She lifts her head and gives me a wobbly smile. "Thanks. It was a long time ago now and she's in a better place. What about you? Is Callie your only sibling?"

I allow her to change the subject, knowing that talking about her biological mam is hard. She was thirteen when she died, and while I'd like to know what happened, especially with her asshole of a father, this isn't the time.

"Yeah, just Callie and I. Mam and Da had more than enough with the two of us. Not to mention, Mam had both Stephen and Freddie at the house more often than not. You met Freddie the night your friend was..." I trail off and she nods. "Then Emmanuel was there. It was a full house constantly."

She's watching me with rapt attention, her hands firmly pressed around the cup. "Really? What was it like? I never had that. Although, once I moved in with Orna, we met Tammy and Clodagh and we became inseparable."

"Tammy's Clodagh's foster mam, right?" I ask, remembering when I dropped her home that night. Also noting that her parents are dead.

"Yeah, it's easier to bond when you've both been through shit," she mumbles. "I think Orna wanted me to have someone I could talk to, but neither Clodagh nor I were ready. Instead, we got drunk, partied, and had fun," she says with a smile. "Poor Orna and

Tammy... I swear, they aged about a decade in the span of six months."

I watch her. She's good at hiding what she's feeling and I fucking hate that. There's a lot that I don't know about her. I want to ask. I want to pry. But I know that's not going to happen right now. If I push, I could end up sending her running. That's not fucking happening. I've just got her. There's no way I'm letting her go.

She's watching me. She has so much sadness in her eyes that she's trying to mask, and I want nothing more than to erase it. I reach out and gently tuck a strand of hair behind her ear.

"Sounds like you and Clodagh gave them a run for their money," I say with a smirk, trying to lighten the mood.

She laughs softly. "Oh, we definitely did. But they never gave up on us. Orna and Tammy are saints, truly."

I can see the love and gratitude in her eyes when she talks about her foster mother. I want to know why her dad left, what the fuck happened, and why he would up and leave. He's a bastard, that's for sure. Ain't no man worth shit if he runs from his kid. I know Lisa will tell me everything when she's ready.

"So, what time do you need to head out to see

Orna and Devin?" I ask, wondering how much time we have.

She glances at her phone and I hear her sigh. "In a while. I need to go home and shower before I go to them." She lifts the coffee to her lips and takes a drink. "Thank you for an amazing night, Mav. I really had the best time."

I narrow my eyes. "Why does it sound like you're about to leave and never come back?"

She stares at me with big, wide eyes. "I don't know," she confesses softly. "I'm not used to this. I have no idea what to expect."

"Expect that I'm going to be around, that I'm going to be present. Today you're spending time with your family. Tomorrow night you're mine."

Tonight I have a job to do. This isn't for Jer, but for The Agency. I have a fucker who's trafficking women into the country and he's not going to leave. I'll make sure he doesn't get to take any more women. So tonight is off-limits. I don't want that shit around Lisa. I don't want any of my jobs to blow back on her. Not fucking ever.

"Okay," she says with a smile as she pushes her phone in my direction. "You never gave me your number," she tells me.

I quickly input my number and call my phone

from hers. "Where do you want to meet tomorrow?" I ask.

She flashes me a grin. "My place. Your house is nice and all, but my house is home," she says softly with a shrug. "Anyway, I'd better get moving. I need to get dressed and get going."

I watch as she rushes toward my room. I'm smiling because she's crazy if she thinks I'm letting her get home by herself.

I follow her into the bedroom, leaning against the doorframe as she gathers her clothes from last night. She's still wearing my T-shirt, and I'm not in any hurry for her to take it off. She's adorably flustered, her cheeks flushing pink as she realises I'm watching her.

"I'll drive you home," I say, my tone leaving no room for argument.

She pauses, looking up at me with those big brown eyes. "You don't have to do that, Mav. I can grab a taxi."

I shake my head. "Not happening, babe. I'm taking you."

She bites her lip, considering, then nods. "Okay, thank you."

She hesitates, clearly unsure about changing in front of me. It's adorable how shy she still is, even after last night. But I don't move. I watch as she gets dressed, and I can't help but admire her body. The curves, the softness—all mine now. I've never been possessive before, but with Lisa, everything feels different. Once she's ready, we head out to my car.

The drive to Lisa's place is quiet, but not uncomfortably so. I keep stealing glances at her, admiring her profile as she looks out the window. She catches me once and gives me a shy smile that makes my heart skip a beat. Fuck, I'm in deep already. I reach over and rest my hand on her thigh, giving it a gentle squeeze.

As we pull up to her building, I put the car in park but don't turn it off. Lisa turns to me, her hand on the door handle.

"Thanks for the ride, Mav," she says softly.

I reach out and gently grasp her chin, turning her face toward me. "I meant what I said. Tomorrow night, you're mine." I need her to know that I'm serious, that I'm not stepping back and letting her go.

Her breath catches and she nods. I lean in and kiss her, soft at first but then deepening it, tasting the coffee on her tongue. When I pull back, her eyes are glazed and her lips are swollen.

"Go on," I tell her, my voice gruff. "I'll see you tomorrow."

Lisa nods, still looking a bit dazed from our kiss. She opens the door and steps out, turning back to give me one last smile before shutting it. I watch her walk to her building, making sure she gets inside safely before driving off.

As I head home, my mind is racing. There's so much I still don't know about Lisa, about her past. The foster care, her dead mother, her absent father—they're all pieces of a puzzle I'm determined to solve. But I know I need to be patient. Push too hard and I might scare her off. For now, I need to focus on tonight's job. I've got a human trafficker to deal with, and I can't afford any distractions.

CHAPTER
EIGHTEEN
LISA

I'M SITTING at my dresser, the one I had custom built for me after I moved back into my ma's home when I turned eighteen. It was hard at first, especially with what happened here, but my ma is someone I loved with my entire heart and soul. I've missed her so much, and being home feels right. I've updated the house as it was abandoned for years while I was living with Orna. It's no longer the same house, but I can still feel my ma's presence, and I'm happy here. I'm currently scrolling through my phone, reading up on the man I've got for tonight's target. I lied to Maverick about meeting with Orna and Devin today. I have a job with The Agency that needs to be done today. As in right fucking now. From what Travis has told me, Leon Manthin is one of Europe's leading traffickers, and he specializes in little boys. Motherfucker has managed to escape for years without anyone getting their hands on him. He was supposed to be taken out last month while he was in Spain, but whoever had the job fucked up and the bastard's still walking the streets. So tonight is my turn. I'm the one who's been tasked with taking him out.

It's been five years since my first kill and I've lost count of how many I've done now. They don't all happen here in Ireland. I do travel, especially now that I'm over eighteen. I've learned the best technique for what I do, and while I'm still not as powerful as Ciarán would like, I'm damned good at what I do. I've earned the moniker the Hanging Reaper for my methods. Only two people know my true identity, and I know I can trust them both with my secret. Hell, those two are the ones who helped mould me into who I am. Without them, I doubt I'd have the skill sets that I possess now.

I usually wait until the dead of the night to do this, and usually on a bridge, but that's not happening today. Fuck no. The man's too powerful, too well known for me to be able to get him out of his hotel room, where he has multiple online meetings, and get him hanged from a bridge. No, today calls for something a little different. Leon usually is in town to get boys and sell them, but thanks to Ciarán's information, we know that he's in town for girls. He's selling them to the Bratva to keep in their whorehouses. So today, I'm going to be 'auditioning' to become one of those women. Thankfully, I have a good disguise that'll keep my real identity from being shown. I have less than an hour to get to the shitty hotel he's staying at close to the airport. The fucker didn't want to go any further into town. Everyone who knows of him wants to kill him, and with Ireland having so many different criminal organizations, it's safe to say that he wouldn't make it out alive.

He won't. I'll make sure of that.

I stand up from my dresser, my heart rate steady despite what I'm about to do. This isn't my first rodeo, after all. I move to my closet, pulling out the carefully selected outfit for tonight's "audition." A tight black dress that leaves little to the imagination, paired with sky-high heels that I can run in if needed. I've learned that lesson the hard way.

As I apply my makeup, I transform myself into someone unrecognizable. I slip on the blonde wig, adjusting it carefully in the mirror. It screams "desperate and naive." Perfect for luring in a predator like Leon. The blue contact lenses complete the transformation. I barely recognize myself, which is exactly the point.

I grab my small purse, double-checking that I have everything I need. The rope is coiled neatly inside, alongside a few other tools of my trade. I take a deep breath, centring myself. This is just another job. Just another monster to remove from the world.

Travis put me in touch with a guy named Jason who boosts cars for a living. It's easy; you contact him with a time and a place, pay him the money, and he'll deliver. Never once showing his face. It's the perfect way to do business.

It doesn't take me long to get to the arranged place, and the car's already waiting for me. I slide in, and the engine purrs to life as I turn the key in the ignition. I love the feeling of the engine revving. It centres me. Taking a deep breath, I pull out onto the street, my mind focused on what lies ahead.

The drive to the hotel is uneventful, giving me time to run through the plan one last time. I've memorized every detail of Leon's schedule, every weakness in his security—there's very little, just his best friend and business partner who will be sampling the local brothel right about now. I know exactly how it's going to go down. Not to mention the tracks that have already been laid by Travis' daughter, Melissa. The woman is amazing at what she does and has managed to make it look as though Leon is a wanted man by the very people he employs. We have the perfect plan. He's a desperate man, one who has no other option. His time is up, and he takes the only way out that he knows how. Ending his own life.

I park the car a two-minute walk away from the hotel, making sure to choose a spot without security cameras. As I walk toward the building, I feel the familiar rush of adrenaline coursing through my veins. My heels click against the pavement, a steady rhythm matching my heartbeat. Since the first kill, I've never felt the panic grow as I do this. I'm always calm and centred. It terrifies me that I'm this way, but there's nothing I can do to change it. While it's terrifying that I'm so at ease, I know I'd actually hate it to be any other way.

I enter the hotel lobby, my eyes scanning the area discreetly. Melissa has also worked her magic on this and the cameras have been out for the past forty-eight hours. The receptionist barely glances up as I walk past, heading straight for the elevators. Leon's room is on the fourth floor, room 412. As the elevator doors close, I take one last deep breath, slipping fully into character.

The hallway is deserted when I step out. Good. I

approach room 412, my hand steady as I knock on the door. There's a pause, then the sound of heavy footsteps. The door opens, and I'm face to face with Leon Manthin. He's older than his pictures, with lines etched deep into his face. His eyes are cold and calculating as they rake over my body. I force myself to smile, playing the part of the eager, naive girl.

"Mr Manthin?" I ask, my voice pitched higher than usual. "I'm here for the... audition," I say, making my voice sound uneasy and a little frightened.

Leon's eyes narrow slightly, a mix of suspicion and interest flickering across his face. "Ah, yes," he says, his accent thick and guttural. "Come in, come in."

He steps aside, allowing me to enter the dimly lit hotel room. The air is thick with the stench of stale cigarette smoke and cheap aftershave. I suppress a shudder as I feel his eyes on me, undressing me with his gaze. He's a sleazy man who uses people in the worst ways possible. He deserves everything that's coming to him.

"You're early," he remarks, closing the door behind us. The lock clicks into place, a sound that would make most girls in my position tremble with fear.

But not me. This is what I wanted.

"I hope that's not a problem," I say, turning to face

him with a coy smile. "I just couldn't wait to meet you."

Leon chuckles; a harsh sound that grates against my ears. "Eager. I like that." He moves closer, his bulk looming over me. "What's your name, sweetheart?"

"Lily," I lie smoothly, batting my eyelashes at him. "I've heard so much about you, Mr. Manthin. They say you can make a girl's dreams come true." I'm laying it on thick and he's eating it up.

His ego visibly swells at my words. "That I can, Lily. That I can. But first, let's see what you have to offer, shall we?"

He gestures toward the bed, and I force myself to giggle nervously. "Of course, Mr. Manthin. Whatever you say." God, being so naive actually makes me hurt. I know there are girls and women out there who are actually like this, and I hate that people like this animal will hurt them due to it.

As I perch on the edge of the bed, I watch him pour himself a drink from the mini-bar. Perfect. I slip my hand into my purse, fingers closing around the small needle in there. This is the drug that I've been using since my second kill. It's the perfect concoction.

"So tell me, Lily," Leon says. "What makes you special?"

I swallow hard, playing up the nervousness. "I...

I'm willing to do anything," I whisper, letting a tremor enter my voice. "Anything at all."

His eyes light up with sick pleasure. "Is that so?" He moves toward me, glass in hand, a predatory gleam in his eyes. "Well then, let's see just how willing you are, shall we?"

As he reaches for me, I make my move. I take a hold of his hand and watch the smile play on his lips. I pull out the needle and plunge it into his finger. His eyes widen in shock and confusion as the drug takes effect almost instantly. Since that first kill with Ciarán and Travis, we upped the dose a little. Now I don't have to wait for it to kick in. It's instantaneous.

"What... what did you..." he slurs, stumbling backwards.

I stand up, dropping the naive act entirely. "Justice, Mr Manthin. That's what I just did."

He tries to lunge at me, but his movements are uncoordinated. He slides into the chair, gripping a hold of the edge, watching me with fearful eyes. "Who... who are you?" he manages to gasp out.

I laugh a little. "They call me the Hanging Reaper."

His eyes widen in recognition, fear replacing the confusion. "No... it can't be..."

I smile coldly, pulling the rope from my purse.

"Oh, but it is. Your time's up, Leon. You've hurt your last child."

He tries to stand, to fight, but the drug has rendered him helpless. His limbs are heavy, uncooperative. I move swiftly, efficiently. It's a routine that has become second nature, no matter who the target is. The rope coils smoothly around his neck, a familiar act that doesn't bring back the memories of that terrible day.

Fortunately, Leon is not one of the larger men I've had to kill, so hoisting him up is not as much of a struggle as it has been with others. I use the window and a sturdy metal beam meant for holding up heavy curtains to secure the rope. It's a simple task, effortless even.

Leon's feet hang limply just inches from the floor. His face turns first red, then purple as he struggles for air. I watch with detached indifference, my mind filled with thoughts of all the lives he's ruined. All those innocent children he's stolen and sold like mere commodities.

I move with purpose and reach for the chair, bringing it under his feet but knocking it over before he can use it for leverage to end this torture. I watch as he continues to struggle, every inch of him turning red as he struggles for air. It's over within a matter of minutes. He stops moving, stops fighting. It's just done.

"This is for them," I whisper to myself, once again reminding myself why I do this. I give Leon's lifeless body one last look before I exit the hotel room, keeping my head down and ensuring I stay out of sight.

Exiting the hotel is easy. I pull in a deep breath as I walk toward my car. It's done. He's dead. But I know there are so many more men and women out there who are exactly like Leon or even worse. They're all ready to prey on unsuspecting innocent children and women. They're bastards. It doesn't matter how many we take out, more of them seem to appear. I won't stop doing this. I see how happy and free Devin is, and I know that it's the right thing. There are others out there who don't have someone like me who can kill their demons.

I slide into the car and take yet another deep breath. I reach for the key to switch the ignition on, when I see a motorcycle enter the street and park three cars in front of me. My heart pounds against my chest as I recognise who it is.

Maverick.

God, what the hell is he doing here?

CHAPTER NINETEEN

MAVERICK

Entering the hotel, I flash Judy, the woman on reception, a smile. She nods her head and slides the keycard to me. We've been using this hotel for years to conduct a lot of our business. With it being close to the airport, it made sense to get close to the owner, Judy's father. He knows what we do and has no problem with that, seeing as having us associated with him gives him a certain level of protection, along with status. It's a win-win for us all.

I take the keycard and see that Judy's written the room number on it for me. Room 412. Leon Manthin.

I got a call from Cole James, Travis's son. In recent years, Cole has taken over from Travis and started to hand out more assignments to me and Stephen. We both tend to take them on as we get paid well, and the

James' are people who know what the hell they're doing. Although, word on the street is that Travis hasn't taken a backseat; that the person he had been training is taking on so many jobs that he's with them. I'm not sure if it's something I believe or not as Travis James isn't a man who will train someone for years. He gives them the basics and lets them fly.

I wonder if that new girl he had years ago panned out for him. He was insistent on having someone help him train her.

As I climb the stairs, my mind drifts back to that girl Travis was so keen on. I can't remember her name. Hell, I'm not even sure if he gave me one. I remember Travis being uncharacteristically excited about her potential. He said she had a natural talent for the work, but needed refining. That was unusual for Travis—he typically preferred recruits who had their shit together already.

I reach the fourth floor landing, slightly winded. Getting old, I chide myself. I should take the damn elevator next time. The hallway stretches out before me, plush carpeting muffling my footsteps as I make my way to room 412.

Outside the door, I pause and listen. Silence. I slide the keycard into the lock, wait for the green light, and enter swiftly, closing the door behind me. The room is dark. The curtains drawn but there's a dim light in the corner slightly illuminating the room. My gaze, however, is drawn to the man who's hanging from the fucking window. Leon Manthin. Shit, someone took the fucker out already. Or did he commit suicide?

I approach the body cautiously, my hand instinctively reaching for the gun holstered at my hip. The room is eerily quiet, save for the soft hum of the air conditioning. As I get closer, I can see that Leon's face is purple, his eyes bulging grotesquely. A thick rope is knotted tightly around his neck, the other end secured to the curtain rod above the window.

This wasn't part of the plan. Leon was supposed to be alive when I got here. This wasn't a suicide. The knot is too intricate, too professional. Someone got to him before I could, and they knew what they were doing.

I scan the room, looking for any signs of a struggle or forced entry. Nothing seems out of place. The bed is still made, the mini-bar untouched. There's no way this was a suicide or done by someone by mistake. No amateur leaves a scene this clean.

I pull out my phone and snap a few quick photos of the scene, making sure to capture the knot and Leon's face. Evidence, just in case. Then I start a thorough sweep of the room, checking for any clues the killer might have left behind.

Nothing. Not a fucking thing. This is definitely a professional that's done this job. So why the fuck was I recruited to do it?

It's time to get the fuck out of here.

Just as I'm about to leave, I notice something. A faint scent in the air, barely perceptible but familiar. Jasmine. It triggers a memory, but I can't quite place it.

I shake my head, filing away the information for later. Right now, I need to focus on getting out undetected. I crack open the door, peering into the hallway. It's clear. I step out, letting the door click shut behind me, and make my way to the stairwell.

As I descend, my mind races. Who could have known about this job? Was I set up? And why leave the body for me to find? It doesn't make sense.

I exit through a side door, avoiding the lobby. Once outside, I take a deep breath of the cool night air, trying to clear my mind. But I'm pissed. Beyond fucking pissed. My feet move quickly as I hit dial on Cole's number.

"Done already?" he asks, amusement filling his voice.

"It's done alright," I snarl. "But not by me. What the fuck, Cole? Want to tell me why the fuck you recruited me when someone else was tasked with the job?"

Silence spreads through the line. "You're the only one who had that job. What the hell?" he mutters. "What happened?"

I give him a quick rundown of what I saw and listen to him let out a low whistle. "I've heard about the Hanging Reaper. They say that they're meticulous at what they do. Tell me, do you think it was them?"

It makes sense. Fuck, it's the person Jer was talking about. "Whoever took out Leon knew what the fuck they were doing. They're damned fucking good at it too. It looked like a suicide. Everything was in its proper place, not a hair out of place."

"I'm going to have to dig and see what the hell happened. Let me talk to Melissa and see if she knows anything about it. I'll call you back when I know more," he says and ends the call.

As I walk briskly away from the hotel, that faint scent of asmine tickles my memory again. Something about it feels important, but I can't quite grasp why. It's as though my mind is trying to figure out why it's triggering me. Fuck, I don't know. I shake it off, focusing on getting to my bike parked a few streets away.

This job was supposed to be straightforward. Get

in, take care of Leon, and get out. Now I'm left with more questions than answers. Who is the Hanging Reaper and how did they know about Leon?

More importantly, why did they leave the body for me to find?

My phone buzzes as I'm leaving Jer's home. He's currently in Spain. He'll be home in a few weeks, maybe sooner if Tommy Jennings starts his shit up again. Tommy had been lying low, but the past few days there's been a lot of chatter about that bastard's operation moving back into Dublin. There's been more movement from his men. They're fucking everywhere once again. However, since Tommy hasn't come out of the woodwork, we're not too worried. We'll just be keeping a close eye on things.

Glancing down at my phone, I'm surprised to see Lisa's name on the screen.

Lisa: Hey, not sure if you're busy tonight or not. I'm home and about to order takeout and put a movie on if you want to join?

I smile at the message from Lisa and quickly reply: **I'm never too busy for you. Count me in. What movie are we watching?**

I hadn't expected to hear from her tonight. She's shy, and I know it's because she's not had a relationship and is unsure of what to do. I fucking love that I'm her only one and I'm determined to keep it that way.

As I make my way to Lisa's place, my mind starts to wander back to Tommy Jennings. Despite the temporary calm, I knew it was only a matter of time before he resurfaced. It's just waiting to see what he plans next. I've no doubt that he's been licking his wounds and figuring out what he's going to do next. It doesn't matter what he's got planned, we're ready for him.

My fingers tighten around the steering wheel and I take a deep breath. Today has been a fucking weird day, from the shit that went down with Leon to finding out that Tommy's back. It's always one thing after another, but now I have a woman that I'm going to spend the night with. I have to admit that it feels good to have that. To have someone I want to spend my life with.

As I turn off the engine, the outside light flickers on, illuminating the pathway to the front door. And then, like magic, she appears in the doorway. Her hair cascades in loose curls around her face and down past her breasts. She's dressed in a short pyjama set; a light pink tank top that shows off her toned arms and shorts that reveal her long legs. She's fucking gorgeous.

I step out of the car, drinking in the sight of her.

With every step I take toward her, my cock thickens. Christ, I'm like a fucking teen again. As I get closer, she gives me that soft as fuck smile.

"Hey, handsome," she says softly as I reach the doorway. Her voice is honey-sweet, sending a shiver down my spine.

I lean in, wrapping my arms around her waist. "Hey, babe," I reply, pulling her close to me. "You have a good day?"

She nods as she rises on her tiptoes, pressing her lips to mine. The second our mouths touch, I take over and deepen the kiss, my tongue sliding against hers as I back her into the house. Her fingers thread through my hair, tugging lightly as a soft moan escapes her.

I pull back, breathless, taking in her flushed cheeks and swollen lips. "God, fuck, I needed that," I murmur, trailing kisses along her jaw.

"Mmm," she moans, her breath hitching as I nip at her earlobe.

My hands roam down her sides, gripping her thighs. In one swift motion, I lift her up, and she wraps her legs around my waist as I walk us into the house, kicking the door closed with my foot. "Maverick," she says with a laugh. "Put me down."

With a teasing nip at her lips, I obey her request and

slowly lower her down my body. I relish in the hitch of her breath and the way her stomach presses against my already hardened erection. "Gotta say, babe, I was pleasantly surprised by your text. I thought for sure you would need some time to work up the courage."

A playful sparkle dances in her eyes as she rolls them at me. "You're such an ass," she sighs. "I don't know why, but I always feel shy around you when we're together. It's highly annoying, especially since I know how comfortable I am with you." Her voice softens and she reaches up to run her fingers through my hair. "But I also know that you weren't lying when you said I was yours. So, I took a chance and sent that text." A blush rises in her cheeks. "And here you are," she says as she steps back from me. "So thank you for answering."

I follow her into the kitchen, my eyes never leaving her sexy body. As she reaches into the fridge, the hem of her tank top rides up, revealing a tantalizing strip of smooth skin. I can't resist anymore. In two quick strides, I'm behind her, my hands on her hips, pulling her back against me.

"Fuck," I growl into her ear, my voice low and husky. "I want you."

She gasps, arching her back, pressing her ass against

my growing erection. "Maverick," she breathes, her voice a mix of surprise and desire.

I spin her around, lifting her onto the kitchen counter in one fluid motion. Her legs part instinctively, and I step between them, my hands running up her thighs. "You have no idea what you do to me," I murmur, leaning in to capture her lips in a searing kiss. Her hands find their way to my chest, fingers curling into my shirt as she pulls me closer. I can feel the heat radiating from her body.

Breaking the kiss, I trail my lips down her neck, savouring the soft whimpers that escape her. My hands slide under her tank top, caressing the smooth skin of her stomach, inching higher. She arches into my touch, silently begging for more.

"Tell me what you want, baby," I breathe against her collarbone, nipping gently.

She shivers, her legs tightening around my waist. "You," she whispers, her voice thick with desire. "I want you, Maverick."

Hearing my name on her lips, dripping with need, nearly undoes me. I capture her mouth in another passionate kiss, swallowing her moans as my hands finally reach her breasts. I palm them roughly, feeling her nipples harden against my touch. She gasps into my mouth, her hips rocking against me instinctively.

"Fuck, you're so responsive," I growl, breaking the kiss to trail my lips down her neck. "So fucking perfect."

Her hands fumble with the buttons of my shirt, desperate to feel my skin. I help her, shrugging it off quickly before returning my attention to her body. In one swift motion, I pull her tank top over her head, tossing it aside.

"God, look at you," I breathe, drinking in the sight of her bare chest. Her breasts are perfect, full and perky, nipples pebbled and begging for my touch. I don't hesitate, lowering my head to take one into my mouth. She cries out, her back arching as I swirl my tongue around her nipple, teasing and sucking. My hand finds her other breast, kneading and pinching gently.

"Maverick," she moans, her fingers tangling in my hair, holding me to her chest. "Oh God, yes."

I switch sides, lavishing attention on her other breast as my hand slides down her stomach, dipping beneath the waistband of her shorts. She's so wet already, her arousal coating my fingers as I tease her entrance.

"Fuck, baby," I groan against her skin. "You're soaked for me."

She whimpers, rocking her hips against my hand. "Please," she begs, her voice breathy and desperate.

I can't deny her. Slowly, I slide two fingers inside her, relishing the way she gasps and tightens around me. I curl my fingers, searching for that spot which will make her see stars. When I find it, her whole body jerks, a strangled moan escaping her lips.

"That's it, baby," I murmur, setting a steady rhythm with my fingers. "Let me hear you."

Her head falls back, eyes fluttering closed as pleasure washes over her. I can't take my eyes off her face, watching as each stroke of my fingers brings her closer to the edge. Her hips move in time with my hand, chasing her release.

"Maverick," she pants, her voice high and breathy. "I'm so close... Please..."

I increase the pace, my thumb finding her clit and circling it firmly. "Come for me," I growl, nipping at her collarbone. "Let go, baby. I've got you."

Her body tenses, back arching as she cries out my name. I feel her walls clench around my fingers as she comes undone, trembling in my arms. I work her through it, slowing my movements as she comes down from her high.

"That's it, baby," I murmur, pressing soft kisses to her neck. "You're so beautiful when you come."

She slumps against me, breathing heavily. I withdraw my hand, bringing my fingers to my lips and sucking them clean, savouring her taste. Her eyes widen as she watches me, pupils dilated with renewed arousal.

"Fuck," she breathes, pulling me in for a deep, hungry kiss. She can taste herself on my tongue, and it seems to ignite something within her. Her hands fumble with my belt, desperate to get me naked.

I chuckle against her lips, gently catching her wrists. "Easy there, babe," I murmur, nipping at her bottom lip. "We've got all night."

She whines, and it's a needy sound that goes straight to my cock. "But I want you now." She pouts, her eyes dark with desire.

"Oh, you'll have me," I promise, my voice low and husky. "But first, I want to taste you properly."

CHAPTER
TWENTY
MAVERICK

Before she can respond, I drop to my knees, hooking my fingers into the waistband of her shorts. I look up at her, silently asking permission. She nods eagerly, lifting her hips to help me slide them off.

"Fuck," I breathe, taking in the sight of her completely naked on the kitchen counter. "You're so fucking beautiful."

I start at her ankles, pressing soft kisses up her legs, savouring the taste of her skin. Her breath quickens as I get closer to where she needs me most. I can smell her arousal, and it drives me wild.

When I finally reach the apex of her thighs, I pause, looking up at her. Her eyes are hooded with desire, her chest heaving. "Please," she whimpers, her hips shifting restlessly.

I smirk, running my tongue along her inner thigh, so close but not quite where she wants me. "Please what, baby?" I tease, my breath hot against her sensitive flesh.

She groans in frustration, her fingers tangling in my hair. "Please, Maverick," she begs. "I need your mouth on me."

I can't resist her any longer. With a low growl, I dive in, my tongue parting her folds and licking from her entrance to her clit. She cries out, her hips bucking against my face. I hold her steady with my hands on her thighs, keeping her spread open for me.

"Fuck, you taste so good," I groan against her, before diving back in with renewed vigour. I alternate between broad strokes of my tongue and quick flicks against her clit, revelling in the way she writhes and moans above me.

Her fingers tighten in my hair, pulling me closer as her thighs tremble around my head. "Oh God, Maverick," she pants. "Don't stop. Please don't stop."

I have no intention of stopping. I slide two fingers inside her, curling them to hit that spot which makes her see stars, while my tongue focuses on her clit. The combination of sensations seems to overwhelm her, and I can feel her getting close again.

"Fuck, fuck, fuck," she chants, her hips rocking

against my face. "I'm gonna come, Maverick. Oh God, I'm gonna—"

Her words cut off in a strangled cry as her orgasm hits her hard. Her thighs clamp around my head, her body shaking as waves of pleasure wash over her. I don't let up, working her through it, prolonging her pleasure until she's gasping and pushing at my shoulders, oversensitive.

I pull back, wiping my mouth with the back of my hand as I look up at her. She's a vision—flushed and panting, her hair tousled, eyes glazed with pleasure. I can't help but grin, feeling a surge of pride at having reduced her to this state.

"You okay there, babe?" I tease, pressing a soft kiss to her inner thigh.

She lets out a breathless laugh, running her fingers through my hair. "More than okay," she murmurs, her voice still husky with desire. "Come here."

I stand, and she immediately pulls me in for a deep, passionate kiss. Her tongue explores my mouth, tasting herself on me. The kiss grows heated quickly, her hands roaming over my chest and down to my belt.

This time, I don't stop her. My own need is becoming unbearable, my cock straining against my jeans. She makes quick work of my belt and zipper, pushing my pants and boxers down in one swift motion.

I step out of them, kicking them aside as she wraps her hand around my length. I hiss at the contact, my hips jerking forward involuntarily.

"Fuck," I groan, resting my forehead against hers as she strokes me slowly. "Baby, you keep that up and this is going to be over real quick."

She smirks, a mischievous glint in her eye. "Maybe that's what I want," she purrs, her thumb swiping over the head of my cock, spreading the pre-cum gathered there.

I growl, capturing her lips in a bruising kiss as I bat her hand away. "Not a chance," I murmur against her mouth. "I'm not done with you yet."

I position myself against her entrance, and with one swift movement, I thrust deep into her, groaning long and hard as I do.

She gasps, her body arching as I fill her completely. For a moment, we're both still, savouring the feeling of our bodies joined. Then I begin to move, setting a slow, deep rhythm that has her moaning with every thrust.

"Fuck, you feel so good," I growl, my hands gripping her hips tightly. "So tight, so wet for me."

Her legs wrap around my waist, pulling me in

deeper. "Maverick," she whimpers, her nails digging into my shoulders. "More, please. Harder."

I can't deny her. I pick up the pace, my hips slamming into hers with increasing force. The sound of skin slapping against skin fills the kitchen, mingling with our moans and gasps. I can feel her walls starting to flutter around me, signalling her approaching orgasm.

"That's it, baby," I growl, feeling her walls start to flutter around me. "Come for me again. I want to feel you come on my cock."

Her eyes lock with mine, dark with desire. "So close," she pants, her hips meeting my thrusts. "Don't stop. Please don't stop."

I slide a hand between us, my thumb finding her clit. I rub tight circles, matching the rhythm of my thrusts. Her breath hitches, her back arching as she teeters on the edge.

"Let go," I command, my voice rough and demanding. "Come for me, now."

She shatters. Her body goes taut, a cry tearing from her throat as her orgasm crashes over her. Her walls clamp down on me, and the sensation is overwhelming, pushing me closer to my own release. I groan, burying my face in her neck as I struggle to hold on, to prolong this moment.

"Fuck, baby," I pant against her skin. "You feel so good. So fucking perfect."

She whimpers, her body still trembling with aftershocks. Her hands roam my back, nails scraping lightly as she urges me on. "Come for me, handsome," she breathes in my ear. "I want to feel you."

With a growl, I increase my pace, my hips slamming into hers. The pressure builds, coiling tighter and tighter in my lower belly until I can't hold back any longer.

With a guttural moan, I bury myself deep inside her as my orgasm hits. Wave after wave of pleasure washes over me as I empty myself inside her, my body shuddering with the intensity of it.

For a long moment, we stay like this, breathing heavily. Christ, she's so much more than I could have ever expected. Once I'm able to gather myself, I lift my head from her shoulder. Her eyes are half open and filled with warmth. My cock's still semi-hard, but I pull out of her, keeping my arms locked around her.

"That's not why I invited you over," she says huskily. "I just wanted to spend time with you."

I can't help but chuckle, pressing a soft kiss to her forehead. "I know, babe. But can you blame me for not being able to keep my hands off you?"

She smiles, a light blush colouring her cheeks. "I

suppose not," she murmurs, her fingers tracing lazy patterns on my chest.

"What do you want for dinner, babe? I'll order for us while you clean up."

Her cheeks flush a deeper red. "Anything," she says softly. "I'm not fussy."

I press a kiss to her lips and help her off the counter. I watch my cum leak down her thighs and my cock stirs. Christ, she's going to be the death of me. I know it.

"I'll clean the kitchen too," I tell her when I see the grimace on her face as she stares at the counter.

"Thank you," she says, ducking her head and walking from the kitchen.

I watch her leave, wondering how the fuck I got so deep so quick, but realising that I don't fucking care. She's mine and that's all that matters.

MY PHONE RINGS and I reach for it on the coffee table, trying not to disturb Lisa, who's curled up at my side. We've had dinner and are currently watching The Green Mile, something that Lisa says is her favourite film and one I hadn't watched before. I've got to say, it's a good movie.

"Yeah?" I answer, keeping my voice low.

"Mav, you good?" I hear Cole ask.

"I'm sound. I take it you have some news for me?"

Lisa lifts off me and hits pause on the movie. I watch as she starts to clear away the plates and glasses as Cole speaks. "I've spoken with Dad. He didn't realise I'd been hired out for that job, but he didn't put the hit out. We're still unsure as to who it was."

I grit my teeth. "Are you sure Travis didn't give the job to someone else?"

"I swear, Mav. Dad had nothing to do with it. Whoever killed Leon did a damn good job covering their tracks. Things went haywire right after you left."

I scrub my hand over my face. "What happened?"

"He was found by one of the hotel staff. He'd asked them to change the sheets and make the room up for six that evening. The maid took one look at his body hanging and screamed bloody murder."

I let out a heavy sigh, pinching the bridge of my nose. "Shit. So, the cops are going to be all over this now?" Fucking cops are involved in everything.

"Yeah," Cole confirms. "They're treating it as a suicide. Whoever killed him did a fucking great job of ensuring that it looks like a suicide. Especially as there are threats against Leon."

Now that's news. "Who was threatening him?" I

ask as I glance over at Lisa, who's quietly loading the dishwasher, giving me privacy for my call.

"Seems like everyone. His closest allies found out that he was planning on taking their daughters and selling them."

I let out a low whistle. "Whoever killed Leon knew what they were doing. None of our research came up with any signs he was doing that."

Cole laughs. "That's exactly it, Mav. He wasn't. It's all a set up to show that suicide was his only option."

Fuck. "So, the Hanging Reaper is definitely not someone to mess with. My question is, how the hell does no one know the identity of them?"

There's always someone who'll know. But this Hanging Reaper, they have their cards close to their chest. Whoever they have on their side is loyal.

"I'm looking into it. Dad doesn't seem bothered by it, but there's just something about it that doesn't sit right with me. I'll let you know what I uncover. Stay safe out there, Mav. Whoever it is, they were close to you today. You missed them by minutes."

"I will do. I'll talk to you soon, Cole." I end the call and toss my phone onto the coffee table, leaning back into the couch with a groan. Lisa finishes in the kitchen and comes back, curling up next to me again.

"Everything okay?" she asks softly, her hand coming to rest on my chest.

I wrap my arm around her, pulling her close. "Yeah, just some work stuff," I say, not wanting to worry her with the details. "Nothing for you to be concerned about."

She nods, but I can see the curiosity in her eyes. "You know you can talk to me about anything, right?" she says, her voice gentle.

I smile, pressing a kiss to her forehead. "I know, babe. And I appreciate that. But trust me, this is nothing you need to worry about."

She seems to accept this, settling back against me. "Okay," she murmurs. "Should we finish the movie?"

"Absolutely," I say, reaching for the remote. As the film resumes, I can't help but think about Cole's words. The Hanging Reaper was close. I missed them by minutes.

My gut is screaming at me that something is going to happen and it's not going to be good. Fuck.

CHAPTER
TWENTY-ONE
LISA

"Travis," I sigh as he answers the phone. "We've got a problem."

It's been over a week since I killed Leon and I've been waiting, watching, and listening. Maverick's hell bent on finding out who killed Leon, and I understand the need for him to know, but crap, he'll be getting dangerously close to uncovering me if he does.

Maverick left twenty minutes ago after I cooked us breakfast. It's crazy how much I enjoy spending time with him. I'm falling so hard for him. Am I crazy? Probably. If he ever finds out what I do, he'll probably leave.

"What's wrong?" Travis asks, his voice alert.

I take a deep breath, trying to calm my racing heart. "Someone came to take Leon out after I did."

"Yeah, the fucking Cleaner did. I had no idea that he was also hired. Did he see you?"

Wait? Maverick's moniker is the Cleaner? Fuck, how did I not know this? He's one of the most feared men in Dublin. He's known for making people disappear without a trace. He's the go-to if you want someone to vanish and never be seen again.

"No," I say softly. "But I saw him. Everything is just complicated now."

"How so?" he practically barks at me.

"Maverick's angry that someone took Leon out. I heard him talking to your son last week. Everyone's tangled up in this and honestly it's giving me a headache."

I don't want to hurt anyone. I kill people to protect the young girls and boys they're trying to exploit and hurt. Now my personal life and business life are colliding and I don't like it.

There's a long pause on the other end of the line. I can almost hear Travis' brain whirring. "Shit," he finally mutters. "What did you mean, last week? Fuck, Lisa, are you and Maverick dating?"

I release a nervous laugh. "Dating? I don't know. We're getting to know one another."

He chuckles loudly. "Is that what you kids are

calling it these days? But yeah, you being tangled up with Maverick makes things messy, to say the least."

"You're telling me," I reply, running a hand through my hair. "What do we do now?"

"We need to tread carefully," Travis says, his voice low and serious. "If Maverick finds out you were involved, it could blow everything wide open. And if he's as angry as you say..."

I sigh. "I'm not sure if he's pissed that someone got to Leon before him or what, but he's angry."

"Probably," Travis murmurs. "But not much we can do about it. I gave you the target. Cole must have gotten the same notification and given the mark to Maverick. I've got to say, kid, you did a good job last week. It went smoothly."

I feel a mixture of pride and unease at Travis' compliment. "Thanks, but that doesn't solve our current problem. What if Maverick starts digging into who took out Leon?"

I'm actually scared that he'll find out it's me, and then what'll happen? He'll leave, and I'm already so deep with him that it'll break my heart.

"He will," Travis says grimly. "That's what the Cleaner does. He's meticulous, and thorough. If there's a trail to follow, he'll find it."

My stomach churns. "So, what do we do? I can't exactly tell him it was me."

"No, you definitely can't do that," Travis agrees. "For now, act normal. Don't give him any reason to suspect you. I'll reach out to some contacts, see if we can muddy the waters a bit, create some false leads."

I nod, even though he can't see me. "Okay. And what about future jobs? I don't want to lie low, Travis. I'm good at what I do. Not to mention, the money is good."

I was able to completely renovate my house. It needed it. It had been left alone for over five years and was in dire need of fixing. With the money I had earned from The Agency, I was able to do that and so much more.

"I hear you, Lisa," Travis says, his tone softening. "But we need to be smart about this. Maybe we can arrange for you to take jobs outside of Ireland for a while. It'll keep you busy and earning, but away from Maverick's radar."

I bite my lip, considering his suggestion. It's not as though I haven't travelled before to do a job. I just hate that I'll have to be cautious about what jobs I take. But I know Travis is right. It's the safest option.

"Alright," I concede. "But not for too long. I can't just disappear on Maverick without raising suspicion."

We've been practically inseparable since we met again. I have a feeling that if I were to tell him that I'd be leaving for a few days, he'd want to know why, but I'm not sure what I'd tell him.

"Of course not," Travis agrees. "We'll play it by ear. For now, just keep your eyes and ears open. If Maverick mentions anything about the hit or his investigation, let me know immediately."

I sigh. "I will do, but I'm hoping that it'll blow over."

He's quiet for a beat. "Lisa... be careful. Maverick isn't just some guy. He's dangerous."

I swallow hard, remembering Maverick's gentle touch this morning, the way he makes me happy, and the way he makes me believe I'm the only woman in the world. "I know," I whisper. I'm not stupid. Knowing now that he's the Cleaner, makes me realise just how deeply entwined our lives are. But I'm able to separate the person from the moniker, and I pray that if the time comes, he'll be able to do the same for me.

"Do you?" Travis' voice is sharp. "Because falling for someone like him... it's not just risky for the job. It could get you killed."

His words hit me like a punch to the gut. "I'm not stupid, Travis," I snap, hating that we're even having this conversation. "I can handle myself."

"I hope so," he says, his tone softening slightly. "Look, I care about you, kid. You're like a daughter to me. I just don't want to see you get hurt."

I feel a lump forming in my throat at his words. Travis has been more of a father to me than my own ever was. "I know," I say softly. "I appreciate that. But I can't just... turn off my feelings."

There's a long pause on the other end of the line. "No, I suppose you can't," Travis finally says with a sigh. "Just be careful. And remember, if things go south, you call me. Day or night, I'll get you out."

"I will," I promise, though I hope it never comes to that. "Thanks, Travis." I hang up and sigh. God, this is a damn mess.

I sit on the couch, my mind racing with everything Travis just told me. The weight of the situation feels like it's crushing me. Maverick is the Cleaner. He's investigating Leon's death. And I'm the one who killed Leon.

My phone buzzes, and I jump. It's a text from Maverick.

Maverick: You've ruined me, babe. You're all I can think about. I'll see you soon.

I stare at the message, my heart pounding. How can something so simple make me feel so conflicted? On one hand, I'm thrilled that he's thinking about me.

On the other hand, I'm terrified of what might happen if he discovers the truth.

I type out a response, delete it, and type again. Finally, I type something simple, hoping I can get my head on straight before he gets here.

Me: Can't wait. See you soon.

As soon as I hit send, I toss the phone aside and bury my face in my hands. What am I going to do? I can't lie to Maverick, but I can't tell him the truth either. The weight of my secrets feel like it's crushing me.

I force myself to take a deep breath. I need to pull myself together before Maverick arrives. I can't let him see how rattled I am. I head to the bathroom, splashing cold water on my face and staring at my reflection in the mirror.

"You can do this," I tell myself firmly. "He'll never have to know."

But as I look into my own eyes, I see the doubt there. The fear. The guilt. I've never felt this conflicted about my job before. Then again, I've never fallen for someone either. Maverick makes me feel alive, makes me feel wanted and beautiful. Something I've never felt before.

I hear a knock at the door and my heart leaps into

my throat. He's here. Earlier than I expected. I take one last deep breath and dry my face and hands.

I pull the front door open with a bright smile. But that smile soon fades when I see who's standing on my doorstep. "What the hell are you doing here?" I snarl.

"Lisa," he says, his voice low and filled with regret. "I've missed you."

I stare at the man I once called my dad. He's changed, gotten older since I last saw him. His hair is now more grey than brown, and there are deep lines etched around his eyes and mouth. But he's still the same man. He broke me and I hate him.

"You can't be here," I finally manage to say, my voice trembling slightly. "You need to leave. Now." I can't deal with him, not now, probably not ever.

He takes a step forward, and I instinctively back away. "Please, Lisa," he pleads. "Just give me a chance to explain. I know I've made mistakes—"

"Mistakes?" I laugh bitterly. "Is that what you call abandoning me, leaving me lying on that hospital bed —a mistake?" I shake my head, my anger bubbling to the surface. "I don't know what the hell happened to you. We were happy and you ruined it. That whore of yours hated me so much that she gave me that rope and you left me for her."

His face crumples at my words, but I can't bring

myself to care. Years of anger and hurt are pouring out of me now. I can't stop it. It's been built up for so long, and now I finally have the outlet to let it all out.

"Lisa, please," he begs, his voice breaking. "I know I can never make up for what I did, but I know what I did. I just... I needed to see you, to tell you how sorry I am."

I shake my head, fighting back tears. "Sorry doesn't cut it, *Ben*. You left me when I needed you most. Do you have any idea what I've been through? What I've had to do to survive?"

He flinches at my words, and I see genuine pain in his eyes. But it's not enough. It will never be enough.

"I don't want your apologies," I say, my voice cold. "I want you to leave. Now."

"Please," he pleads. "Just give me a chance to explain."

Is he for real? "You left me for dead," I spit out. "Do you have any idea what that did to me? How long it took me to recover, physically and mentally?" I shake my head, tears forming in my eyes. Why does he always hurt me? "I needed you. I laid in that hospital bed, my throat burning. I couldn't speak, I couldn't move, and all I wanted was my dad."

I hear footsteps but ignore them. I need to get rid of this man in front of me.

"Because of you, I have no parents. Not biological ones anyway. I hate you for what you did."

He shakes his head, his eyes filled with tears. "Please," he whispers. "Please, Lisa, give me a chance."

"Is she still with you?" I ask, needing to know if he stayed with that bitch.

He looks down at his hand, and I see the wedding ring nestled on his finger. I guess that answers my question. "Leave," I hiss. "Go. I don't ever want to see you again."

He reaches out for me, but before he can touch me, Maverick's there, his hand gripping Ben's wrist and twisting it away from me. "I believe the lady asked you to leave," Maverick says, his voice low and dangerous.

Ben's eyes widen as he takes in Maverick. Being over six feet with broad shoulders and muscles, Maverick is an intimidating sight.

"Who the hell are you?" Ben demands, trying to pull his arm free from Maverick's iron grip.

"I'm the man who's going to make sure you walk out that door and never come back," Maverick replies coolly. "Now, are you going to leave on your own, or do I need to assist you?"

BEN'S EYES dart between Maverick and me, a mixture of confusion and anger on his face. "Lisa, who is this guy? You can't be serious about this."

I step closer to Maverick, drawing strength from his presence. "This is Maverick," I say, my voice steadier now. "He's my...." I pause, unsure of what to call him.

"Her boyfriend," Maverick says smoothly. "She's asked you to leave, so do so, otherwise you won't like the way I remove you."

Ben's jaw drops, his eyes widening in shock. "You're dating *him*?" he practically sneers.

"That's none of your business," I reply coldly. "You lost the right to know anything about my life the day you walked out on me."

Maverick's arm wraps protectively around my waist, and I lean into him, grateful for his support. "You heard her," he says to Ben. "It's time for you to go."

Ben's face contorts with a mixture of anger and pain. "Lisa, please. I know I screwed up, but I'm still your father. Doesn't that mean anything to you?"

His words hit me like a punch to the gut, and I feel tears stinging my eyes.

"A father doesn't abandon his child," Maverick hisses. "Now fucking leave," he snaps.

He pulls me closer to his body, wrapping me tightly in his arms as he pushes me further into the house and slams the door closed.

The sound of the door slamming echoes through the house, and I collapse against Maverick's chest, my body shaking with sobs I can no longer hold back. His arms tighten around me, one hand gently stroking my hair as he murmurs soothing words into my ear.

"It's okay, baby," he whispers. "I've got you. He's gone now."

I cling to him, burying my face in his shirt as years of pent-up pain and anger pour out of me. Maverick just holds me as I fall apart.

Just when I thought I had overcome everything that happened, he shows up and tears apart everything I've worked hard for.

CHAPTER
TWENTY-TWO
MAVERICK

She's trembling in my arms and it's taking everything in me not to go and follow that motherfucker. I heard enough for me to understand that he's her father, but I also heard what she said. That he left her for dead. It's bringing up a fucking lot of questions for me, and right now, the way that she's trembling and struggling to breathe tells me that she's not ready to answer them. I hold her tighter, feeling the tension in her body slowly ebb away as she clings to me for support. Her sobs quiet down to soft hiccups, and I stroke her hair gently, trying to offer some sort of comfort when all I want to do is kill that motherfucker.

Once her tears subside and she's able to breathe again, she lifts her head from my chest and looks up at me with tear-streaked eyes. My heart clenches at her tears. Fuck, I hate them.

"You okay, babe?" I gently run my hand over her hair, feeling the silky strands slide between my fingers.

"Yes," she says on a shaky whisper. "I'm sorry," she apologises, her voice quivering with emotion.

"You never have to apologise," I reassure her. "Never. You up for talking?"

Her body stiffens against mine and she takes a deep breath, steeling herself before speaking. "I... I don't know if I can talk about it yet," she admits, her voice still shaky.

I nod understandingly, pressing a gentle kiss to her forehead. "That's okay. You don't have to tell me," I reassure her. "But I'd like to know what you meant when you said he left you for dead."

She closes her eyes briefly, and I get the feeling that she's not going to share the details with me. But when she opens them again, they hold a mixture of determination and vulnerability. "If I do, you'll see me differently."

"That's not going to happen," I growl. No fucking way.

"We had a happy family. Or so I thought. Everything was going so well, until my dad had an affair and broke our family apart," she whispers, her voice laced with heartache. "I don't know what happened, but my dad changed. He became distant and absent. My parents got divorced, and my ma spiralled into depression. She had always struggled with mental health issues, but after my dad left it got worse."

My gut clenches. Fuck, is she going to say what I think she is?

"One day, I came home to find my ma happy and upbeat. It had been months since I'd seen her like that. I was relieved and proud that she had pulled herself out of the depths of her depression." She begins to tremble again, and I hold her tighter, offering comfort. "That night, I was supposed to go to my dad's house, but he was—is—an asshole and his affair partner was even worse. I couldn't bring myself to go, so I stayed home. And then..." Her voice breaks and tears start streaming down her face. "My ma took her own life."

Christ, I knew that's what she was going to say, but fuck.

"I'm so sorry," I whisper, feeling utterly useless as I watch the tears stream down her face.

"I found her," she confesses. "She slit her wrists. I was so engrossed in reading that I didn't even hear."

Fuck, she was thirteen when her mam died. "You were just a kid. You couldn't have known," I murmur against her head.

She shakes her head, tears flowing freely down her cheeks. "But I should have known. It was so hard, so damn hard. I couldn't sleep. I couldn't function. Every time I closed my eyes, I saw my ma's dead body. I just wanted it to stop. I needed a break. I just wanted it all to stop." Her voice breaks, choked with sobs. "The doctor came and gave me sleeping pills," she cries, pulling in a ragged breath. "I took them all. I just needed it to stop. I wanted to sleep and not think about anything."

I feel my heart drop to the pit of my stomach as she reveals the depth of her pain. I can't imagine what she must have gone through. I hold her close, feeling the tremors wrack her body.

"You were just a child trying to cope with something no one should ever have to face," I whisper, my voice thick with emotion. "It's not your fault. None of it is."

She clings to me as if I'm her lifeline, soaking my shirt with her tears. "Twice I did it. Both times I failed," she chokes out between sobs. "I miss her every single day."

Fuck. Fuck. She's been through so fucking much. So fucking much. How the hell has she survived?

"I know, baby. I know," I murmur, pressing a kiss

to the top of her head. "You're so strong, baby. So fucking strong."

She bucks against me, her tiny body shaking in my arms, and I tighten my grip, holding her closer to me. "It's going to be okay," I whisper, stroking her hair, trying to calm her down. I'm completely shattered by what she's told me. I would never have known the shit she's been through. She's so fucking strong. She's managed to hide just how much she's hurting.

I remember the first time I saw her. Christ, she looked so broken, and now I know why.

She glances up at me. Her eyes are still red-rimmed from crying, but there's a look of relief in them. "Thank you," she whispers, her voice barely above a whisper.

"For what?" I ask, genuinely confused.

"For listening to me," she says, her voice barely audible. "For not judging me. For just... being here."

"You don't ever have to thank me for that," I reply softly, pressing my lips against her forehead. "I'll always be here for you, no matter what."

She presses closer to me and releases a yawn. "Come on, baby. Let's get you to bed."

She wrinkles her nose. "It's still early."

"You need some rest," I tell her as I lift her into my

arms and carry her to the bedroom. She protests weakly but eventually melts into my embrace. I tuck her into bed, pulling the covers up to her chin as she curls up on her side.

She looks so fucking beautiful, even with the red, puffy eyes and tear streaks on her cheeks. I press a kiss to her head and leave the room.

My anger has been simmering on the surface, ready to explode at any moment. I want to track down her fucking father and hurt him. That motherfucker doesn't deserve the title of father. Fuck no.

Once I'm in the sitting room, I pull out my phone and call Freddie. The man is good at getting information. If anyone can get me what I want, it's him.

"Maverick, it's been a while. What's the craic?"

"Not much, but I need your help," I say through clenched teeth. "I need you to find someone called Ben Turner." I heard Lisa call him Ben while she was arguing with him.

"Are you finally taking a pop at Jennings' son-in-law?" he laughs. "About fucking time."

My brows knit together. "What the fuck are you talking about?"

"Ben Turner," he begins, "is the husband of Tanya Jennings—or Turner now. Tommy's daughter. If that's not what you're doing, then what is?"

I take a deep breath and let out a sigh. "He's my

woman's father. I need to find out everything I can about him."

"Alright, Maverick. I'll see what I can dig up," Freddie agrees. "But just so you know, with both Tommy and Tanya running the show, it's not a long shot to conclude that Ben is too. You might not like what you find about Turner."

I scoff. "I already don't. Trust me, Freddie, Ben Turner is a motherfucker and I'll enjoy taking the fucker out. I just need to know anything you can find."

"You got it, but I'm pretty sure that Jer knows about him—well, Tanya at least."

I run a hand down my face as I remember having the conversation with Jer about Tanya years ago. Fuck.

"That woman broke up a marriage. They both did. Her now husband was already married, had a kid and a family. They fucked up the mam and daughter with their bullshit. His ex-wife had bipolar and was struggling to find the right medication to help her through her depression. From what Niall found out, Tommy's daughter was switching her pills. The poor woman couldn't even get the help she needed."

Lisa believes her mam died due to her depression, but the truth is, she wouldn't have been in a deep depression if it hadn't been for Tanya. That fucking bitch played with her medication, which eventually led to Lisa's mam's death.

"I'll talk to Jer, but I'd appreciate you digging for me."

"You got it. How long are you going to keep your woman hidden?"

I scoff. "For as long as possible. I know what you fuckers are like."

It's been just over a week. I'm nowhere near ready to share her with these assholes, but I know eventually they'll meet properly. Lisa isn't going anywhere.

But right now, I need to focus on ensuring her father stays away from her. She's been in foster care since she was thirteen. That means that asshole hasn't been a father to her for over eight years. He can get fucked if he thinks he can show up and things will go back to how they were before he abandoned her.

Freddie laughs. "Can't blame you, man," he says, clearly amused. "I have a feeling that this shit with Ben isn't merely an information finder. You're going to do what the Cleaner does best. When the time comes, remember you're not alone."

"I know. I appreciate it, Freddie. Thanks, I'll speak to you soon," I say, ending the call.

I need to call Jer, and then decide what I want to happen. I respect my uncle. I'd do anything for him.

He's the boss. But right now, with the way that I'm feeling, I can't obey him if he tells me to stay away from Ben Turner. No fucking way. Not after knowing what I do now.

I pace the room, my jaw ticking with each step I take. I won't let him hurt her again. I won't let him bring her down as she fights the memories of what happened eight years ago. He fucked up, and I'll be damned if he gets close to her again.

I'm falling so fucking hard for this girl. I'll do whatever it takes to ensure that he dies for what he's done to her.

CHAPTER
TWENTY-THREE
LISA

My phone buzzes on the nightstand and I groan, reaching over for it. The harsh brightness of the screen stings my eyes as I squint to read the message. It's from The Agency.

> The Agency: 6 a.m. Dublin city. Male, aged 48.

That's all the message says, but it's enough for me to know what it means. I have another target. It's been a month since I killed Leon, and tonight I have one more person to take out.

I quickly respond, letting The Agency know I'll be taking the job. My gaze moves to the time on the screen and I see that it's a little after three a.m. I don't have much time to get organised and make sure everything is in place.

Thankfully, tonight is the first night in three weeks that Maverick and I haven't spent together. Which means I don't have to have any awkward questions about where I'm going.

I jump out of bed and start packing the essentials into my bag. Black leather gloves, along with a thick black snood. I crouch in front of the safe in my wardrobe and open it, pulling out the needle filled with the toxin I need, along with a thick rope.

My phone buzzes again, this time with the full details of my intended target and where to find him. Thankfully, this asshole will be by the river as it is, meaning it will be a quick and easy death for him.

I read through the text as I quickly get dressed. It's going to take me at least thirty minutes to walk to the location—I don't have time to contact Jason and get a stolen car— not to mention sifting through each idea and coming up with the best plan of action to ensure that nothing goes wrong with this hit.

It's over an hour later when I'm leaving the house. I wanted to be gone a lot sooner than this, but I needed to ensure I had everything. It's always better to be over prepared rather than under prepared.

I slip into my black leather jacket, zipping it up as I

head out the door, making sure everything is locked behind me. The wind wraps around me as I move quickly down the street, trying my hardest to not be seen.

As I approach the location, I glance at my watch. Fuck, it's now almost five a.m. I should have been here sooner, but fuck, I'm here now. I keep to the shadows, keeping an eye out for any potential threats. I need to remain hidden until the time is right.

It doesn't take long until the man I'm here for appears, a young drunken woman on his arm. She's stumbling around, trying to free her arm from his tight grip.

Fuck. Fuck, this isn't good. He's early. This changes everything. I need to act quickly and stay calm. My heart pounds hard and fast. I stay in the shadows, watching, wanting to see what happens next.

"Get off me, asshole," the girl screams, her voice shrill and filled with fear. I watch with sickening fascination as she brings her knee up and hits him in the balls. He stumbles backwards, releasing her arm and gripping a hold of his manhood.

The girl wastes no time and rushes away, sprinting as fast and as far away as she possibly can.

Now is my time to shine.

I move silently from the shadows, the leather of my

boots barely making a sound on the cold, damp pavement. I've done this a hundred times before. I take a deep breath, focus on the task at hand, and allow the adrenaline to course through my veins.

As I approach the man, I hear him groaning and cursing about the girl. She's already long gone. The girl ran away as fast as she possibly could. When you've got adrenaline coursing through you, you can do anything you put your mind to, including running faster than you ever dreamed possible.

My hand slides into my bag, my fingers tightening around the syringe. He turns to me, his eyes wide and filled with fear. I lunge at him, pushing the syringe into his palm that he has held upwards as though that's what's going to keep me at bay.

His body tenses for a moment as the toxin starts to take effect. His eyes widen in fear, no doubt from feeling his body start to numb. I watch, waiting for him to collapse to the ground, glad that's the hardest part of my job. He slumps to the ground, his eyes wide and filled with fear.

I take a deep breath and reach for him. I've learned the best way to carry someone heavier than me. It's not easy, but I'm able to do it. It takes a while, but with him not being able to move, it means that he doesn't fight me, making it easier to position him where I need him to be.

Wrapping the noose around his neck takes mere seconds.

Tying the other end to the bridge, I make sure it's secure, knowing that the next part will only take seconds. The wind picks up, rustling through the nearby trees. It's now or never. I push him off the edge of the bridge, the noose tightening around his neck as it catches as he drops.

Taking a deep breath, I stand back, watching his body swing.

Three minutes later and it's finished... Another target eliminated.

My phone rings and I groan. Pulling it out of my jacket pocket, I'm surprised to see it's Travis calling me. "What's wrong?" I ask.

"You need to abandon the mission," he tells me on a growl. "Fuck, Lisa, Maverick's on his way. Yet again. Fucking Cole is handing out targets without checking."

"But I've already done it," I whisper. "I'm about to leave."

Silence spreads between us but it's soon broken by Travis' laughter. "Christ, he's going to get paranoid," he says. "He'll think you're leaving him presents."

"What should I do?" I ask, glancing around to make sure no one is nearby.

"Get out of there, Lisa. Go home and wait for me to call," Travis says, his voice now serious. "And for fuck's sake, be careful."

I nod, even though he can't see me. "Got it. Keep me updated on what's going on."

"Will do. Stay safe," Travis replies before ending the call.

Glancing at the bridge, I see the noose still wrapped around it. My gaze moves to the ground and I spot a red ribbon. It belonged to the girl the asshole had as he walked up earlier. She no doubt dropped it trying to get away from him.

I pick it up and make a quick decision. If Maverick thinks I'm leaving him presents, why not do so?

I quickly tie the red ribbon to the noose, making sure it's secure. Giving it one last look, I turn on my heel and start to make my way home. I don't want Maverick to find me still in the area. I'm not ready for him to know about what I do. I'm not sure how he'll take it.

It takes me almost forty minutes to get home, the adrenaline still pumping through my veins. I strip out of my clothes and jump into the shower. God, my heart is still racing, but the job is done and that asshole is dead. He'll never be able to hurt another woman again.

As I sit at the kitchen counter, facing my phone, waiting for Travis' call, I can't help but think about Maverick finding the ribbon. Will he be angry? Probably, but I need to give him a sign that I'm not coming for him. We just seem to have been given the same target. Again.

The phone vibrates on the counter, the screen lighting up with Travis' name flashing across it. I answer the call, my heart once again pounding in my chest.

"Lisa, did you get out of there?" Travis asks, his voice filled with concern.

"Yeah, Travis. I'm safe at home, waiting for you to call," I reply, trying to sound calm. "Did Maverick find him?"

"Yes. Did you have to leave a fucking red ribbon on the noose?" he says, his tone more serious than I've ever heard it.

"That was your fault," I hiss. "You said he'd think I was leaving him presents. So that's what I did."

Laughter fills the line. "Christ, Lisa, I didn't expect you to do that. Don't worry, Maverick took the ribbon. He's on the warpath though. You've only fuelled him to find out who's doing it."

I sigh. I knew it would. "So, what happens now?"

"That's up to you. I take it you're not ready to tell him it's you."

"No," I say quickly. God no, I'm not ready for that. I'm not sure if I will ever be.

"Okay, then lie low. You're good at what you do. For what it's worth, I don't think Maverick would care."

I laugh. "He's overprotective as it is. I have no doubt him finding out what I do will send him over the edge."

"Probably. He's always been intense. I've always seen that part of him, no matter how hard he hides it behind his laid-back attitude."

"Travis," I begin softly. "My dad showed up a few weeks ago. It was..." I pause, trying to find the right word to describe it. "Intense. I didn't know he was back, and I have no idea where he disappeared to. Can you find out for me?"

"I will. I'll have Melissa look into it. We'll uncover everything; even find out where that motherfucker has been hiding these last few years. As soon as I have the information, I'll let you know," Travis promises. "Stay safe, Lisa."

"You too, Travis," I murmur and end the call.

I've fought against myself about whether or not I'd

find out where my dad's gone, but the past three weeks, no matter how hard I try to forget about him, I can't. I can't get past everything that's happened.

I sit in silence, running my fingers over the edge of the countertop, lost in thought. My father, the man who abandoned me when I needed him the most. The man who left me without a single goodbye, without a single explanation. I needed him. I was so lost, so hurt, so broken, and he left. He chose Tanya over me, just as he did every time before that.

I thought I could move past it, that I could forget about him. But the moment he showed up, I realised I had only buried the feelings deep down inside of me.

Why can't I forget about it? Why does it still make me sad whenever I think of him leaving? He made his choice and I wasn't it. I hate him for that. I hate him for all the stupid choices he's made. He ruined so many lives, and mine was one of them.

CHAPTER
TWENTY-FOUR
MAVERICK

Eight Months Later

FOR FUCK'S SAKE. Yet another hanging body, another red ribbon. Who the fuck is leaving this for me?

"Maverick, you done already?" Cole asks when he answers the phone.

"No, it was already done, Cole. Yet another fucking present. This makes the sixteenth one in the span of fucking eight months," I growl.

It's been eight months and we've yet to uncover who the hell is behind this shit. It makes no sense to me. How the hell have they been able to keep their identity hidden? How does no one have any fucking idea who the hell is doing the killings? I'm fucking impressed, that's for sure. They've managed to make a name for themselves without doing anything other than hanging men and women. They're a fucking legend. Everyone knows of the Hanging Reaper, yet no one knows their true identity.

"Maverick, you're beginning to sound like a paranoid old man. Just because someone is leaving red ribbons on the nooses, it doesn't mean it's a conspiracy to get to you," Cole attempts to reason with me. "Maybe they're helping?"

"Helping?" I scoff. "Sixteen times in eight months isn't helping, Cole. It's a fuck of a lot more than that. If it's so innocent, why haven't they shown their face?"

"I know. I was just trying to help. I'm looking into it," he sighs. "But don't go jumping to conclusions, alright? You never know what the hell this is. I'm just glad they haven't come for you. The way the Hanging Reaper operates, you won't see them coming until it's too late."

"I know. That's why I want to know who the fuck is behind it all," I snap. "There's so much more to this than meets the eye."

"Alright, alright," Cole says, sounding frustrated.

"I'll get to the bottom of it. Just try to stay calm, alright?"

"I will," I assure him. "Just keep me updated on it." I end the call and turn to Emmanuel. "We'd better go. Jer will be waiting on us."

"This shit is creepy, Mav. You sure Cole doesn't know who the fuck it is?" he asks, his voice hard.

"Trust me, Eman, I've been on him for the past eight months to figure this shit out. No one has any idea who's behind it."

He shakes his head. "It's fucked up," he sighs. "Melissa is one of the best hackers. She's one of the best at finding information, and yet nothing? It doesn't add up. Something is fishy about this."

He's not wrong. I've been thinking the same thing since the beginning.

As we drive to meet Jer, I can't shake the feeling that there's more to these red ribbons than just a signal from the Hanging Reaper. It's like there's some other meaning, some hidden message in the act.

But what could it mean? Who would be bold enough to orchestrate such a plan? To leave a calling card like this? I know without a doubt that it's for me, that whoever's doing it is leaving the ribbon for me.

"Tell me that we're actually going to do something about this fucker Jennings?" Emmanuel asks. "He's been grating on me over the last few weeks and there's only so much I can take before I snap."

He's not wrong. Tommy and his cronies have been back in full force, spouting their bullshit in The Hanged Man, the pub that they own. We know all that they have planned, including setting fire to Jer's pubs here in Dublin and in Spain. Thankfully, they didn't do much damage as we knew the plan was in place but not the date and time. Jer had managed to up security, and when the blaze was lit, it was put out before any permanent damage could be done.

"I fucking hope so," I grunt. "This shit has been going on for too long."

"Not to mention the ties that those fuckers have to Lisa," he says. "Has her dad been in contact since that day?"

Just thinking about that motherfucker makes my jaw clench. He went to ground that day and hasn't resurfaced since. Something he no doubt learned from Jennings.

"No, Lisa's dad hasn't reached out since the incident. And frankly, I don't want that bastard anywhere near her," I reply, my voice laced with anger. If I get my hands on him, I'm going to enjoy killing him.

Lisa still hasn't told me everything about what went down with her dad and her, but the little I do know is enough for me to fucking hate the prick. When I told her what Jer had said about what Tanya had done to her mam's medication, she broke down. She told me she'd thought Tanya had something to do with it but could never prove it.

Things between us have been great. I'm so fucking in love with her, I can't think straight. We're practically living together now. A few months ago, shit went down with Thomas Grace, Jessica, and Stephen. My cousin was suffering and had been for years without anyone knowing. Stephen uncovered it, and now the two of them are married and Thomas is dead. The fucker burned Jess when she was a fucking kid. Bastard deserved everything he got and so fucking much more. Right now, Jess is still trying to recover from the burns he gave her two months ago. But she's healing well and is with Stephen as she recovers.

As we pull up to Jer's house, my thoughts are suddenly interrupted by Emmanuel. "Seems as though it's a private party," he muses.

I glance around the driveway and see Stephen's car parked out front, along with Freddie's and Jer's. "Guess so," I grunt as I slide out of the car. I'm hoping this means that Jer's finally gotten his head out of his ass and will give us the go-ahead to take out one of the Jennings' crew.

As we enter the house, the sound of low tones hits me. I guess they're waiting on us. We make our way into the living room, where everyone is assembled. Stephen's standing beside the fire, and Freddie's in the corner, a drink in hand, watching as Jer paces around the room, obviously agitated about something.

"Maverick, Emmanuel," Jer greets us, his eyes darting between the two of us. "Glad you could make it," he says thickly.

"We're here," I say as I take a seat on the sofa. "What's up?"

"I know that you've all been wanting to go at the Jennings' and I've held you back. It was necessary for us to let them implode and that's what they've done."

"Meaning?" I snap.

"It means, Maverick, that Tommy's daughter has fucked up and instructed Tommy's men to come after us. The fires and shit are all her doing, and Tommy's pissed. He's out for blood, and any of his men who are seen to be taking orders from his daughter are dead."

Now that's news. But Christ. What the hell is Jer doing? "Fuck's sake, Jerry," I growl. "This shit's been going on for months and nothing from you, and now all of a sudden you're forthcoming with details?"

"Calm down, Maverick," Jer says, raising his hands in defence. "I've been working behind the scenes to gather information and plan our next move. I needed to make sure we had all the pieces in place before we made our move."

"And what exactly are we going to do?" Emmanuel asks, crossing his arms over his chest.

"We're going to strike first and hard," Jer replies, his eyes burning with intensity. "We're going to take down the Jennings', once and for all. We've been patient, waiting, and now it's time to act."

"And how are we going to do that?" I ask, unable to keep the scepticism out of my voice. "We've been wanting to do this for ages and you've held back."

"For a good reason. Now it's time to strike," Jer assures us. "I have the perfect plan, one that you're going to love, Mav."

Emmanuel raises an eyebrow. "So what's this plan of yours?"

Jer rubs his hands together, looking almost gleeful. "Word is Tanya and her fucked up husband are in town for the weekend. There's a Jennings family reunion of sorts. Not only is that asshole in town, but so is Tommy's youngest. It's up to you who you take out."

"It's clear who I want to be taken out," I growl. I've been wanting to get my hands on that bastard since the moment I laid eyes on him.

"Fuck yeah," Emmanuel agrees. "I'd love to take out the whole fucking family if I'm being honest."

Jer nods, clearly pleased with our enthusiasm. "I thought you might feel that way. The plan is simple." He pauses, glancing between the three of us. "While Tommy and his goons are drinking the night away, I'll have James and Tony orchestrate a distraction to draw them away from the pub. That's when you'll go in and take whoever the fuck you want. We need to do this fast, before they can realise what's going on."

Stephen grins, and it's sadistic and filled with anger. The past two months, he's been helping his wife recover. He's not unleashed his anger since he killed Thomas Grace. "It'll send a clear message to the Jennings that they can't continue with their operations," he snarls. "We get these fuckers and send a direct message."

"But what about Tanya?" I question. "I want her to know who did it. I want her to live in fear, knowing she could be next. I want her to know that she's the reason this is going down."

Jer grins. "Oh, don't worry about that, Mav. We'll ensure she fucking knows. We'll be sending a message directly to Tommy and Tanya."

I nod, glad that we're finally taking a stand against these fuckers. I understand why Jer kept them at a distance. He's biding his time, ready to strike when the moment is right. Not to mention all the shit that went down with Stephen, Jess, and Thomas.

We leave Jer's house and enter Emmanuel's car. It's bigger than the others. Emmanuel and I exchange looks as I slide into the front seat.

"This is the night we end it," Emmanuel murmurs, his voice low and filled with determination.

I nod. He's right, it fucking is. More so for Lisa. She's been hurt by that bastard for long enough. It ends now. "It is," I say low.

Arriving at the pub, we're greeted by James and Tony, both looking gleeful and excited. It's been a while since we've all let loose and tonight we finally get to play.

"We've got a petrol bomb," James laughs. "We're going to set fire to both Tommy's and Tommy Junior's cars. When they exit the pub due to the noise, Tony and I will be waiting. When they notice us, we'll drive off and they'll follow us, giving you all the time you need."

Fuck yeah, now this is what I call playtime. "Nice," I comment. "You two good to escape?"

Tony grins. "We've got Jason and some of the other guys on standby. The moment we're on the move, they will be also. Don't worry about us; focus on what you need to do."

I nod, shaking their hands. "Have fun, guys," I tell them, grinning. "Let's get this show on the road."

Stephen, Emmanuel, and I split up to form a triangle, each targeting a different entrance into the pub. The idea is to strike fast and hard, not giving them the chance to react. As we move, I can feel my heart pounding, the adrenaline rushing through my veins.

I reach the back room first, where Tommy and his men are gathered, drunk and oblivious. I stay, waiting for the sound of the cars going up in flames.

It doesn't take long until I hear the sound of the car alarms, along with a bang. The Jennings' men scramble, all heading for the front door. There are shouts of anger as they realise their cars are being set ablaze.

I hear the rev of the car and know that James and Tony are gone.

Within minutes, the pub is cleared out, and I know it's time to get this done. It's down to Emmanuel, Stephen, and I.

Pushing open the door, I'm not surprised to see Ben Turner sitting down sipping on his drink. Right beside him is Tommy Junior. Damn, now isn't this a great fucking surprise.

Moving toward the bar, I grab a bottle of whisky and a glass, pouring a generous drink. Walking toward them, I put the glass down, and with a sneer, I say, "You two seem to be enjoying yourselves, but I'm afraid your night is about to take a turn."

Both Ben and Tommy Junior's eyes narrow at the sight of me, their expression quickly changing from amused to alarmed. But it's too fucking late.

"Have you met my friends?" I ask, gesturing toward Emmanuel and Stephen, who have now entered the bar. "We've come to send a message."

Ben and Tommy Junior's eyes widen in fear as they realise the situation they're in. I can see the desperation and the realisation in their eyes. There's nowhere to run.

"You?" Ben grunts as he finally realises who I am. I merely grin at him. He's going to be in a world of hurt when I'm finished with him.

"We've got a message for your father and sister," Emmanuel growls, his eyes burning with anger as he glares at Tommy Junior. "You thought we were going to let this shit slide?"

"Not a fucking chance. We bided our time. Now we're done waiting," Stephen adds, his voice just as menacing.

"Let's get this shit done," I snarl, my voice rough.

Both Emmanuel and Stephen move forward. Stephen lunges at Tommy Junior and lands a haymaker of a punch on his jaw, knocking him out cold. Meanwhile, Emmanuel quickly draws his gun and uses the handle to hit Ben across the face with a loud thud. The sound echoes in the room as Ben falls to the ground, knocked out.

Both men are unconscious and it's time to get the fuck out of here and send the message we've been dying to send for months.

CHAPTER
TWENTY-FIVE
MAVERICK

I'm scrolling through my phone as I wait for Lisa to be ready. Today is Uncle Jer's annual party. He's celebrating his birthday, and for the first time in years, everyone in the family will be in attendance. It's a huge, extravagant affair; a sit down dinner and then music afterwards. It's not only family who'll be there but anyone who's significant in our lives. Which means the majority of Dublin will be there, including my parents and sister, all of whom are chomping at the bit to meet Lisa.

It's been just over eight months since we started dating and I've not introduced her to my parents, knowing that she wasn't ready. I still don't think she is, but the party is happening and she's coming with me, so she'll meet them either way, but at least she'll be surrounded by other people that she can escape to if she needs. Thankfully, Callie and Chloe will also be in attendance and she knows them both, so it'll help. Not to mention, Clodagh's coming too. Lisa's not going to be alone.

My phone rings and I see Stephen's name on the screen. "You good?" I ask as I answer.

"Yep," he replies. "Jess is getting ready and I've probably got another hour to wait," he sighs.

"Same here. I don't know why it takes Lisa so long. But we'll be there at some stage this evening," I mutter.

"I can hear you, you know?" I hear her yell from the bathroom, and I chuckle.

"Tanya Jennings is on the warpath," Stephen tells me, and I tense. "She's lost her damn fucking mind, Mav. From what Freddie and I have heard, with every limb and body part that the Jennings' are sent, it sends her spiralling even more."

"Good. That fucking bitch deserves this," I snarl. I know what she did to Lisa's mam. I'm not letting Tanya Jennings off lightly. No, that bitch is going to suffer just as her husband is.

"Yep, and it makes it even sweeter that she's not sure if it's her husband or brother who's being sent to them."

I grin. "That's the plan," I say, revelling in the

despair that bitch is feeling. "Keep her guessing, keep her scared. She deserves every bit of torment coming her way." She has no fucking idea that I have her husband still, that he's alive and kicking—for now at least. I'm nowhere near finished with him. He deserves everything he gets. He hurt Lisa, and that's not something I'd ever allow to happen or let slide.

The woman is the love of my life. I know how special it is to find the one who makes everything make sense and feel natural, and that's what I've found with Lisa. She's the calm to my storm, and I won't tolerate any person or thing that tries to cause her harm. I'll kill anyone who even tries to hurt her.

"Agreed," Stephen replies. "But listen, Mav, we need to be careful. Tanya's unpredictable on the best of days. This shit is going to send her over the edge. She's unhinged as it is. There's no knowing what she'll do next."

I run a hand through my hair. It's why I've not been far from Lisa. I don't want any backlash to come at her. "Any word on increased security for the party?"

"Jer's doubled it. Says he's not taking any chances with the whole family there," Stephen says, and I know that he's more than pleased about that, especially as his wife will be in attendance.

"Smart move," I mutter, glancing toward the bathroom, where I can hear Lisa humming softly. "Look, I gotta go. We'll see you there."

I hang up just as Lisa steps out of the bathroom looking stunning in a deep emerald green dress that hugs her curves perfectly. Her long, dark hair cascades down her back in soft waves, and her eyes sparkle as she smiles at me.

"How do I look?" she asks, running a hand down her dress to smooth out an imaginary wrinkle.

It takes me a while to swallow. Fuck, she's beyond beautiful, and she has no fucking idea just how stunning she is. Those fucking cunts Ben and Tanya made her doubt herself. I know they did. Whatever shit they pulled with her, they broke her confidence, and I'm going to do whatever the fuck it takes to show her just how beautiful she truly is.

"Absolutely breathtaking," I finally manage to say, standing up and walking over to her. I place my hands on her waist and pull her close. "You're so fucking beautiful, Lisa. Christ, I'm rock hard just looking at you."

Lisa blushes and looks down, still not used to compliments. I tilt her chin up gently, forcing her to meet my gaze. "I mean it, baby. You're stunning."

She smiles shyly and leans in to kiss me softly. "Thank you," she whispers against my lips.

I deepen the kiss for a moment before reluctantly pulling away. As much as I want to take her right here and now, we have a party to attend. "We should get going," I say, my voice husky with desire. "As much as I'd love to stay here and show you exactly how beautiful you are, we can't be late to Uncle Jer's party."

Lisa nods, a flash of disappointment dancing across her face. I know she's nervous about meeting my family, especially my parents. I squeeze her hand reassuringly. "It'll be fine, babe. Everyone's going to love you."

She takes a deep breath and gives me a soft smile, but it doesn't hide the fear in her gorgeous eyes.

"Trust me, Lisa. It's going to be okay." I draw her close once more and kiss her. This time, it's hard and deep. When I pull back, her eyes are dark with lust and her lips swollen. My cock is thick and hard. I want her so fucking much, but I don't have the time to show her just how much I do.

I rest my forehead against hers. "We'll be late if we don't leave now," I say, my voice husky with desire.

Lisa grins, a mischievous glint in her eye. "We can always continue later," she says, stepping backwards and reaching for her purse that's on the sofa.

I groan, adjusting myself in my trousers. "You're killing me, woman."

She laughs, and the sound is music to my ears. I love seeing her like this, carefree and happy. This is all that I want. Her like this, happy and smiling.

I keep her hand in mine as we walk out of her house and toward my car. She keeps her head down as we walk, and I fucking hate how nervous she is. As I open the door for her, I notice her hands trembling slightly. Once we're both inside, I turn to her before starting the engine. "Hey," I say softly, taking her hand in mine. "It'll be okay."

She takes a deep breath and nods. "I just want to make a good impression. I want them to like me."

"They will," I assure her, giving her hand a gentle squeeze. "How could they not? You're fucking amazing."

Lisa gives me a small smile, but I can see the doubt lingering in her eyes. I lean in and kiss her softly. I fucking hate just how much she doubts herself. She rarely shows her vulnerability and only when we're alone. She trusts me. I'm fucking glad that I earned her trust and that she's comfortable to show me how she truly feels, but I know the moment we step into my uncle's home, she'll plaster on a fake smile and show everyone that she's fine, when she'll be anything but.

As we pull away from her house, I can feel the tension in her body. I don't know how to help her. I wish I didn't have to bring her, but I know that she wants to come, and everyone's dying to see her. I keep one hand on the wheel and the other intertwined with hers, my thumb tracing soothing circles on her skin.

As we approach the gates of Uncle Jer's property, I feel Lisa's hand tighten around mine. The driveway is already lined up with cars. It wasn't that long ago that part of it was blown up thanks to that motherfucker Thomas Grace. He kidnapped both Jessica and Callie. He deserved the horrific death he suffered for what he did to Jessica.

"Breathe, baby," I say softly and listen to her suck in some oxygen.

Parking my car at the side of the house that's reserved for family only, I squeeze her hand reassuringly before stepping out of the car and moving around to open her door. She takes a deep breath before stepping out, smoothing her dress nervously.

"You've got this," I whisper, placing a gentle kiss on her temple. She gives me a small smile, but I can see the fear still lingering in her eyes.

As we step through the door, I feel Lisa's grip on my hand tighten, but the fear is gone from her eyes and she's got a big bright smile on her face.

The foyer is packed with people, all dressed to the nines. I scan the room, looking for familiar faces. I spot

Stephen and Jessica near Callie and Denis. I don't hesitate; I make my way over to them, knowing that Callie will instantly put Lisa at ease.

"Maverick," Callie says loud enough to be heard over the music. "You're here. Lisa, it's so good to see you again. How are you?"

I can feel some of the tension leaving her body as Callie speaks to her. "I'm good. How are you?" she asks, and is surprised as my sister steps forward and pulls her into an embrace.

"I'm good, thanks, hon. Have you met my husband, Denis?" she asks, pulling back from the hug. I tug Lisa's hand and press against her as Lisa shakes her head. "Denny, this is Maverick's girlfriend, Lisa. Lisa, this is my husband, Denis," she introduces them.

"I've heard a lot about you." Denis grins. "It's nice to meet you."

"Same," she says softly.

"This is Stephen," I tell her, pointing at the man. "And his wife, who is also our cousin, Jessica."

"Hey," Lisa says, and I watch Jess' eyes soften as she takes my woman in. "It's really nice to meet you."

"And you. I know that Stephen and the other guys have been dying to meet you," Jess says with a small grin. "Do you want a drink?"

"I'll get you one," I tell her, pressing a kiss to her head. "Stay here with Callie, okay?"

I get a nod from Lisa as both Stephen and Denis say the same thing to their wives. Once they agree, we head toward the makeshift bar Jer has organised for the evening.

"You good?" Denis asks. "I know a little from what Jer told me about Lisa's situation. You know if you ever need anything, I'm only a call away."

One of the great things about having a brother-in-law who is the head of the Irish Mafia is having him on speed dial whenever I need him. "Appreciate that," I mutter.

"Let's try and not have a repeat of the last time," he says, giving Stephen a pointed look. When shit went down with Jessica, Stephen didn't want anyone else involved. He's a paranoid fucker and I get it. It's hard to know who to trust when the woman you love is in danger.

"There won't be," I assure him. I won't let Lisa out of my fucking sight.

We order the drinks and rejoin the women, all of whom are deep in conversation. Lisa smiles up at me as I hand her a glass. Out of the corner of my eye, I catch sight of my parents making their way toward us. Shit, I was hoping we'd have more time before this moment.

"Mav," my da's deep voice calls out as he approaches, my mam at his side. "There you are, Son."

I feel Lisa stiffen beside me, and her hand reaches out and grips mine. I squeeze Lisa's hand reassuringly as my parents approach. My mam's eyes are already fixed on Lisa, studying her intently.

"Da, Mam," I greet them, trying to keep my voice casual. "This is Lisa. Lisa, these are my parents, Eric and Nichola."

Lisa puts on a bright smile, though I can feel her trembling slightly beside me. "It's lovely to meet you both," she says, her voice steady despite her nerves.

My da gives her a warm smile. "The pleasure's all ours. We've heard so much about you."

My mam, however, is a bit cooler in her reception. "Yes, Maverick's been quite tight-lipped about you," she says, her tone carrying a hint of disapproval. "It's nice to finally put a face to the woman my daughter's told us about."

Lisa tenses beside me at my mother's words. I squeeze her hand reassuringly, shooting my mother a warning glance. "Mam," I say, my tone laced with anger.

"Are your parents here tonight?" Mam asks. "Jer did say he invited everyone. I'd like to meet them."

I'm about to lose my fucking shit with my mam

when Lisa speaks up. "Ma's in St. Fintan's if you want to visit with her, and if you happen to find my dad, then I applaud you," she says coolly, her eyes spitting fire. "If you'll excuse me," she says, releasing my hand and moving away.

"Mam," Callie hisses, shaking her head. "What the hell?"

"It was just a question," Mam says, acting innocently. "How was I supposed to know that her mam was dead and her dad wasn't around?"

I clench my fists, trying to control my anger. "It's not your fucking business to know," I growl. "The hell is fucking wrong with you? Didn't you learn not to fucking interfere with Callie and Jess?" I snarl, beyond pissed that she's acting this way.

My da places a hand on my shoulder, his eyes sympathetic. "Go after her, son. We'll deal with your mother."

I nod, shooting one last glare at my mam before walking away in search of Lisa. I'm not surprised to have Stephen and Jess at my back. Stephen had enough of my mam's shit when she found out about him marrying Jess. My mam doesn't know when to back off. She's all about appearances but doesn't care about people.

My jaw clenches when I see who Lisa's standing

beside. Fucking Cowboy. What the hell is wrong with that man and why the hell is he sniffing around my woman?

I stride over to where Lisa is standing with Cowboy, my blood boiling. As I approach, I catch the tail end of their conversation.

"I'm fine. You know better than that," Lisa says, her voice a little hard.

Cowboy grins, leaning in a bit too close for my liking. "I do, but I also saw the anger on your face. You only get that way when someone pisses you off, and Lisa, you know I won't stand for someone upsetting you."

I clear my throat loudly as I reach them, sliding an arm possessively around Lisa's waist. "Everything okay here?"

Lisa relaxes against me, offering a small smile. "Yeah, we're good. Cowboy was worried about me."

Cowboy straightens up, his easy grin fading slightly as he meets my hard stare. "Maverick." He nods in greeting. "Just wanting to make sure your ma didn't let her inner bitch out again."

I can't lie, having him so close to Lisa pisses me the fuck off, but he's her friend. There's not a lot I can do about it, but he's pushing his luck.

"Cowboy," I growl, my arm tightening around

Lisa's waist. "I appreciate your concern, but I've got this handled."

Lisa looks between us, sensing the tension. "It's fine, really," she says, placing a hand on my chest. "Cowboy was just being a friend."

Cowboy's eyes flick to Lisa's hand on my chest, and I see a flash of something—jealousy?—in his eyes before he masks it with another easy grin. "Of course," he says, taking a step back. "I'll leave you two be. Lisa, always a pleasure. You know where I am if you need me. Maverick." He nods at me before walking away.

I watch him go, my jaw clenched. When he's out of earshot, I turn to Lisa. "You okay?" I ask, my voice softening as I look at her.

She nods, giving me a small smile. "I'm okay. Your mam just caught me off guard, that's all."

I sigh. I'm beyond pissed off at Mam. "I'm sorry about her. She can be... difficult sometimes."

I hear Jess' soft laughter. "Difficult is putting it mildly," she mutters. "Aunt Nichola is a handful and doesn't know when to hold her tongue."

Lisa waves her off. "It's fine. I can handle it."

I pull Lisa close, pressing a kiss to her forehead. "You shouldn't have to handle it. I'll talk to her."

"Mav, don't," Lisa says, placing a hand on my chest

again. "I don't want to cause any problems between you and your family."

I shake my head, cupping her face in my hands. "You're not causing problems. My mam is. You're important to me, Lisa. I won't tolerate that shit again."

"Think you won't have to worry about it, Mav," Stephen says thickly. "Your da, Denis, and Callie are losing their shit at her. About fucking damned time too."

"Where's Freddie?" I ask, changing the subject.

"He's not coming. Ava's still not back and he doesn't know if she's ever coming back," Stephen tells me.

Ava went to America about six months ago looking at property for Callie. She works as a manager for Callie in her bars. They're best friends, have been since they were kids. Ava hasn't returned since, and she's also not spoken to anyone except the odd messages to Callie. It's all fucking weird, but not my monkey, not my circus.

"Lisa," I hear a low British accent call out, and turn to see Danny—Denis' eldest son—and his wife Melissa making their way over to us. Lisa pulls away from me, and I watch, shocked and confused, as the two women embrace.

"How the fuck does she know Melissa Gallagher?" Stephen questions.

"No fucking idea," I grunt, unable to pull my gaze away from the woman I love.

There are a fucking lot of questions that I have about Lisa, things that need answers, and this is just another one to add to the list. There's so much more to her than meets the eye.

I'm not going to hold back any longer. I need answers.

CHAPTER
TWENTY-SIX
LISA

"Lisa," I hear the familiar voice call out to me. Turning, I'm unable to keep the smile off my face when I see Melissa Gallagher—Travis' daughter—walking toward me. I pull away from Maverick and move toward her, so damn happy to see her.

"Hey you, I didn't know you'd be here," I say as we embrace. It's been a few years since I've actually seen her but we speak often.

"Danny's dad is married to Jerry's niece," she explains.

"Oh, which one? I met two," I say, smiling, glad that I have some knowledge of who's here.

"Callie, Maverick's sister," she tells me. "How are things going between the two of you? It's been a while now, hasn't it?"

I nod, glancing back at Maverick, who's now talking with Stephen, Jessica, and Melissa's husband Danny. "Yeah, about eight months now. It's... good. Really good, actually."

Melissa's eyes light up. "I'm so happy for you, Lisa. After everything you've been through, you deserve some happiness."

A twinge of guilt flickers through me at her words. I still have that fear that when Maverick finds out the truth about me, he'll up and leave. I won't survive it. I know that. I haven't loved someone so fiercely in my life. I'm so afraid to tell him how I feel. The only people I've loved have left me. What happens if I tell him and open myself fully to him and then he does the same? Then he walks away and never looks back.

"Thanks, Mel," I say, pushing those thoughts aside. "How about you? How's Danny and the girls?"

Her smile falters slightly. "All good. We're all good. Dad was talking about you this morning."

I raise a brow. "Oh? And what was Travis saying?" I ask, not knowing what that man could be talking about.

"Your dad," she says softly. "He was meaning to call you but he's watching the kids for me."

I feel my chest tighten at the mention of my father.

"My dad? What about him?" I ask, trying to keep my voice steady.

Melissa glances around then leans in closer. "He's disappeared. There's been no sight of him over the past week. He was in Dublin with his wife and then poof, he vanished."

My heart races, and I'm not sure what I'm feeling right now. Relieved, scared, concerned, indifferent? "Oh, okay," I murmur.

She nods sympathetically. "Dad wanted you to know as you had asked him about Ben. He was planning on coming over to visit, but wasn't sure how that would go down with Maverick. We know that he doesn't know about what you do."

I bite my lip. "Yeah. I'm just scared that he'll leave if he finds out."

Her eyes flash with anger. "Trust me, Lisa, if a man can't handle who you are and what you do, they're not the man for you. Danny supports me even though I can be slightly deranged at times. We match each other perfectly, and from what I know of Maverick, the two of you match also."

"He's protective," I say. "Like way over the top with it. He's jealous of Cowboy even though I've told him we're just friends."

She laughs. "Oh, girl, trust me, Danny's the exact

same way, and I wouldn't have it any other way. They can be protective and supportive. You just have to find the strength and courage to tell him. Once you do, you'll feel free."

She's right, I know she is, but it doesn't stop the fear of rejection lingering in me.

"Lisa?" Maverick's deep voice cuts through my inner thoughts. "You okay, babe?"

"Yeah," I reply softly as he slides his arm around my waist. I sink into his embrace. I love that he shows me just how much he cares for me.

"Hey, Maverick," Melissa says as Danny joins us. "We were just talking about you."

"So, how do you two know each other?" Maverick asks, looking between Melissa and me.

"Ah, that would be down to Cowboy," Melissa says with a smile. "He knows Dad, and when Lisa was looking for her dad, he put her in contact with me."

Maverick glances down at me. "Are you looking for your dad, babe?"

I freeze, my heart racing. God, why is this happening now? I look up at Maverick, seeing the confusion and concern in his eyes.

"I... yeah," I say softly, my voice barely above a whisper. "I wanted to know where he was."

Maverick's arm tightens around me. "Why didn't you tell me?"

I take a deep breath, steeling myself. "You were angry when he showed up to the house. I knew you'd be pissed that I would be asking. I didn't know why I wanted the information. I just knew that I wanted it."

"That fucker doesn't deserve your kindness," he snarls low. "He fucked up your life, baby. He doesn't deserve any of your compassion."

I nod. "He's still my dad," I whisper, hating that I'm so bloody weak when it comes to Ben. He'll always have this power over me.

Maverick's arms tighten around me. "Fuck," he whispers.

"I hate him. He hurt me. I think I just needed to ensure that he wasn't here in Dublin. I don't want to see him ever again."

That's something I know for sure. I don't want to see him or talk to him. I just need to make sure he's away from me and won't hurt me again.

Maverick's jaw clenches, and I can feel the tension radiating from his body. He takes a deep breath, clearly trying to calm himself. "I understand, baby. I just wish you'd told me. You don't have to face these things alone anymore."

I nod, my throat tight with emotion. "I know. I'm sorry, I just... It's hard for me to open up sometimes."

Melissa and Danny exchange a glance, and Melissa clears her throat. "We'll give you two a moment," she says, gently touching my arm before they walk away.

Once we're alone, Maverick turns me to face him, his hands cupping my face. "Lisa, I need you to understand something. I'm here for you, always. No matter what it is, no matter how difficult or painful, I want to be there for you. I know that it's going to take time for you to open up fully, but you've got to trust me and let me in."

I look up into Maverick's intense brown eyes, seeing the sincerity and concern there. My heart swells with emotion, and I feel tears prickling at the corners of my eyes. God, I love this man. I really fucking love him.

"I do trust you, Maverick," I whisper, placing my hands over his. "It's just... I've not had someone that I trust fully in such a long time, someone I would trust my life with. I'm not used to having someone to lean on, someone who cares this much."

He leans down, pressing his forehead against mine. "Well, get used to it, baby. Because I'm not going anywhere."

I don't know what I did to deserve him. I just pray

that when the truth comes out, he'll stay by my side. I can't lose him. I won't make it if I do.

Walking into Orna's home, I can see that she's freaking out. The house smells of fresh linen, and I know she's got her favourite candles burning, as she does whenever she has people over. She's meeting Maverick tonight, as I met his family last night. Something that didn't start off too good, but by the end of the night, I had a blast. His mam apologised, and she was actually really lovely. Stephen and Denis told me that Nichola tends to open her mouth without thinking and is just extremely judgemental until she knows you, although Stephen says that doesn't actually change; she's still an asshole. But she apologised and was really sweet afterwards so I'm not holding any grudges.

"Mamaí, we're here," I call out, pulling Maverick along with me.

"Coming!" Orna's voice echoes from upstairs, a hint of panic evident in her tone.

I turn to Maverick, who's got a smirk on his face. Nothing ever seems to faze him. "She's nervous."

"Just like you are," he says quietly, pressing a kiss to my lips. "Chill, baby, it's going to be okay."

We hear Orna's footsteps rushing down the stairs, and suddenly she's there, her cheeks flushed as she watches us. "Oh, hello!" she exclaims, a bright smile on her face. "You must be Maverick. I'm Orna, it's so lovely to finally meet you!"

She extends her hand, and Maverick takes it, his charm kicking in as he greets her warmly. "The pleasure is all mine. Thank you for having me over," Maverick says, his voice smooth and confident. God, why is he so charming and unaffected by meeting new people?

I can see Orna visibly relax at his politeness. I know she was worried about us dating, especially as she knows about who he works for. She ushers us into the living room, where I notice she's gone all out. She's set the table with her finest china and glasses, the ones she never brings out as she's worried they'll break.

"Please, make yourself comfortable," she says, gesturing to the couch. "Can I get you anything to drink?"

As Maverick and I settle on the sofa, I glance to the kitchen, smelling burning.

"Ugh, Mamaí, I think you forgot about something," Devin says as he waltzes in from the kitchen.

I stare at my brother. It's been a few weeks since I

last saw him and he's grown so much. Gone is all the childness he had when he first came to live with us. He's come out of his shell and grown so much.

"Oh, the roast!" she exclaims, dashing off to the kitchen.

I turn to Maverick, rolling my eyes. "See? Nervous."

He chuckles, squeezing my hand. "I think it's sweet," he replies.

"What are your intentions with my sister?" Devin questions, sitting across from us on the armchair.

My cheeks flush with embarrassment at Devin's words. "Dev!" I hiss, shooting him a warning glare.

But Maverick just laughs, seemingly unfazed. "Well, Devin," he says, leaning forward slightly, "my intentions are to treat your sister with respect, make her happy, and be there for her no matter what. To love and cherish her, always."

My heart melts at his words. God, Maverick is so good with words. He always knows the best things to say to make me fall even harder for him.

Devin narrows his eyes, studying Maverick intently. "Hmm," he mumbles, clearly not entirely convinced. "And what about your job? It's dangerous."

I tense up. Maverick and I haven't discussed his job. I haven't brought it up and neither has he. I'm too scared to in case it turns back on me. I pull in a shaky breath as Maverick's hand grasps mine.

"I understand your concern," he says softly. "My job does come with risks, but I always prioritise your sister's safety. I won't let anything happen to her."

Devin stares at him. "You'd better not. My sister is the best person in this world. I'll kill you if you ever hurt her."

I feel my face flush. I've never heard Devin be so serious or protective before and I love that he is. He's an amazing brother.

Before I can say anything to lighten the mood, Maverick leans forward, his expression serious. "I appreciate your protectiveness, Devin. It shows how much you care for your sister," he says, his voice steady. "I promise you, hurting her is the last thing I'd ever want to do. She means everything to me."

Devin doesn't back down. No, my little brother stares at Maverick almost as though he's searching for something. After what feels like an eternity, Devin's face softens slightly. "Alright," he says, nodding. "I'll hold you to that."

Orna rushes into the room looking harried. "I hope everyone's getting along," she says, her voice a little too cheerful, betraying her nerves.

"We're fine. Is everything okay with dinner?" I ask,

taking in her flushed face and heavy breathing. She's beyond stressed out. I didn't intend for her to be like this. I just wanted her to meet Maverick, not send her into a full blown panic.

"Well, the roast is... well, it's a bit more well-done than I intended," she says with a nervous laugh. "But I've salvaged what I could. Dinner will be ready in just a few minutes."

I quickly get to my feet. "Do you need any help, Mamaí?"

"Oh, no, no," she waves me off. "You stay here with your boyfriend. Devin will help me."

I hide my laughter as Devin glares at her but gets up and follows her out of the room. "It would have been better if we had met at a restaurant," I murmur. "Thank you for coming with me," I whisper, tilting my head to look up at him.

His brown eyes meet mine, a soft smile playing on his lips. "I wouldn't be anywhere else."

"Dinner's ready," Orna yells from the kitchen.

We make our way to the kitchen, where Orna has set out the slightly charred roast alongside an array of side dishes that look much more appetizing. As we take our seats, I can't help but feel a mixture of nervousness and excitement. This is it—my family and Maverick, all together. All the people I love dearly in one place.

"I hope everyone's hungry," Orna says, her voice still a bit shaky as she begins to serve the food.

"It looks delicious," Maverick says smoothly, flashing that charming smile of his. "Thank you for having me over."

Orna visibly relaxes at his words, a genuine smile spreading across her face. "It's our pleasure to have you here."

During dinner, Orna keeps glancing between Maverick and me, her eyes full of questions she's too polite to ask. Devin, on the other hand, is eating his weight in food. I've never seen someone eat as much as he does.

Maverick is determined to break the ice. "So, Orna," he says, his voice soft. "Lisa speaks highly of you. How long have you been a foster parent?"

Orna's eyes light up at his question. "Oh, about eight years. Lisa was my first foster child until Devin came along a few years later," she says, but I can see the pride in her eyes. "Giving children a home is one of the most rewarding things in this world. Being able to watch these two grow up into beautiful and amazing people is without a doubt the best thing ever."

God, Orna's the fucking best. She's always been sweet and welcoming. I shouldn't have been worried about her meeting Maverick.

"That's truly admirable," Maverick says, his voice filled with genuine respect. "It takes a special kind of person to open their heart and home like that."

Orna beams at his words. "Thank you, Maverick. It's been a blessing, really. These two have brought so much joy into my life."

"Even when Lisa was being a little shit?" Devin pipes up, a mischievous grin on his face.

"Language, Dev," Orna scolds, but there's no real heat behind it. "But yes, even then. Lisa kept me on my toes, that's for sure. I just pray to God that Devin doesn't follow suit."

I can't help but laugh. "I'll teach him how to joyride," I quip.

Orna's eyes narrow in on me. "You'll do no such thing, young lady. I've had enough grey hair thanks to you and your need to chase thrills. Devin is not going to do that."

Devin chuckles, and I know that he'll push the limits, but he's been with Orna for a long time now. He's been able to heal from what that monster did to him. He won't need to find an outlet for the rage and hurt he feels.

Maverick leans back in his chair, a grin on his lips, and starts to ask question after question about Devin and me to Orna. Mamaí smiles and answers every single one. She's so relaxed now that it makes it easier for me to breathe.

Maverick's hand finds mine under the table, entwining his fingers with mine as he talks to my foster mam. He has no idea just how much I love him. God, I got so lucky finding him. I couldn't imagine my life without him.

I'm praying that when the truth comes out, we can work through it.

CHAPTER TWENTY-SEVEN
MAVERICK

Five Months Later

I AM JOLTED awake by a sharp kick to my leg, and my eyes snap open to see Lisa writhing in distress. She clutches at her throat, gasping for air as tears stream down her face. Her body shakes with sobs, the sound of her ragged breaths filling the room. I knife up from the bed, my heart pounding in my chest as I watch Lisa trying to fight off the imaginary assailant.

I gently shake Lisa awake, watching as her chest rises and falls with ragged breaths. Her eyes snap open and widen in fear as she realises where she is. Tears stream down her flushed cheeks as she tries to catch her breath. I wrap my arms around her trembling body, feeling the heat of her skin burning against mine.

"You were having a nightmare," I whisper, trying to calm her. But as she clings to me, her grip tight and desperate, I can feel that there's something more going on than just a bad dream. "Talk to me, baby. What's going on?"

"I didn't want to do it," she whispers. "I was so lost after Ma died, so fucking lost, but she hated me," she sobs, her body bucking against mine. "Dad didn't give a shit. He only cared about himself and her."

My body tenses at her words. Fucking Ben and Tanya. "What happened?" I ask, glad that my voice isn't as hard as I had expected it to be.

"Are you going crazy like your mam did? She laughed when she asked me that. She hated me. She said that the world would be a better place without either me or Ma. She told me I should do something about it."

I rock her against me, her tears soaking through my skin as I try to soothe her. My rage is boiling just beneath the surface. That fucking bitch. God, I can't even put it into words how much I hate her. I swear I'm going to kill her and relish every single second of it.

"I just wanted everything to be quiet," she sobs. "I took the pills, hoping to find some peace in sleep," she confesses.

I close my eyes and press a gentle kiss to the top of her head. "It's okay, baby," I whisper soothingly.

"I got help," she cries, clinging to me desperately. "I went to an in-care psychiatric facility and was able to work through the pain. I was healing, I was getting better, but she wouldn't let me," she sobs, her hands clawing at my arms.

"What did she do, baby?" I ask, my voice rough and raw with emotion.

"She handed me a rope," she whispers, her body trembling. "She wouldn't stop. She kept telling me how awful I was. She wanted me dead. I didn't want to do it but I had no choice." She breaks down again, her sobs shaking her entire body.

"I'm so sorry, Lisa," I whisper against her head. "So fucking sorry that you went through that. What about your dad? Where was he? Did he know?"

Lisa continues to cry, her body shuddering in my arms. I stroke her hair, trying to provide some small comfort in this nightmarish situation. "Yes, he knew. I think he did anyway. It doesn't matter. He left me in the hospital and I didn't see him again until the day he showed up at my home," she cries.

"None of them will hurt you again," I promise her, my voice laced with anger.

She continues to cry against me and I feel helpless, unable to help her right now. All I can do is offer her comfort and promise her that she's going to be okay.

Tomorrow, I'll be able to end some of her suffering. That motherfucking dad of hers is finally going to meet his demise. I've held him for five months now, tortured him mercilessly, and yet it's not enough. He abandoned the woman I love when she needed him the most, and now I know the truth, nothing will hold me back from killing him.

Lisa's breathing evens out and I lay her down on the bed and pull her against me. I'm not wanting to let her go, not now, not after I know the truth about what happened to her. We've still got a lot to talk about, but she's opening up to me. We're finally getting there.

I close my eyes, listening to her soft breathing. It takes a while before I'm able to find sleep, and when I do, my dreams are filled with images of Lisa with a rope around her neck, hanging.

I STARE at the man who was supposed to protect and love Lisa. The man who was to care for her and ensure her safety. He failed her. Fuck, he failed her miserably and fucked up her life due to his selfishness.

The burn marks on his feet are ugly and blistered. I smile at the sight. I caused that, along with the jagged, raised scars along his chest and arms. Every inch of them are deserved.

The man, now cowering in fear, glances up at me with wide, terrified eyes. He knows what's coming next. I can see it in his expression; the realisation that this is his last moment reflects in the depths of his eyes.

"Lisa... she... she's my daughter. Please don't do this," he begs, stammering his words.

I scoff. "Since when did you care about her? I mean, wasn't it you who left her alone when she needed you? Or better yet, wasn't it you who let that fucking bitch give her the rope that she used to try and hang herself?"

"Tanya—" he begins, his body trembling. "She made a mistake."

My laughter is cruel as it fills the room. "A mistake?" I repeat. "A mistake? Leaving your own daughter to be manipulated when she was at her most vulnerable by a psychopathic bitch is a mistake? Letting her try to take her own life because that cunt called her worthless is a mistake? No, you piece of shit, that was a calculated decision, one you made to save your own pathetic self from facing the mess you created!" I'm breathing heavily, my anger coming to the forefront. "You did this. You fucked up and continued to do so by putting that fucking cunt ahead of your own daughter."

"Please," he begs. "Don't do this."

"Why?" I ask. "Why shouldn't I do this?"

He doesn't answer, because the truth of the matter is, he hasn't got an answer. He made his bed years ago and now he's going to lie in it.

"I'll be sure to let Lisa know just how much of a useless fucking asshole you are. She's better off without you."

The man's eyes fill with tears as he continues to plead for his life. But I won't let him live. He doesn't deserve to. "No," he whispers, shaking his head as I reach down and pick up the sledgehammer, feeling the weight of it in my hands. The satisfaction of seeing the terror in his eyes is almost enough to make the adrenaline rush worth it.

I stalk toward him, a sadistic grin on my face. "This is for Lisa," I say, before bringing the hammer down with all my force onto his chest. The crack of the blow echoes through the room, and I can feel the satisfaction of my revenge coursing through my veins.

As I continue to take my time in inflicting every

last bit of pain on him that he deserves, memories surface of Lisa struggling to breathe as she relived that awful night when that cunt tried to have her kill herself. I remember how she clung to me while she sobbed as she relived the pain this cunt and his bitch of a wife caused her.

I unleash every ounce of rage that I have. Lisa will never have to see him again. She'll be free from his neglect. She can start to heal without the shadow of her father looming over her. I know it'll be tough for her to know I'm the one who killed her father, but I can't let her continue to suffer because of his actions.

Tanya is next on my list. I'm not going to let her get away with what she's done to Lisa. When it's finally her turn, I will slowly peel back her skin until her body is nothing more than a bloody, agonising mess. She's not going to get off lightly just because she's a female. Fuck no.

As each blow lands on his broken, trembling body, I can feel the rage inside me dissipating. It's almost over. I'd do it over and over again if I needed to. All that matters is keeping Lisa safe and this fucker couldn't do that. In fact, he did the opposite and put her in danger.

Finally, I stop, standing back to admire my work.

The man is lifeless, his eyes so wide you can still see the hint of fear in the deadness of his orbs.

I'm not finished yet. Now, I have to have the body delivered to his cunt of a wife and wait for the fireworks. She's going to lose her ever-fucking-loving mind and I'm going to enjoy every fucking second of it.

I reach for my trusty saw. It's one of my more preferred ones. I start it up, listening to the engine rev and the saw's blade start to churn. I start sawing into her father's body, the sound of the blade tearing through flesh and bone echoing throughout the room.

I work methodically, cutting the body into smaller and smaller pieces. Each pass of the saw brings this shit closer to the end. As I finish dismembering the man, I take a step back to survey my handiwork. The sight is gruesome, but it's what he deserves. I can't help but feel a sense of satisfaction wash over me. Tanya will get her turn soon enough, and I'll make sure she remembers this day for the rest of her life.

With the body now in manageable pieces, I carefully wrap each one in thick plastic wrap and then place them into a box. I load the box into my truck, excited for what's about to happen.

It takes me a while to get changed and cleaned up.

Once I'm ready, I climb into the truck and drive. Excitement courses through me. The Jennings' have lost their son and now son-in-law. Soon they'll lose their daughter.

I can't fucking wait. Let the games begin.

CHAPTER
TWENTY-EIGHT
LISA

I'm giddy with excitement. Tonight, Maverick is taking me on a date. We tend to do one every month. I love being with him even though we practically live together. We spend almost every night at my house. The only nights we don't are when we have a job to do. Thankfully, my jobs seem to coincide with Mav's, so it's easy to hide what I'm doing.

I'm currently cleaning. I do this when I've got built up energy to burn. I strip the sheets off the bed and toss them into the laundry hamper. The windows, floors, doors—all receive a thorough scrubbing and polishing. The smell of lemon cleaner fills the air as I move around the room dancing to the music blasting from the speakers.

Once that's done, I make my way to the pantry.

With determination, I begin organising and throwing out expired items. As I reach for a can of soup on the top shelf, there's a sudden knock at the door. My brows knit together in confusion. Who could that be? I'm not expecting anyone.

"Hey," I say to Ciarán when I see him standing on my doorstep. "Is everything okay?" I ask when I notice his hardened expression.

He enters my home and shuts the door behind him. "Travis wanted to be here," he tells me. "He's on his way, but he wants you to know."

I feel a chill run down my spine at Ciarán's words. "What's happened?" I ask, needing to know what he's not telling me.

He sighs. "I hate to be the one to tell you, but your father's body was found early this morning. He's gone, Lisa."

I stare at Ciarán, my mind struggling to comprehend his words. My father, gone? My world tilts, like the ground has been shifted beneath me. God, he's gone? I blink back the tears, willing them not to fall. How the hell did this happen?

"I'm sorry. I know this is probably the last thing you want to deal with right now," Ciarán says softly, his gaze filled with worry.

My eyes burn with unshed tears, and I cling to the

counter in front of me for support. "Thank you for letting me know," I whisper, barely able to get the words out. My stomach drops as reality sinks in. "What happened? Do you know who did it?" I ask, needing to know.

Ciarán's face darkens. "He was tortured. It looks like it was long and brutal. It looks as though it was the Cleaner."

My breath catches in my throat. It feels like I've been punched in the gut. "No... no, it can't be," I gasp, hoping that I misheard him or that this is all some sick joke.

"I wish I could say it was a joke, Lisa," Ciarán says solemnly, his eyes filled with sorrow. "But it's not. The Cleaner is notorious for his method of killing and your father is a victim of the Cleaner."

My heart sinks and a sob breaks from me. Why would he do this? Why would Maverick hurt me like this?

Ciarán reaches out a hand to steady me as I sway on my feet. "Lisa, I know this is a lot to take in. Travis will be here soon. He's worried about you. I'm not leaving. Do you want me to call Maverick?" he asks.

I'm unable to find my voice as tears finally spill down my cheeks. The pain of loss grips my heart in a vice-like hold, squeezing the breath out of me. What the hell is going on? Why would he do this? I know my dad wasn't the greatest, but killing him? I don't understand.

The front door opens and my entire body tenses. Maverick's home.

"What the fuck is going on?" he rumbles.

I spin on my heel. "Why?" I rasp, anger and hurt etched in the word. "Why did you do it?"

"What?" Maverick returns, glancing between Ciarán and me. "What the fuck is going on?"

I take a step back, my voice trembling with raw emotion. "My dad, Maverick. He's...he's dead," I choke out, the words heavy with grief.

Maverick's expression darkens as realisation dawns on him. His jaw tightens, his fists clenching at his sides. "Lisa—" he says gravely, stepping closer to me.

I shake my head in disbelief, tears streaming down my face. "How could you? Why would you do this to me?" I cry out, my heart torn between the love I have for him and the pain of his betrayal.

"What am I missing?" Ciarán asks.

"Meet the Cleaner, Ciarán." My voice drips with venom. I'm so hurt and angry. I never expected this from him.

"Shit," Ciarán grunts, his face slack with shock. "Fuck, I didn't know."

"How long have you known?" Maverick questions, shoving his hands into his pockets and clenching his jaw.

"Months," I reply, my tears falling thick and fast. "I didn't care. You're more than the Cleaner. You were my Maverick."

Maverick's eyes soften as he takes a step closer to me, his hand reaching out tentatively, but I step away. I can't let him touch me. "Lisa, I never wanted this life to touch you," he begins, his voice pained. "I kept you separate to protect you."

"How can you say that?" I choke out, my voice barely above a whisper. "You killed my dad!"

"That fucker hurt you. He let that cunt almost destroy you. I'm not a man who'll let that slide, baby. I fucking love you. I won't ever let that happen. Someone hurts you; they'll pay for doing so."

Pain slashes through me. No, he can't love me. Everyone who has loved me has gone, has left me.

"I can't—" I breathe, my heart pounding, my body trembling with fear. "Please," I beg, unsure of what I'm pleading for.

"Baby, listen to me," he rasps torturedly. "Please, just hear me out."

"You killed him, Maverick. You killed my dad. How do we get past that?"

He shakes his head. "I don't know, but I do know that we can."

I find myself staring at Maverick, my eyes wide with disbelief. Could he really be so heartless? My dad was a piece of shit, but he was still my dad. How could Maverick take that away from me?

"Maybe we can't," I say finally, my voice barely a whisper. "Maybe some things can't be forgiven."

Maverick's face is a mixture of anger and pain. "I know you don't agree with what I've done, but I can't change it," he says, his voice full of pain. "I'd do anything to ensure no one ever hurts you. When you love someone, baby, you want to protect them. You want to make sure that they're safe."

"Stop saying that," I scream. I can't listen to it. I don't want to fucking hear it. It's too much. All of this is just way too much.

"What?" he asks with a raised brow. "That I love you?"

"I don't want to hear it!" I yell, my voice breaking with emotion. "Don't you get it? I'm not worthy of love. I fuck up everyone's life."

His face contorts with rage and pain. "Fuck no," he growls. "You don't fuck up anyone's life. Your father was a cunt, Lisa, one of the biggest fucking assholes I've ever come across. Killing him was a fucking privilege, baby. I'd do it over and over again. That motherfucker made you doubt how amazing you are."

"Stop," I beg, sinking to the floor, unable to take this anymore.

Maverick crouches in front of me, his touch soft as he runs his thumb along my cheek, swiping away the tears that won't stop falling. "You are more than worthy of love, baby. I fucking love you. My world was bleak until you walked into it. I fucking love everything about you."

"Please," I rasp. "Stop. Please, Mav, please go. I can't do this right now." My body bucks as sobs rip through me, tears streaming down my face. I can't take this. The pain is too much. I feel like I'm going to shatter into a million pieces.

Maverick's face is a mixture of pain and anger, but he nods, wiping his hand across his face, trying to regain control. "I'll go, just for now, but I'm not leaving you, baby. Not now, not fucking ever. I'll be back," he promises me. He presses a kiss against my head. It's soft and lingers for a moment. "I'll be back soon," he whispers.

I close my eyes as he stands up. I hear low whispers and know that he's talking with Ciarán, but I can't hear what they're saying. My body is still trembling as my sobs continue. The moment the door closes, my cries get harder.

He's gone. God, he's gone. What have I done? I sit here, broken and lost, sobbing, trying to catch my breath as I try to hold on to that tiny glimmer of hope that he'll be back. That I haven't ruined everything. That I haven't pushed away the only man I've ever loved and lost him forever.

CHAPTER TWENTY-NINE

MAVERICK

Sweat drips from my body. Every punch to the punching bag is filled with power and anger. Images of Lisa crumbling on the floor, looking broken, haunt me. I fucked up. Christ, I fucked up badly. Killing her dad was always going to happen. I did it to protect her. He's tied to the Jennings', and they're all going to pay for the shit they've caused. Tanya Jennings is one of the more prominent figures within that family, meaning that Lisa's dad was always a target, even before I knew what that cunt did to her.

My fist connects with the bag again, and I imagine it's Ben's face. The satisfying thud echoes through the empty gym. I've been here for hours, trying to beat away the pain I'm feeling. But it's not working. Lisa's tear-stained face keeps flashing before my eyes. The way she looked at me when she found out what I'd done will haunt me forever. It was a mixture of horror, disgust, and love. There was also a hint of fear in her eyes.

I never wanted her to be afraid of me. Everything I've done, I've done for her. To keep her safe. To make those bastards pay for what they did to her. But in doing so, I've become the very thing she was trying to escape.

The irony isn't lost on me as I pummel the bag harder, my knuckles raw and bleeding. Have I lost her forever? That's what I'm afraid of. What if she doesn't want to see past what I've done?

I sink to the floor, my back against the cold wall, and bury my face in my hands. The adrenaline fades, leaving me hollow and aching. What am I going to do?

Lisa's words echo in my head: *Don't you get it? I'm not worthy of love. I fuck up everyone's life.* She has no idea just how much she means to me; how much I truly fucking love her. She's so used to people giving up on her and leaving her be that she's afraid I'll do the same. She can't see that she's it for me, has been since the moment she walked into Callie's pub last year.

Rising to my feet, I know it's time to prove to her that I'm all in. We'll get past this. I know it. Right now,

I need to get to her. Leaving her was a mistake. What if she thinks I'm gone?

I don't bother changing out of my sweat-soaked clothes. Instead, I make my way to the front door and out of the house, nabbing my phone and keys from the table as I do. The cool night air hits me as I burst out of the house. All I want to do right now is find the woman I love and hold her. I fucked up by leaving. That's not what she needed. Fuck.

My finger hovers over the button on the key fob, ready to unlock my car. Suddenly, a sharp crack echoes through the air behind me, causing my muscles to tense and my heart to race. Before I can even turn around to see what caused the sound, a heavy object slams into the back of my head. A wave of dizziness washes over me and I feel myself losing consciousness as everything goes black. The last thing I hear is feminine laughter as I crash to the ground.

THE MOMENT I REGAIN CONSCIOUSNESS, I tense up as I remember what happened. Some motherfucker hit me over the head. Fucking bastard. Opening my eyes, I see I'm in a dimly lit room. The room spins as I try to focus, my head throbbing from the blow I suffered. I'm tied to a chair, my wrists and ankles bound tightly. The air is stale and musty, as though the room hasn't been aired in years. As my vision clears, I make out a figure standing in the shadows.

"Well, well. Look who's finally awake,' I hear the feminine voice say, and her words are filled with amusement.

I strain against my bonds, anger surging through me. "Who the fuck are you and what do you want?"

The figure steps into the light, and I glare at the cunt standing before me. It's Tanya Jennings, her red lips curved into a cruel smile. "Oh, I think you know exactly who I am. And as for what I want? Well, that's simple. Revenge."

I spit at her feet, my voice a low growl. "You'll die for what you've done."

She raises a brow at me. "What I have done? You killed my husband, my brother, and mutilated my other brother, and I'm the one who's going to die?" Her laughter is forced. "No, you'll die, Maverick. You'll die for killing them."

I glare at Tanya, my jaw clenched tight. "Your husband and brother deserved what they got. Your husband especially."

Tanya's eyes flash with rage. She steps closer, her heels clicking on the concrete floor. "What did my husband ever do to you? You fucking Houlihan Gang members should come for me or Da, not my husband."

"I would have," I snarl. "But after I found out what you had done to my woman, there was no way in hell that I was going to leave it alone."

"What woman?" she sneers. "Don't tell me that the mighty Maverick has fallen for some stupid girl?"

Fucking bitch. The moment I get free of these bindings, I'm going to kill this bitch. "Lisa Turner. You know her, right, Tanya?"

Her eyes darken with anger. "Lisa was weak," she spits. "Just like her mam was. Useless and fucking crazy. She tried to come between my husband and I, even wanted me to leave the house I lived in. She was delusional. No one puts me second, not even to a fucking crazy bitch like Lisa."

My vision goes red. I strain against the ropes, wanting nothing more than to wrap my hands around Tanya's throat. "You sick bitch. You manipulated a thirteen year old girl into trying to commit suicide."

Tanya's eyes narrow, a flicker of surprise crossing her face before she quickly masks it. "How do you know about that?" she hisses, leaning in close.

"Lisa told me everything," I growl, meeting her gaze with sheer hatred. "How you tormented her, made her believe she was crazy. How you pushed her to the brink."

A cruel smile twists Tanya's lips. "Oh, poor little Lisa. Always the victim, isn't she? She was nothing but a nuisance, getting in the way of my perfect life. I did what I had to do."

My muscles strain against the ropes, fury coursing through my veins. "You cunt," I spit. "I'm going to make you pay for every tear Lisa ever shed because of you."

Tanya smirks. "I'd love to see you try. What are you going to do? Hmm? You're tied to the chair. You're pathetic. You were unconscious for hours. You didn't even wake when I dragged you into the house."

"Where did you manage to get this house from?" I snarl, my fingers trying to undo the rope. "What poor fella did you burn to get it?"

Tanya's smile is filled with glee. "You think you're so clever, don't you? This house was the house where Lisa tried to take her own life. It's fitting really." She circles behind me, her fingers trailing across my shoulders. I resist the urge to shudder at her touch. "You know, Maverick, I almost admire your dedication. Killing for the woman you love... It's almost romantic. Stupid, but romantic."

"Fuck you," I growl, still working at the ropes.

They're tight, but I can feel them starting to give. I just need to keep her talking. "You don't know the first thing about love."

Tanya laughs, a harsh, brittle sound. "Oh please. Love is for the weak. Power, money, respect, that's what really matters in this world."

"That's 'cause no one would ever love your psycho ass. You're a toxic bitch, Tanya, and the only way you can get someone to even stay with you is by manipulation."

Tanya's eyes flash with rage. She leans in close, her breath hot on my face. "Is that so? Then tell me, Maverick, where is your precious Lisa now? Does she know what you've done? Does she still love you after learning what a monster you really are?"

Her words hit me like a punch to the gut, but I refuse to let her see how much they affect me.

"Oh, this is priceless." Tanya grins. "I'm sure she just loves the idea of her man killing her dad. What will she do? Hmm? Cry to mammy? Oh wait, she can't; she's dead too."

"You're a fucking bitch," I snarl, feeling the rope start to loosen. "I'm going to enjoy killing you, and when I'm done, I'm going after your dad and mam."

"Not going to happen," she laughs. "But don't worry, Maverick, once I'm finished with you, I'll be sure to let Lisa know just how much you loved her. That's, of course, right before I kill her. It's been a while since I last saw her. I wonder if she's still crazy?"

"Well, you don't have to wonder for much longer," I hear Lisa's voice say, her tone hard.

"Get the fuck out of here," I growl, my heart racing. She can't be here. Fuck no, she needs to leave.

Tanya whirls around, her eyes wide with shock as she sees Lisa standing in the doorway. Lisa's face is slack and filled with shock, but she quickly recovers. "Lisa," Tanya sneers. "How nice of you to join us. We were just talking about you."

"I heard," Lisa says coldly, taking a step into the room. Her gaze flicks to me, concern flashing across her face before she turns back to Tanya. "But don't worry, bitch, I won't be staying long."

I've never heard Lisa's voice sound so cold or hard. What the fuck is going on?

CHAPTER
THIRTY
LISA

Five Hours Earlier

"Lisa," Ciarán says, his voice gentle as he crouches in front of me. "Come on, girl, let's get you up."

I take a steady breath and let him help me off the floor. "He's gone?" I ask, needing to know if I was right and he left.

Ciarán nods. "Yeah, he left, but you won't have long until he'll be back again."

I close my eyes. It's so fucking stupid, so damn stupid, but I miss him. After everything that's happened, I actually want him to come home to me. I love him, but how can I forgive him? He killed my dad.

"Do you want me to stay with you?" he asks, his words laced with concern. "Travis will probably be here soon."

I sigh. Fuck, I forgot that he told me that. "I'll be fine. I'm going to have a shower and then curl up in bed and rest for a bit."

Ciarán hesitates, his brow furrowed with worry. "Are you sure? I don't like leaving you alone after... everything."

I force a weak smile. "I'm sure. Thanks for being here, but I just need some time to process."

He nods reluctantly and heads for the door. Before leaving, he turns back. He's unsure of whether or not to leave me. He's a great friend, and I truly appreciate that he's worried, but I need some space. "Call me if you need anything, okay?"

"I will," I promise, even though we both know I won't. I hate relying on anyone and it's something that Ciarán knows. I rarely call him, and when I do it's just to check in with him and make sure he's okay.

As soon as the door clicks shut, I slump against the wall. The silence in the house is deafening. I cleaned everything this morning, and right now I'm really wishing I hadn't. There's no trace of him right now and I hate that. God, I'm such an idiot. One minute I hate him and the next I'm wishing he was here. What the hell is wrong with me?

I drag myself to the bathroom, shedding clothes as I go. The hot water stings my skin, but I welcome the pain. It's a distraction from the ache in my chest. As I stand under the scalding spray, memories of him flood my mind. His smile, his touch, the way he'd hold me at night. But then, like a cruel twist of fate, I see my father's face. The betrayal, the shock, the life fading from his eyes. I choke back a sob, my hands trembling as I brace myself against the shower wall.

The water runs cold before I finally step out, wrapping myself in a towel. Once again, the house is filled with silence and I hate it. I fucking hate it. I quickly get dressed and pad into the bedroom—our bedroom—and curl up on his side of the bed. It's pathetic, I know, but I can't help myself. I bury my face in his pillow, wishing that I hadn't washed his scent earlier on. Tears threaten to spill, but I hold them back. I've cried enough. I can't keep crying.

My phone buzzes from the kitchen but I ignore it. I don't want to talk to anyone. I close my eyes and pray that sleep will come. Anything to take away this pain I'm feeling.

Two Hours Earlier

Loud knocking at the door wakes me up. Groggily, I slide out of bed. As I walk out of my room, everything hits me.

God, my dad's dead and Maverick's gone. A sob bubbles up in my throat, but I swallow it down. I can't fall apart now. The knocking continues, more insistent this time.

"Lisa? Lisa, are you in there?" Travis yells, his voice tight and filled with anger.

I take a deep breath, trying to compose myself, before I open the door. Travis stands there, his eyes wild, his jaw tight as he watches me with concern. "Thank God," he breathes, pulling me into a tight hug. "I've been trying to reach you for the past thirty minutes."

"I was asleep," I mumble as I step back, gesturing for him to come inside. "What's wrong?"

Travis' eyes scan the room then settle back on me. "Maverick's gone."

I shake my head, trying to understand what he means. "Gone?"

"Someone snuck up behind him, hit him over the

head, and took him," Travis tells me, his gaze focused on me, his eyes filled with worry.

My heart stops. "What?" I whisper, my voice barely audible. "How... How is that possible? Who would..."

Travis runs a hand through his hair, frustration evident in every movement. "We don't know yet. The security footage doesn't show their face. Whoever did this knew what they were doing."

I stumble back, my legs suddenly weak. Travis catches me before I fall, guiding me to the couch. My mind is reeling, trying to process this new information. Maverick... This can't be happening. I can't lose him. I love him. God, I love him so much. I can't lose him. How could this happen?

"Lisa, I need you to focus," Travis says, his voice firm but gentle. "Did Maverick mention anything to you? Any threats, any enemies?"

I shake my head, trying to clear the fog in my brain. "No, nothing. We never spoke about what we do," I confess. "I didn't want him to know who I was, what I did. I thought it was easier not to mention his job so it wouldn't come back to me." I run my hand through my hair. "I should have done. If I had—"

Travis rests his hand on my shoulder. "Don't do this to yourself," he urges. "We're going to find him. I have Melissa doing what she does best, and when she has that information, we'll find him."

I nod, trying to hold on to Travis' reassurance, but my mind is racing. Maverick's face flashes before my eyes—his cocky grin, his intense gaze, the way his eyes softened when he looked at me. And now he's gone. Taken. My stomach churns with fear and guilt. Would they have taken him if I hadn't kicked him out?

"What can I do?" I ask, my voice stronger than I feel. "There must be something." I need to find him.

Travis hesitates, his eyes searching my face. "Lisa, I know you want to help, but it might be best if you stay here. We don't know who took him or why. You could be in danger too."

I shake my head vehemently. "No. I can't just sit here and do nothing. He's out there somewhere, probably hurt. Maybe..." I can't finish the thought. "I need to help. Please, Travis."

He sighs. "We're waiting on Melissa's intel. Once we have that, we'll make a plan."

"Have you spoken to his uncle?" I ask, hoping he may give us a lead.

"Yeah, I spoke to Jerry while I was on the way here. From what he said, they have had run-ins with Tommy Jennings and his crew."

I grimace, thinking back to when Maverick and I

first met when I was sixteen. The goons I ended up running over belonged to Tommy. "That still going on?" I ask, wondering how long a feud lasts. Surely being part of the Houlihan Gang would mean that it wouldn't have gone on that long.

Travis' mouth tightens. "Yeah, and that fucker's daughter has risen in the ranks. From what I understand, Tanya Jennings is practically running the show."

No, surely not. My blood runs cold at the mention of Tanya Jennings. I beat back the memories that flood back. I had hoped I would never hear that bitch's name again.

"Lisa?" Travis' voice cuts through my panic. "You okay? You look like you've seen a ghost."

I swallow hard, trying to compose myself. "I... I know Tanya," I admit, my voice barely above a whisper.

Travis' eyes widen. "What? How?"

I take a deep breath, steeling myself for the conversation I never wanted to have. "Remember when we met, you knew about me?" I ask and he nods, his brow furrowed. "Did you happen to see who my dad was dating?"

Travis' brows deepen as he frowns harder. "No, I didn't delve too deeply. Why?"

"Tanya Jennings was the woman my dad cheated on my ma with," I tell him and then launch into the whole sordid details I've hidden for so fucking long. I've been chained by the shame I felt when I tried to take my own life, but the truth is, I was a child, one who was lost and needed direction. Instead of getting what I needed, I ended up being abandoned by my father and left to deal with that whore of a girlfriend of his. I did nothing wrong. I know that now.

"Fuck," Travis growls. "Why the fuck didn't you tell me?"

I lift my shoulders and shrug. "That was a time in my life that was painful. I felt shame and alone. I don't like anyone seeing me vulnerable, Travis."

Travis' eyes soften with understanding. He reaches out and squeezes my hand. "I get it, Lisa. But you're not alone anymore. We're family now, and we'll get through this together."

Since the moment I met him, he's always treated me like a daughter. He's always looked out for me and showed that he cares. He lost his oldest daughter to a drug overdose years ago. He's a man who protects those he considers family.

I give him an apologetic smile. "I know. It's hard sometimes. I'm trying," I promise him and take a deep breath. "So, what do we do now? If Tanya's behind this..."

"It changes things," Travis admits, his jaw clenching. "She's dangerous, Lisa. More ruthless than her old man ever was. If she's got Maverick..."

He doesn't finish the sentence, but he doesn't need to. I can see the concern etched on his face. My heart races as I imagine what Tanya might be doing to Maverick right now.

"If she's got Maverick then I'm going to get him back." There are no ifs, buts, or maybes. I love him and I'm not going to let that bitch hurt him.

Travis raises an eyebrow. "I never thought I'd see the day that you'd fall in love. I'm happy for you, Lisa. Really, I am. Maverick may be a little..." he pauses, a smile playing on his lips, "irrational at times, but he's a good man. I couldn't pick someone better for you. In fact, when I first met you and was looking for a mentor for you, he was—" He's cut off by the sound of his phone ringing. "It's Lis," he says as he answers it.

As he speaks to his daughter, I feel my nerves building up and begin to pace back and forth. My heart is pounding in my chest as I pray that she has found something, anything. We are running out of time. All I want is to find the man I love. Every second that passes feels like an eternity as I anxiously await any news.

"She's sending you a video," Travis says thickly, his

phone pressed to his ear. "Did you get it? This was taken two hours ago."

I reach for my phone from the counter and see that I do in fact have a message from her. I hit play on the video and my heart plummets. It's of a car pulling up outside a house that I know all too well. My hand trembles as I see the woman who has haunted my dreams for years step out of the white car.

My mind whirls, and the only thing I can think of is Maverick and what that evil bitch is doing to him. I drop my phone to the ground as I spin on my heel and run out of the house, grabbing the keys from the hook beside the door as I do.

"Lisa!" Travis shouts after me, but I'm already out the door and racing toward my car.

My hands shake as I fumble with the keys, finally managing to unlock the door and slide into the driver's seat. The engine roars to life as I turn the key.

"Lisa, wait! You can't go alone!" Travis yells.

I pull out of the driveway, tyres screeching against the pavement. I can see Travis in my rear-view mirror. He's rushing to his own car, and I know he'll be right on my tail. He's right. I know I shouldn't be doing this alone, but I can't wait. Not when Maverick's life is at stake.

It takes me twenty minutes to make it through the

city. Thankfully, the traffic isn't as bad as it could be. My knuckles turn white as I grip the steering wheel and turn onto the street that holds some of my worst fears. Right now, I'm more focused on saving the man I love.

I pull up outside the house and fight off the onslaught of memories that threaten to pull me down. I quietly walk up to the front door, glad that it's slightly ajar. The stupid bitch really should have locked up. I slip inside, my heart pounding wildly. The house is eerily quiet, but I can hear muffled voices coming from the sitting room. Carefully, I make my way to the door.

"You think you're so clever, don't you? This house was the house where Lisa tried to take her own life. It's fitting really," Tanya sneers. Her voice hasn't changed over the years. She's still a whiny bitch. "You know, Maverick, I almost admire your dedication. Killing for the woman you love... It's almost romantic. Stupid, but romantic."

"Fuck you. You don't know the first thing about love," Maverick growls, and my knees almost buckle at hearing his voice. God, he's alive.

Tanya laughs, a harsh, brittle sound. "Oh please. Love is for the weak. Power, money, respect, that's what really matters in this world."

"That's 'cause no one would ever love your psycho ass. You're a toxic bitch, Tanya, and the only way you can get someone to even stay with you is by manipulation."

"Is that so? Then tell me, Maverick, where is your precious Lisa now? Does she know what you've done? Does she still love you after learning what a monster you really are? Oh, this is priceless. I'm sure she just loves the idea of her man killing her dad. What will she do? Hmm? Cry to Mammy? Oh wait, she can't; she's dead too."

She's a twisted motherfucker. Sick and twisted.

"You're a fucking bitch," Maverick snarls. "I'm going to enjoy killing you, and when I'm done, I'm going after your dad and mam."

"Not going to happen," she laughs. "But don't worry, Maverick, once I'm finished with you, I'll be sure to let Lisa know just how much you loved her. That's, of course, right before I kill her. It's been a while since I last saw her. I wonder if she's still crazy?"

"Well, you don't have to wonder for much longer," I say, unable to listen to her any longer. She's not changed at all. Still the conniving bitch she was eight years ago. I ignore Maverick urging me to leave. The fear in his voice hurts my heart, but I'm not leaving.

"Lisa," Tanya sneers. "How nice of you to join us. We were just talking about you."

"I heard," I drawl coldly. "But don't worry, bitch, I won't be staying long." I step forward, cocking my fist back and letting fly. One thing Ciarán taught me was how to fight hard and dirty. My fist connects with Tanya's jaw before she can react, sending her staggering backward.

She recovers quickly, her eyes flashing with rage. "Oh, sweetie, do you really think you can take me on? You couldn't even kill yourself properly."

Her words sting, but I push the pain aside. I'm not that broken girl anymore. "I'm not here to talk, Tanya. I'm here for Maverick."

I risk a glance at him. He's tied to a chair, blood trickling from a cut on his head. His eyes meet mine, filled with a mixture of relief and fear. "Lisa, get out of here," he pleads.

"Not without you," I reply firmly. I'm not leaving him. I won't do it.

Tanya laughs, and the sound grates on my nerves. "How touching. But I'm afraid neither of you will be leaving here alive."

I lunge at the whore, my hand wrapping around her neck. My fingers dig into Tanya's throat as we crash to the ground. She claws at my face, drawing blood, but I don't let go. Years of pent-up rage fuel my strength as I slam her head against the hardwood floor. I hit her over and over again. She's panting hard as she tries to fight me off, but she's not a match for me. I've worked on being strong. I've learned how to fight and overpower even the strongest of people.

"Baby," I hear Maverick say, and I let his voice wash over me. He's alive and he's safe. But this isn't over. I'm not going to let this bitch get away with this. "Lisa," he whispers. He's right beside me, his lips pressing against my forehead.

I spot the rope he escaped from and smile, the perfect plan forming. This cunt wanted me to kill myself by hanging; well, two can play that game. Only this time, no one will be around to save her from the noose tightening and taking every last breath from her.

I look up at Maverick, his eyes filled with love and worry as he watches me. "Give me that rope," I instruct, my voice cold and determined.

He hesitates for a moment, then nods. He moves quickly, bringing me the heavy rope. She's dazed from the beating, but still conscious, yelling at me, calling me crazy. I ignore her and focus on what I do best. I tie a noose with the rope and slide it around her neck. She stills, her eyes wide as she watches me, and I can't help but smile.

"What are you going to do?" Maverick asks softly.

I stand up, my eyes never leaving Tanya. "I'm going to finish what she started years ago." I drag the bitch to the doorframe, just as she wanted me to die over eight years ago. She's a hell of a lot lighter than my other victims and getting her into position is easy. I've done this a hundred times over. By this stage, it's just going through the motions. Maverick's silent as he watches me. I don't look at him. I don't want to see the horror in his eyes at what I'm doing.

Once she's in position, I let the cunt hang. She gargles as the noose tightens around her throat, her eyes wide as she tries to claw at the rope. I watch as Tanya's face turns red, then purple, her legs kicking uselessly in the air. Her eyes bulge, filled with terror and hatred. For a moment, I'm transported back to that dark day when I was in her position, fighting for my life. But this time, I'm in control.

"Lisa." Maverick's voice breaks through my trance. His hand slides along my shoulder and he pulls me against him. "It's done, baby. She's gone."

I blink, realising that Tanya has stopped moving. Her body hangs limp, swaying slightly. I feel... nothing. No satisfaction, no relief; just a hollow emptiness.

Maverick turns me away from the sight, pulling me into his arms. I bury my face in his chest, inhaling his scent, feeling the steady beat of his heart. He's alive. He's safe. That's all that matters.

I hear the crash of the front door being thrown open. "Fuck, did we miss it all?" I hear Ciarán ask with laughter in his voice.

"Shit, the Hanging Reaper's got to her," I hear a low voice say. "But damn, what a way to go. She looks like she was viciously attacked. But where are they?"

Maverick's body tenses against mine. "Fuck," he growls. "It's you? You're the Hanging Reaper?" he asks.

I swallow hard. I knew this day would come. Shit.

CHAPTER
THIRTY-ONE
MAVERICK

I HOLD HER CLOSE, needing to have her in my arms. Christ, seeing her walk into the room, knowing that crazy bitch would hurt her and there was nothing I could do, was truly frightening. Fuck.

"Fuck, did we miss it all"?" Cowboy laughs, and I glare at the prick. What the fuck is he doing here?

"Shit, the Hanging Reaper's got to her," Emmanuel comments. "But damn, what a way to go. She looks like she was viciously attacked. But where are they?"

Eman's words hit me like a fucking freight train. Holy fuck. "Fuck," I growl. "It's you? You're the Hanging Reaper?"

Lisa stares up at me, her eyes wide and filled with fear. "Yes," she confesses.

My blood runs cold as Lisa's admission sinks in. The woman I love, the one I've been trying to protect, is the very person I've been trying to locate. I feel her trembling in my arms, but I can't bring myself to let her go.

"Jesus Christ," I mutter, my mind reeling.

Jer lets out a low whistle. "Well, fuck me sideways. Didn't see that coming."

I want to punch him in the face, but I can't seem to move. Lisa's grip on me tightens, her fingers digging into my shirt.

"Please," she whispers, her voice cracking. "I can explain. Please, just let me explain," she says so only I can hear her. "Don't leave," she begs.

Fuck, does she actually think I'd leave? I slide my hand around the back of her neck, pulling her close to me. I lower my mouth on hers and kiss her deeply, desperately. I pour everything I'm feeling into that kiss—my fear, my anger, my confusion, but most of all, my love for her. When I pull back, I see tears glistening in her eyes. The scent of her perfume fills my nostrils and it hits me why the smell of Jasmine has always been so familiar to me. It's become of Lisa. Shit, I should have seen it, I should have realized. Fuck. "I'm not going anywhere," I growl, low enough for only her to hear. "But we need to get the fuck out of here, now."

I turn to face Cowboy and Emmanuel, my arm still wrapped protectively around Lisa. "We're leaving," I announce, my tone leaving no room for argument.

Cowboy raises an eyebrow. "Just like that?" he asks. "She's been beating herself up for months, wondering what the hell you'd say when you found out about who she is, and you don't even have a real reaction."

Oh, I'm furious, but only because she's the woman I love and I don't want her in harm's way. But knowing how prolific she is at what she does, I know that I'll always worry about her. From now on, any job that she gets, she'll not be going alone.

"You heard me," I snarl, taking a step toward him. "We're fucking leaving."

Emmanuel puts a hand on Cowboy's shoulder. "He's not a real big fan of you, man, especially with how close you are to Lisa."

Ain't that the fucking truth. He's too damned close for my liking.

"How about we all go back to mine," Jer says, stepping forward. "There are a lot of unanswered questions that I need answered. Firstly, Maverick, do you need to be seen by the doctor?"

"Yes," Lisa says for me, her eyes spitting fire. "You were knocked unconscious," she hisses. "Do you have a doctor on call?"

"I'll call Grainne," Cowboy says. "I'll have her meet us at Jer's."

I nod, my head still pounding from the blow I took earlier. "Fine," I grunt. "But we're taking Lisa's car, and you can get your own way there."

I guide Lisa toward the door, keeping her close. As we step outside, the cool night air hits us, and I feel her shiver. I pull her closer to me, trying to block the chill from getting to her.

We climb into Lisa's car, and I wait until the others have pulled away before starting the engine. As soon as we're alone, Lisa turns to me, her eyes filled with a mixture of fear and determination.

"I'm sorry," she says softly. "I wanted to tell you, but I was afraid. I didn't know how you'd react."

I grip the steering wheel tightly, my knuckles turning white. "How long?" I ask, my voice gruff with emotion. "How long have you been the Hanging Reaper?"

Lisa takes a deep breath, her hands fidgeting in her lap. "Since before we met," she admits quietly. "It started as a way to protect Devin. But then... it became something more."

"How long?" I repeat, needing to know how long this has been happening for.

"The first one was by mistake. It just happened. I

didn't intend it to. I was so scared, but I'm not sorry I did it. Devin was so scared, and I'd do it all over again if it meant keeping him safe."

Part of me wants to be angry, to demand answers to all the questions swirling in my head. But the larger part of me just wants to keep her safe, to shield her from the danger that comes with her other identity.

"Babe, that's not an answer," I tell her. "How old were you?"

"Sixteen," she answers, turning to look out the window.

"The fuck?" I growl. "Tell me you're joking?"

She shakes her head. "I didn't mean to do it," she whispers. "He hurt Devin, Mav. He hurt him so badly. Devin was terrified he'd hurt him again. I couldn't let him do that. I just couldn't."

I feel the anger and pain radiating off her, and it hits me like a punch to the gut. Sixteen. She was just a fucking kid. I reach over and take her hand, squeezing it gently. "Lisa, look at me," I say softly. She turns, her eyes shimmering with unshed tears. "You did what you had to do to protect your brother. I get that. But Christ, babe, you were just a kid yourself."

She nods, a tear slipping down her cheek. "I know."

"But why continue? Why become the Hanging Reaper?" I ask, needing to make sense of it all.

"At first, it was just about Devin. But then... I saw how many other people were suffering, and how many monsters were walking free. I couldn't just stand by and do nothing. I worked for The Agency and I was able to stop those monsters."

I nod, understanding her motivation even if I don't agree with her methods. "And now? Are you still... active?"

She hesitates before answering. "Yes," she admits. "But I'm more careful now. I've learned a lot and come up with the perfect way to ensure that I'm not caught." She takes a deep breath. "That was until today. Seeing you tied to that chair—" She shakes her head. "I lost it."

I run my thumb over her knuckles, trying to process everything. The woman I love is the notorious Hanging Reaper. She's killed people, multiple people. But she's still the woman I love. I don't give a fuck about what she does; all I care about is that she's safe while doing it, and that's something I'll ensure happens.

"We'll figure this out," I tell her, reaching over to take her hand in mine. "Together. But right now, we need to deal with the immediate situation. Those fuckers back there, how much do they know?"

Lisa squeezes my hand, relief evident in her eyes.

"Ciarán knows everything. He's been my..." she pauses, her lips twitching, "mentor since the very beginning."

Christ, what the actual fuck? "Let me guess, Travis?"

She grins at me. "Yeah. He actually happened across me killing Devin's dad and then propositioned me."

I keep her hand in mine as I drive toward Jer's house. My mind is whirling with all the information I've just learned. "Lisa," I begin cautiously. "I'm sorry that I hurt you when I killed your dad, but I need you to know that I'll do whatever it takes to protect you."

She nods. "I know. When I heard that you were missing—" She presses her lips together and turns to look out the window. "I was so scared. I know why you did it, and yes, I'm hurt and angry that you did, but if the tables were turned, I would have done the same thing."

Relief washes through me. Fuck, I can deal with her being hurt and angry. We can get past that.

I pull into Jer's driveway and park the car, sliding out of the vehicle and running around to reach for Lisa. The moment she's standing, I draw her into my arms. "I've held back," I tell her, my voice low and intense. "But I need you to know that I love you, Lisa.

Everything about you. Even this part of you that I'm just learning about. It doesn't change how I feel."

She looks up at me, her eyes searching mine. "You mean that?"

"Every fucking word," I growl, pulling her closer. "We're in this together now. Whatever comes next, we face it as a team. No more secrets between us."

Lisa nods, a small smile playing on her lips. "No more secrets," she agrees.

I lean down and capture her lips in a fierce kiss, pouring all my emotions into it. When we break apart, both breathless, I rest my forehead against hers.

"Now," I say, straightening up and keeping an arm around her waist, "let's go deal with this shit show on the road."

Her fingers wrap around mine, the pressure so tight I can feel my blood flow stop. Her breath is warm against my cheek as she whispers, "I love you, Maverick." My eyelids squeeze shut in response. Shit. I know what it means to her to say those words. "When I heard you were gone," she continues, her voice thick with emotion, "I thought my world was falling apart." She pauses to take a deep breath, her grip on my hand tightening even more. "I'd tear this whole damn city apart just to find you."

I pull her close, my heart pounding. "I love you too, Lisa. More than anything. And I'd do the same for you; tear apart this whole fucking world if I had to."

We stand there for a moment, just holding each other, before I reluctantly pull away. "Come on, let's get this over with."

As we approach Jer's front door, I hear muffled voices inside. Lisa tenses beside me, and I give her hand a reassuring squeeze. "Remember, we're in this together," I murmur.

She nods, taking a deep breath as I knock on the door. It swings open almost immediately, revealing Jer's concerned face.

"About fucking time," he grumbles, ushering us inside. "Grainne's here. She wants to check you out, Mav."

I nod, my eyes scanning the room. I notice all eyes are on us as we enter. Cowboy is leaning against the wall, his arms crossed, while Emmanuel sits on the couch, looking uncomfortable. Travis is pacing, his phone glued to his ear as he talks low. Grainne, the doctor, is standing by the kitchen counter, her medical bag open beside her.

"Sit down, Maverick," Grainne orders, gesturing to a chair. "I need to check that thick skull of yours."

I comply, reluctantly letting go of Lisa's hand. She hovers nearby as Grainne begins her examination, her fingers probing the spot where I was hit.

"You're lucky," Grainne mutters after a few minutes. "No signs of a serious concussion, but you'll have one hell of a headache for a while. Take it easy for the next few days."

I nod, wincing as the movement sends a spike of pain through my head.

"Thanks, Doc," Jer says once Grainne is finished. "I'll send payment tomorrow."

Grainne nods and quickly exits the house, no doubt not wanting to be around when this shit hits the fan.

"So," Jer says, his voice filled with anger. "Where the fuck do I begin?" He turns to Lisa, his eyes dark with rage. "You've been on a killing spree, young lady. Do you have any idea what could have happened if anyone found out or if any of those men you killed got the jump on you?"

Cowboy scoffs before Lisa can answer Jer. "She's been trained since she was sixteen. Lisa is more than capable of taking care of herself."

I tag Lisa's hand and pull her close to me once again. Jer's eyes narrow as he looks between us. "You're okay with this, Mav? With her being the Hanging Reaper?"

I take a deep breath, choosing my words carefully. "I'm not okay with her being in danger," I admit. "But I understand why she does it. She's good at what she does. And I respect her choices."

"Fuck," Emmanuel mutters from the couch. "This is some serious shit."

Travis, who's finally finished his phone call, joins the conversation. "You're all a bunch of sexist assholes," he says, his voice vibrating with anger. "If this was a man, you wouldn't have this problem. Besides, Lisa is damned good at what she does. Now, I won't have to tell you all how serious it is to ensure that Lisa's identity remains anonymous."

Jer rolls his eyes. "Like I'd tell anyone," he grunts. "I just want to ensure that my new niece isn't in harm's way."

I grin. Jer's smooth as hell, and the soft smile he sends Lisa's way helps her relax. I feel her shoulders sag and she leans against me. "Now, young lady, are you sure—"

"I appreciate the concern, but I've been doing this for years. I know the risks, and I know how to handle myself," she says, cutting him off.

"That may be," Jer counters, "but now you're part of this family. That means we look out for each other. No more solo missions without backup."

I feel Lisa stiffen beside me, ready to argue, but I squeeze her hand gently. "He's right, babe. We're in this together now."

She looks at me, conflict clear in her eyes, but after a moment she nods reluctantly. "Fine. But I'm not giving it up entirely."

"Wouldn't dream of asking you to," Jer says, his tone softening. "Now, let's talk logistics. Travis, who else knows about Lisa's true identity?"

Travis grins. "The six of us in this room, along with Melissa. That's it and that's all it will be." The warning's clear in his voice.

Jer nods. "Good. We'll ensure it stays that way." He turns back to me. "You take Lisa home and rest. While you've been kicking back with that bitch Tanya, Stephen and Freddie were beyond pissed. Along with Denis, they decided it would be best to take out the entire Jennings' organisation."

I raise a brow. "Oh, and how did that go down?"

Cowboy grins. "Perfectly timed hits. The pub went up in flames, not to mention their houses. There are no more assholes with the name Jennings left."

I smile back at the fucker. This is good news. Now I don't need to worry about retaliation against Lisa.

"You're up to speed, so now you're going to go home and get some rest," Jer instructs. "The both of you."

Lisa rolls her eyes. "Am I going to have to listen to him boss me around from now on?" she whispers so only I can hear her.

I chuckle. "Probably," I answer truthfully.

"Maverick, take care of my girl," Travis says, a dark gleam in his eyes. "Darling, I'll call you in the morning," he tells Lisa.

"Now go," Jer says, waving his hand, dismissing us.

I turn on my heel, pulling Lisa with me. It's time to get home and forget about this fucked up day.

As we step outside, Lisa lets out a long sigh. I can feel the tension in her body, coiled tight like a spring. We walk to her car in silence. She's deep in thought so I leave her be for the moment.

Once I pull out of Jer's drive, I turn to her. "You okay?"

She nods. "It's just... a lot. I've been doing this alone for so long. Having people know, having them worry... it's strange."

I grin. I'm glad she's getting it. "You're not alone

anymore, Lisa. We're in this together now, whether you like it or not."

A small smile tugs at her lips. "I think I like it. It's just going to take some getting used to."

I aim my own big smile at the windscreen. The woman I love is happy and there are no secrets between us. I have a feeling that it's going to be smooth sailing from here on out.

CHAPTER
THIRTY-TWO
LISA

Four Weeks Later

Maverick's arms slide around my waist as he holds me close. I love how affectionate he is and the fact that he doesn't mind showing it. Even if it's around his family.

I lean back into his embrace, savouring the warmth of his body against mine. It's been a month since that shit with Tanya happened and it's been blissful.

"You two lovebirds going to help or just stand there looking cute?" Mary, Callie's daughter, asks with a roll of her eyes. "You're worse than Mam and Da."

I feel the rumble of Maverick's chuckle against my back. "We're providing moral support," he quips.

I turn in his arms to face him, unable to hold back my smile. His eyes are crinkled at the corners, that mischievous gleam I adore lighting them up. "Maybe we should actually help though," I suggest, reluctantly pulling away.

Maverick catches my hand, bringing it to his lips for a quick kiss. "Fine," he sighs dramatically, but the grin on his face betrays his feigned reluctance. "What do you need us to do, Mary?"

Mary grins. She's excited that Nichola delegated her to be the one to organise everyone. "Just grab those boxes over there and bring them to the kitchen. We need to sort through the decorations to decorate the house."

I smile. I'm not a huge fan of Christmas, but I have a feeling this year is going to change that. We're spending Christmas Day with Maverick's family here at his parents' house. His uncle Jer, along with Stephen and Jess, and Orna and Devin are also coming. It's going to be a huge festive spread. I can't help but smile at how quickly I've been embraced by Maverick's family. The warmth and easy banter is unlike anything I've ever experienced.

Usually, I'd spend the evening with Clodagh on

Christmas Day but my girl is having a hard time, especially as Emmanuel is around so much. I'm not sure what the hell happened between the two of them, but she can't deal with it and has run to the West Coast, where she's currently living in Galway. We still talk every day. It's just hard not having her around anymore.

We spend the next hour unpacking ornaments, fairy lights, and festive tablecloths. All the while Christmas songs play in the background.

"I know," Callie says as she sinks down on the sofa. "We should go out on Christmas Eve for dinner."

Maverick shrugs. "Sure, sounds good."

Callie wrinkles her nose at him. "I wasn't talking to you, Amadán," she mutters. "I was thinking a girls' night out. What do you say, Lisa?"

I grin. "That does sound good. Who's going?"

"Well, the two of us. I'm pretty sure Melissa will come, Jessica, Chloe, and Ava," Callie tells me as she ticks the names off on her fingers.

I nod, excitement bubbling up inside me. "Count me in. It'll be fun to have a night out with the girls. Plus, it'll be nice to get to know everyone better."

Maverick feigns a pout. "What about us men? Are we supposed to sit at home twiddling our thumbs while you ladies paint the town red?"

Callie snorts. "Oh, please. I'm sure you boys can find something to entertain yourselves with for one night. Maybe you can have your own little gathering, seeing as Mam's offered to babysit all the kids."

Damn, that's a huge task. There are a whole lot of kids to watch over. Callie has four and Melissa and Danny have three. I'm not sure if anyone else has any, but either way, that's seven kids.

Mary pipes up from where she's lying on the floor, currently drawing. "Yeah, Dad's said that he'll be staying close to Mam. You should join him, Uncle Mav."

Maverick's eyes light up at the suggestion. "You know what? That's not a bad idea. I'll give Stephen and Freddie a call, see if they want to join us."

I can't help but laugh at him.

"You can't be serious?" Callie hisses. "It's girls' night, not bring your partner along night."

"We'll be close by, not with you," Maverick says, rolling his eyes. "You're so dramatic, Callie-girl."

"Just promise me you won't get into any trouble," I tease, poking him in the ribs. "I don't want to come back from my night out to find you've all decided to go wild and get picked up by the garda."

He grins that roguish smile that never fails to make my heart skip a beat. "Me? Trouble? I'm wounded by the accusation." He places a hand dramatically over his heart.

Callie snorts. "You were born trouble," she tells him. "As long as you don't interrupt our night, I don't care what you all do."

"It'll be fun," I say with a smile. I'm actually really excited.

Maverick pulls me close again, pressing a kiss to my temple. "Don't worry, baby. I'll behave..."

Callie rolls her eyes but there's a fond smile on her face. "That's what I'm afraid of. Your version of behaving usually involves some sort of shootout or someone dying."

I laugh, shaking my head. "No shootouts or killings, please. I'd like to enjoy my first Christmas with your family without any drama." I'm still not over him being kidnapped by Tanya. I still have nightmares about it. But when I wake from them, he's right beside me and it pulls me from the panic quickly.

Maverick grins, pressing a kiss to my lips. "No promises, but I'll do my best."

I COME AWAKE as his tongue swirls around my nipple, his finger sliding into my pussy. His touch ignites a fire within me, spreading through me like an inferno. I arch my back, pressing against his hand, silently begging for more. His lips find my neck, trailing hot kisses down to my collarbone. I shiver as his stubble grazes my sensitive skin.

"You're so responsive," he murmurs against my throat, his voice husky with desire.

I can only whimper in reply as he adds another finger, stretching me deliciously. My hands grip his shoulders, nails digging into taut muscle. The room fills with the sound of our ragged breathing and the rustle of sheets as we move together.

His fingers curl inside me, finding that perfect spot that makes me see stars. I cry out, my hips bucking against his hand. He captures my lips in a searing kiss, swallowing my moans as he continues to stroke me from the inside.

"That's it, baby," he growls. "Let me hear you."

I'm trembling now, teetering on the edge of bliss. His thumb finds my clit, circling it with precision. The dual stimulation is too much. I break the kiss, throwing my head back as waves of pleasure crash over me.

He doesn't let up, working me through my orgasm until I'm a quivering mess beneath him. Only then does he withdraw his fingers, bringing them to his lips to taste me. The sight makes me whimper with renewed desire.

"We're just getting started," he promises, his eyes dark with lust. I love that look he gets when he's on the edge. The way that he watches me never fails to take my breath away.

He moves between my legs, the broad head of his cock nudging my entrance. I'm still sensitive from my orgasm, but I ache to feel him inside me.

He enters me slowly, inch by delicious inch, stretching me in the best way possible. I wrap my legs around his waist, urging him deeper. We both groan when he plants himself fully inside of me.

"You feel so good," he pants, holding still to let me adjust. "So tight and wet for me. So fucking perfect."

I roll my hips, silently begging him to move. He takes the hint, pulling out almost completely before slamming back in. The force of his thrust pushes me up the bed, and I clutch at his biceps for support.

He sets a punishing rhythm, each powerful stroke hitting that spot deep inside me that makes me see stars. The room fills with the sound of skin slapping against skin, our moans and gasps mingling in the air. I'm lost in sensation, every nerve ending alight with pleasure. His lips find mine again, and he kisses me deeply.

I run my hands down his back, feeling the muscles flex and ripple as he moves above me. His skin is slick with sweat, and I can taste the salt on his lips. I drag my nails up his spine, eliciting a growl from deep in his chest. I love that I can drive him wild, just as he does me.

"Fuck, you're driving me crazy," he pants against my ear. His teeth graze my earlobe, sending shivers down my spine.

I can feel the tension building in the pit of my stomach, that delicious pressure coiling tighter and tighter. He must sense how close I am because he snakes a hand between our bodies, finding my clit. His fingers work in tight circles, perfectly in sync with his thrusts.

"Come for me again, baby," he commands, his voice rough. "I want to feel you come around my cock."

His words, along with his cock and fingers, are enough to push me over the edge. I cry out his name as my second orgasm hits me like a tidal wave, even more intense than the first. My inner walls clamp down on him, gripping his cock as my orgasm washes over me.

He groans, his hips stuttering as he fights to maintain control. "Fuck, you're so tight," he grits out. "So fucking perfect."

I'm still riding the aftershocks of my climax when I feel him swell inside me. With a final, powerful thrust, he buries himself to the hilt and lets go. I feel his cock pulse and fill me with his cum. He collapses on top of me, his face pressed against my shoulder as we both struggle to catch our breath.

His fingers trace lazy patterns on my skin, sending little shivers through me. I run my hands through his sweat-dampened hair, fully sated and in love.

He lifts his head to look at me, a soft smile playing on his lips. "That was..."

"Amazing," I say. "It always is, handsome. Always is amazing."

He chuckles softly, pressing a tender kiss to my lips. "You're amazing," he murmurs against my mouth.

Reluctantly, he pulls out of me and rolls to the side, gathering me into his arms. I snuggle against his chest, listening to the steady thump of his heartbeat as it gradually slows. His fingers trace lazy patterns on my back, and I sigh contentedly. I know I need to get cleaned up, but I'm so happy just lying here with him.

"I love you," I whisper, tilting my head to look up at him. It's easier to say the words now. I never thought I'd ever get to this position where I'd be this happy or in love, but Maverick makes it so easy.

His eyes soften, and he brushes a stray lock of hair

from my face. "I love you too, baby. More than you could ever know."

I can't help but think about how far we've come. How far I've come. I used to be so scared about losing him that I never gave him all of me. Now, he has every single part of me, and I've never felt so at peace.

Maverick shifts beside me, propping himself up on one elbow to gaze down at me. His gorgeous brown eyes are soft and filled with an emotion that makes my heart skip a beat.

"What are you thinking about?" he asks, his voice a low rumble that sends shivers down my spine.

I trace the line of his jaw with my fingertips, feeling the rough stubble beneath my touch. "Us," I admit. "How lucky I am to have found you and how grateful I am that you were so certain about me that you never gave up on me."

He catches my hand in his, bringing it to his lips to press a kiss to my palm. "I'll never give up on you," Maverick says softly, his eyes intense as they hold mine. "You're it for me, baby. The one I've been waiting for my whole life."

His words make my heart swell with emotion. I lean up to capture his lips in a tender kiss, pouring all my love and gratitude into it. When we part, I rest my forehead against his, savouring the closeness.

"I never thought I could have this," I confess, my voice barely above a whisper. "Someone who loves me completely. Someone I trust with my whole heart."

Maverick's arm tightens around me, pulling me closer. "You deserve all of it and more," he murmurs. "I'm the lucky one here."

I frown as he reaches behind him. "Everything okay?" I ask, wondering what's going on.

My breath hitches as I see a blue box in his hands. "I had planned to do this on Christmas Day, but fuck, baby, this right here is the perfect time."

He opens the box, revealing a stunning diamond ring nestled inside. My heart stops as I realise what's happening.

"I love you more than I ever thought possible," Maverick says, his voice thick with emotion. "You've shown me what true happiness feels like. I want to wake up next to you every morning, and fall asleep with you in my arms every night. I want to build a life and a family with you." Tears blur my vision as he continues. "Will you marry me?"

For a moment, I'm speechless, completely stunned by this. "Yes," I whisper, then louder, "Yes, yes, a thousand times yes!"

He slides the ring onto my finger as happy tears slide down my face. "Fuck," he growls, sliding his arms around me. "We'll plan it for Valentine's Day," he says.

"Valentine's Day?" I gasp, my mind reeling. "That's only two months away!"

Maverick grins, his eyes sparkling with excitement. "Why wait? I've waited my whole life for you. I don't want to waste another day not being your husband."

"Valentine's Day," I repeat, testing the words on my tongue. "It's perfect."

He pulls me in for another passionate kiss, his hands roaming over my body. I can feel him hardening against my thigh, and a fresh wave of desire washes over me.

"Round two?" I suggest, arching an eyebrow. I'll never ever get enough of this man, and now he's my fiancé and soon to be my husband. I have no idea when my life turned around and the crap stopped and the good began, but I'm so damn happy that it did. It led me to him. My perfect man.

"God, I love you," Maverick growls, rolling me onto my back.

EPILOGUE
MAVERICK

Four Weeks Later

"Congrats, Mav," Danny says as he slides onto the stool beside me. "Lis is over the moon that you and Lisa are engaged. I swear she pierced my eardrums with the scream she let out when she got the text."

I chuckle, knowing that he's not exaggerating, because after Lisa sent out the text, Melissa called her and was still screaming with excitement. "Thanks, man," I reply, taking a sip of my beer. "Although, I think half the neighbourhood heard Melissa screaming on the phone to Lisa," I say through laughter.

Danny claps me on the back. "Lis adores Lisa.

Though I gotta say, my wife is in a mood. Apparently, she feels neglected that she didn't get a proposal."

A smile tugs at my lips. "So how did you manage to get Melissa to marry you?"

"She was pregnant," Danny says simply. "When's the wedding?"

"The fucker has chosen Valentine's Day," Denis says, laughing. "Now we've got to listen to our wives talk about how romantic this shit is."

Freddie chuckles. "He's only doing it on Valentine's Day so he doesn't forget the date."

I flip him off. That's not the reason. If I could marry her tomorrow, I would, but I know my woman. She'll want to plan something, so I'm giving her time.

"Two months, though, Mav?" Emmanuel says. "You sure that's enough time?"

I share a glance with Stephen. The man married Jess in less than a week and the wedding was exactly as his wife wanted.

"With Lis and Callie involved," Danny sighs, "you'll not need to worry about it. They'll organise everything."

I nod, knowing Danny's right. Lisa's friends are like whirlwinds when it comes to event planning. "Yeah, I'm counting on it. Lisa's already mentioned they've started a group chat for ideas."

"God help us all," Denis groans, taking a long swig of his beer. "Remember Chloe's wedding? I thought we'd never hear the end of it."

"At least this time, it's not your wallet on the line," Stephen chimes in, a hint of amusement in his voice.

My niece had the wedding of her dreams and her dad gave her everything that she wanted. Just like any father would do for their daughter.

My phone buzzes just as four other phones vibrate. I grin, knowing that it means the women have finished their dinner and drinks. I'm hoping Lisa lets loose and has a few drinks. Fucking her anytime is magnificent and the best I've ever had, but I have no doubt that drunk sex with her will be wild.

"Time to go," Stephen mutters as he rises to his feet. He's eager to go to his wife, who's currently five months pregnant. He's protective of Jess, even more so now that she's carrying his child.

I can't lie, I want that. I want to see Lisa pregnant with our child, but my woman needs time to warm up to the idea. Things are moving forward and I need to check to see if she's on the same page yet.

We make our way out of the bar. The chill in the air is fucking cold, and I have no doubt that it'll snow tonight. Something Lisa will be happy about. She's been talking of a white Christmas.

I grin as I look across the street. The women are standing outside the restaurant. Lisa, Melissa, and Callie have their heads bent together talking while Jess, Chloe, and Mallory are locked in conversation. Ava—who returned from America just over a month ago—has her attention on her phone.

I hear the beep of a car and turn to see Raptor—Mallory's man—and Pyro—Chloe's man—smirking as they walk toward the women.

"Oooh," I hear Callie say as we cross the street. "It's time to go home."

Lisa's eyes light up as she spots me approaching. She breaks away from Callie and Melissa, practically skipping over to me with a radiant smile.

"Hey handsome," she purrs, wrapping her arms around my neck. The scent of her perfume mixed with a hint of alcohol envelops me. "Miss me?"

I pull her close, my hands settling on her waist. "Always, baby." I lean in for a kiss, tasting the sweetness of whatever fruity cocktail she's been drinking.

When we part, Lisa's cheeks are flushed and her eyes are sparkling with mischief. "Mmm, take me home, Maverick. I have plans for you tonight."

A low growl escapes me. "Is that so?"

She nods, biting her lower lip in that way that drives me wild. "Yes," she breathes.

My cock thickens against my zipper. Fuck, I need to get her home.

A high-pitched whining sound hits me and I instinctively pull Lisa closer to me. My eyes dart around, searching for the source of the sound. The others have tensed up too, their protective instincts kicking in.

"What was that?" Lisa whispers, her grip on me tightening.

Before I can answer, I hear Callie's muffled scream as she stares down at the ground. My gaze follows the direction and my stomach drops when I see Ava lying on the cold, dirty ground, a bullet wound to the chest.

Fuck. Ava.

My instincts kick in immediately. "Everyone down!" I shout, pulling Lisa to the ground with me and shielding her body with mine. The others follow suit, dropping to the pavement as another shot rings out.

"Fuck!" Denis yells. "Where's it coming from?"

"Over there!" Emmanuel growls. He'd know better than anyone. The man's the best crack shot that I know.

I push Lisa to Raptor as he and Pyro round up the women, along with Denis and Danny. Emmanuel,

Stephen, Freddie, and I take off running toward the source of the gunfire.

Emmanuel leads the way to an alleyway and then up onto the fire escape ladder. My jaw's tight as I push myself up onto the ladder. Right now, I want to turn the fuck around and go and find Lisa, make sure she's safe. Even though I know Denis, Danny, Pyro, and Raptor wouldn't let anything happen to her, I'd prefer it was me who was with her.

"Fuck," Freddie snarls as we get to the top of the ladder and climb onto the roof. "They're gone." He runs his hands through his hair in frustration. "I want that motherfucker found."

I glance around the rooftop, beyond pissed that this fucker managed to escape.

"Shit," Stephen growls, his voice low and filled with anger. "What the fuck?"

I move toward him, my footsteps crunching on the gravel beneath my feet. As I reach him, I can feel the tension radiating off of his body like a tightly wound bow ready to snap.

"What is that?" Freddie asks, peering over my shoulder with wide eyes.

I carefully pick up the objects in question. A single bullet casing and the Ace of Hearts card, now slick with blood.

"Fuck me," Emmanuel breathes out, his voice filled with dread. "They left a calling card."

"Who did?" Freddie snarls, his fists clenched at his sides. "Who the fuck shot Ava?"

Emmanuel shakes his head, clearly just as confused and angry as the rest of us. "I don't know."

"Fuck," Stephen grunts, running a hand through his hair in frustration. "Let's get back to the women and check on Ava."

My gaze slides to Emmanuel's, and I can see the same look of realisation and fear in his eyes. We both know that Ava is gone. I saw her lifeless expression as she lay on the ground.

We make it back to the women and they're all crying. Danny's hunched over Ava's body, his fingers pulling her eyelids closed.

"No," Freddie snaps, his voice cracking with anguish. "No, no, no!" He drops to his knees beside Ava's body, cradling her head in his hands. "Baby," he whispers, pressing a kiss to her head.

The sight of Freddie's raw grief hits me like a punch to the gut. I reach for Lisa and hold her close to me, needing to feel her warmth, her life. She buries her face in my chest, her body shaking with silent sobs.

"We need to move," Emmanuel says, his voice low and urgent. "Whoever did this could still be watching."

Freddie turns his gaze to Emmanuel. "I'm not fucking leaving her," he growls.

"Brother," Danny says low. "I'll stay with you, but the women should go home."

I nod, agreeing with Danny. "Alright, let's get the women out of here. Pyro, Raptor, you take Chloe and Mallory home. Denis, get Callie and Melissa somewhere safe. Stephen, get Jess home and stay with her."

Emmanuel speaks up, his voice tight with tension. "I'll call Jer and let him know what's going on."

I turn to Lisa, cupping her tear-stained face in my hands. "Baby, I need you to go with Callie. I'll be home as soon as I can."

Lisa shakes her head vehemently. "No, Mav. I'm not leaving you."

"Lisa, please," I plead, my voice barely above a whisper. "I need to know you're safe. Go with Callie and Denis, and wait for me."

Lisa's eyes flash with defiance, but I can see the fear lurking beneath the surface. She opens her mouth to argue, but I cut her off with a gentle kiss. "Please, baby," I murmur against her lips. "For me."

She lets out a shaky breath and nods reluctantly. "Okay, but you'd better come home to me, Maverick. Promise me."

"I promise," I say, my voice hard but firm. "Nothing could keep me away from you."

I watch as Denis ushers Lisa, Callie, and Melissa into his car, my heart clenching as Lisa looks back at me one last time before getting in, her eyes filled with tears. The moment they're out of sight, I turn back to the grim scene before us.

Freddie is still cradling Ava's body, his shoulders shaking with silent sobs. Danny kneels beside him, a hand on his shoulder offering support.

Two hours later and the place is crawling with police. They've been asking questions, demanding to know why their witnesses have gone, but after Jer unleashes his anger, they shut the fuck up and get to work.

"We need to find out who the fuck did this," Jer growls.

"Why take out Ava?" Emmanuel asks. "I mean, no offence to her, but she's not dating any of the men. Yes, she means a fucking lot to Freddie, but if you're wanting to hurt someone, you'd take out a wife or significant other."

I can't lie, the thought has run through my mind a few times since Lisa went home. As sick as it is, I'm fucking glad it wasn't my woman who was shot. I'd lose my ever-loving mind if it were.

"The calling card means something," Danny hisses. "Someone's left us a message."

"The Ace of Hearts? It means nothing to me," Jer snaps agitatedly. "It doesn't make sense."

No, it doesn't, but then again, taking Ava out doesn't either. "Where's Freddie?" I ask, glancing around and seeing that he's nowhere in sight.

"Fuck," Jer growls. "I'm on it, don't worry. You all go home and keep the women safe. We don't know who did this or when they'll strike again."

I nod grimly, my jaw clenched tight. The thought of someone targeting Lisa or Callie makes my blood boil. "We need to increase security," I say, my voice low and filled with anger. "Around the clock protection for all of them."

Emmanuel nods in agreement. "I'll make some calls and get our best men on it."

"Good," Jer says, his eyes scanning the area one last time. "Go home, all of you. We'll regroup tomorrow."

As I make my way to my car, my mind races with possibilities. Who could be behind this? Why Ava? And what the hell does the Ace of Hearts mean? One thing's for sure, whoever did this has made a grave mistake. They've awoken a beast in Freddie, and he's not alone. We're a family, and we won't rest until we've hunted them down.

I drive to my parents' house as that's where Denis brought the women. Danny's in the passenger's side on the phone to Melissa, who's been scanning the local security cameras to see if she can come up with anything.

"Anything?" I ask Danny as he hangs up the phone.

He shakes his head, frustration evident on his features. "Nothing yet. Melissa's still combing through the footage, but so far, no clear shots of the shooter or any suspicious vehicles."

I grip the steering wheel tighter, my knuckles turning white. The lack of leads is infuriating. Someone out there knows something, and I'm determined to find out who.

As we pull up to my parents' house, I see Lisa waiting on the porch, wrapped in a blanket. The moment I step out of the car, she's running toward me. I catch her in my arms, holding her close as she buries her face in my chest.

"Thank God you're okay," she whispers, her voice muffled against my shirt.

I stroke her hair, pressing a kiss to the top of her head. "I'm right here, baby. I'm okay."

Lisa pulls back slightly, her eyes searching my face. "What happened? Did you find out anything?"

I shake my head, frustration evident in my voice. "Not much. Whoever did this knew what they were doing. They left almost no trace."

Lisa's eyes widen with fear. "But why? Why Ava? It doesn't make any sense."

"I know, baby. We're trying to figure that out." I cup her face in my hands, my thumbs gently wiping away the tears that have started to fall. "But right now, I need you to focus on staying safe. We're increasing security for everyone."

Lisa nods, her lower lip trembling. "Okay. What about Freddie? How is he?"

I sigh heavily. "Freddie's... not good," I say, choosing my words carefully. "He's disappeared. Jer's looking for him now."

Lisa's eyes widen with concern. "Oh no. Should we be out looking for him too?"

I shake my head firmly. "No, baby. It's not safe. Jer will find him. Right now, we need to focus on keeping everyone protected until we figure out what's going on."

We make our way inside, where my parents, Callie, and Melissa are waiting anxiously. My mother immediately pulls Lisa and me into a tight embrace.

"Oh, thank goodness you're alright," she says, her voice thick with emotion.

My father's face is grim as he looks at me over my mother's shoulder. "Any news?"

I shake my head. "Nothing concrete yet. We're working on it."

Danny joins us, Melissa tucked into his side. "We'll find out who's done this. They won't get away with it."

We're all determined to find out who the fuck did it. It was too fucking close for comfort. Too close to our women. The fucker who did it knew what they were doing and they'll pay for it.

Lisa's grip on my shirt is tight and I know that she's worried about me, but right now, all we can do is sit tight and wait for information. This is unlike anything we've ever dealt with before. This isn't some regular asshole looking for a fight. This is a skilled professional. Someone out there is sending us a message. The question is, what the fuck is it?

"I'm taking Callie to bed," Denis says, and I see that my sister is sobbing against his chest. Ava has been her best friend since they were kids. She's feeling this deeply. Fuck.

"You all should go to bed," Mam says softly. "I'll check on the kids."

I pull Lisa toward our bedroom. She's trembling as I help her out of the sexy as hell black dress she wore tonight. I had plans to fuck her while she was wearing it, and then again in only those fucking shoes she's got on, but right now, that's nowhere on my mind.

I gently lie Lisa down on the bed, her eyes still full of tears. She sniffles and wipes her face, trying to hold back her emotions. I sit beside her, stroke her hair, and say, "You're safe, baby. I promise you that nothing will ever happen to you." I'd fucking die if it did. Lisa is everything to me. I can't even bear the thought of losing her.

Lisa takes a deep breath and looks up at me, her eyes soft and grateful. "It's you that I'm worried about," she whispers.

I lean in and kiss her gently on the forehead. "Christ, baby, I'm fine. We're getting married in two months. Nothing is going to happen," I reassure her.

"I love you," she says softly, her eyes filled with love and fear.

"I love you too, baby," I reply, my voice thick and gravelly. "Never doubt that." I press a hard kiss to her lips, loving the little moan that escapes her. My cock thickens at the sound, and Lisa's hands begin to roam south. "Baby," I groan.

"Love me," she pleads. "I want you to love me."

I can't deny her anything. My hands skim along her body and I watch her eyes dilate with lust. "I love you, Lisa," I growl as I push her onto her back, my hands running along her curves.

Her lips pull into a soft smile. "And I love you."

I sink into her tight, hot pussy and groan. Fuck, there's nothing better than being with her. I'll do whatever the hell it takes to ensure her safety. Whoever the hell shot Ava won't have a chance at getting to Lisa.

I need her more than anything. She's my dream come true, and I can't and won't lose her.

ARE YOU READY FOR MORE?

Up next is The Silencer: Are you ready for Emmanuel and Clodagh's story? https://geni.us/TheSilencerHMOD

Cowboy's story is coming soon in the Fury Vipers MC: Dublin Chapter. You can start the series with Preacher's story: https://geni.us/FVDPreacher

Denis and Callie's story takes part in the Made series. Shattered Union is an age gap romance: https://geni.us/ShatteredUnion

BOOKS BY BROOKE:

The Kingpin Series:
Forbidden Lust

Dangerous Secrets

Forever Love

The Made Series:
Bloody Union

Unexpected Union

Fragile Union

Shattered Union

Hateful Union

Vengeful Union

Explosive Union

Cherished Union

Obsessive Union

Gallo Famiglia:
Ruthless Arrangement

Ruthless Betrayal

Ruthless Passion

The Houlihan Men of Dublin:

The Eraser

The Cleaner

The Silencer

The Thief

The Fury Vipers MC NY Chapter:

Stag

Mayhem

Digger

Ace

Pyro

Shadow

Wrath

Reaper

The Fury Vipers MC Dublin Chapter:

Preacher

Raptor

Bozo

Cowboy

Saint's Outlaws MC Boston Chapter:

Ghost's Redemption (prequel)

Rogue's Reckoning

Standalones:

Saving Reli

Taken By Nikolai

A Love So Wrong

His Dark Desire

OTHER PEN NAMES

Stella Bella

(A forbidden Steamy Pen name)

Taboo Temptations:

Wicked With the Professor

Snowed in with Daddy

Wooed by Daddy

Loving Daddy's Best Friend

Brother's Glory

Daddy's Curvy Girl

Daddy's Intern

His Curvy Brat

His Curvy Temptress

Daddy's Devilish Girl

Twisted Daddy

Seduced by Daddy's Best Friend

Stepbrother Seduction

Taboo Teachings:

Royally Taught

Extra Curricular with Mr. Abbot

Forbidden Bosses:

Conveniently Yours

Bred by Daddy

Gilded Billionaire

Maid for Love

One Night Forever

The Mistletoe Promise

Strings Attached

His Dark Desire

ABOUT BROOKE SUMMERS:

USA Today Bestselling Author Brooke Summers is a Mafia Romance author and is best known for her Made Series.

Brooke lives with her daughter and hubby on the picturesque west coast of Ireland. There's nothing Brooke loves more than spending time with her family and exploring new cities.

Want to know more about Brooke? www.brookesummersbooks.com
Subscribe to her newsletter: www.brookesummersbooks.com/newsletter
Join Brooke's Babes Facebook group.

Printed in Great Britain
by Amazon